SECOND CHANCES

SECOND CHANCES

REMI DAYLE

TO MY DAUGHTERS, FAWN AND FEATHER,
WHO ENDURED SO MANY STRUGGLES WITH
ME AS THEIR SINGLE MOTHER, AND CAME
OUT ON THE OTHER SIDE OF THEM AS
STRONG, INDEPENDENT WOMEN.
THANK YOU FOR BEING MY AMAZING
DAUGHTERS, FOR SURVIVING ALL THE
TOUGH TIMES, AND LOVING ME THROUGH
THEM ALL.
THANKS FOR HELPING ME BELIEVE I COULD
ONE DAY ACHIEVE MY GOAL OF BEING A
PUBLISHED AUTHOR.
I DID IT!
TO MARY VARNADEAUX, ONE OF MY ELDER
CARE CLIENTS, WHO, AT THE AGE OF 95, WAS
THE FIRST PERSON TO READ MY ROUGH
DRAFT AND ENCOURAGED ME TO PUBLISH BY
ASKING ONE QUESTION:
"WHY ARE YOU DOING ELDER CARE?"
FLY FREE IN THE SPIRIT REALM, MISS MARY!
TO MY DAUGHTER, FAWN, THANK YOU FOR
YOUR ASSISTANCE.

1

Warehouse Worker - Local warehouse needs a shipping and receiving dock hand. Experience not required. Will train hard worker. Starting Pay $15 per hr. E.O.E. Apply in person, Fenton Warehouse.... Breezy Jo reads the job search advertisement, saves the link and inputs the address in her GPS.

"Well, that offers the highest pay of anything I've found. I'll apply for that one first thing in the morning."

BJ's desperation is about to reach maximum overwhelm. The meager insurance money ran out weeks ago, and the money she's been making at various odd jobs she picked up along the way, traveling from town to town during the past few months, has barely been covering daily essentials and fuel. The surprise money she received from a bond left by her mother, listing BJ as the beneficiary, is what she's using to pay for the motel room she finally splurged on last week after so many nights sleeping in their car or tent at campgrounds. A job at those wages will be helpful, no matter how hard she needs to work.

Looking over at her two darling daughters napping on the bed, Breezy Jo whispers, "I promise, things will get better."

With the following bright sunny morning bolstering her confidence, BJ listens to the GPS directions, taking the final turn; she pulls into the parking lot of Fenton Warehouse. BJ takes in the huge, imposing gray cement structure before her. She parks near the front double glass doors, she exits her car, squares her shoulders, draws a fortifying breath and gives herself a firm talking to. "You've got this! I sure hope the people are more welcoming than the place appears."

Brady glances at the stack of applications that Cheryl, the Administrative Assistant, hands him. "Hmm, the one part of my job I dislike is hiring and firing," the older man mumbles. "Call these four, and have them come in for an interview as soon as possible."

Cheryl takes the documents he indicates, glancing at them. "This one, Sir," she says, holding up one sheet, "is still here. Would you like to do the interview right now?"

"Still here?"

"Yes, Sir," she replies, smiling shyly, glancing down at the application. "BJ McCallister just finished filling this out. When I saw you coming, I said that you might be doing some interviews today, so..." she finishes sheepishly.

"I see. Anything special about this one in your opinion?" Brady is suspicious that this particular applicant made an impression on his young secretary. Maybe he's good-looking?

"Well, actually...." Cheryl hesitates.

"What, then? Go on," he encourages.

"Just that we talked a bit, and there seems to be an urgent need for a good-paying job and appears to be a real hard worker too." She does her best not to reveal too much. BJ will have to do any explaining if the manager accepts the interview. She graces the man with an encouraging smile.

"Oh, all right. Give me a minute in my office to get organized, then send in this McCallister." He turns and walks away, grumbling under his breath. She doesn't quite catch it all, something about *young people* and *only looks, count.*

Cheryl hurries into the break room, where she told the applicant to wait. Smiling brightly, she tells her about the conversation. "I didn't tell him anything except that you are seriously in need of a good job," she giggles shyly, "I think he believes I have *an eye for you.*" They both laugh. "Well, I think it's been long enough, you should go in now," she directs BJ toward the Dock Manager's office.

"Here goes nothing," she states, shoulders squared to help with confidence.

"You'll do fine," Cheryl encourages.

"Come in," the gruff reply from the other side of the door responds to her light knock. Opening it carefully, filled with determination, she enters.

A full head of coarse, wavy salt and pepper hair is bent over a cluttered desk. The body it is attached to, rises without looking up at the entrant. "BJ stand for Billy Joe or someth..." Brady stops mid-sentence as his head raises to greet the newcomer. His mouth drops open, and he nearly falls back into his chair as the applicant answers the unfinished question.

"Or something." Seeing the shock on the man's face produces mixed feelings: those of laughter bubbling up at the older gentleman's expression are added to those of fear that he might start laughing at her and summarily dismiss her without giving her a chance.

"Um, ah, well," the flustered man stutters and stammers as he tries to regain his normal gruff composure. "Well, then, what does it stand for?" he asks a bit grumpily.

"I generally don't tell people, Sir. I prefer BJ," her answer polite, yet firm.

"Have a seat," he invites, seating himself at his desk.

The man across from her studies her application more thoroughly, noticing for the first time the box marked 'F', spurring his deeper perusal of the document in his hand.

She sits in the only other chair in the room. She glances around the man's small office and at the man. They seem to blend well. She guesses the man is at least in his late 50s or early 60s. Though his manner is gruff, his eyes are clear blue and friendly. They give away the true man inside. When they are standing, he is slightly taller than her own 5'10", and despite the fact that he carries a bit of a jelly belly, he is burly and still fit for his age.

The man clears his throat, bringing BJ's wandering mind back to the matter at hand.

"Mrs. McCallister..." he begins.

"Please drop the Mrs. I don't need the reminder," she interrupts.

"I see. Well, although my secretary said you are desperate for a good-paying position, this job entails loading and unloading trucks, very heavy lifting. It's dirty, sweaty work, and all the other dock men are, well, exactly that...men. From the looks of you, I don't believe you could lift even the smallest boxes of the shipments we receive. I'm sorry, but I don't think we can help you."

"Your employment posting states that you'll 'train hard workers', which I am. It also says E.O.E. Equal Opportunity Employer. Give me the opportunity to prove myself."

Under the thick gray beard, BJ glimpses the man's jaw tighten and mouth pucker as he draws a deep breath. "I don't know," he drawls.

"I'm begging you, Sir." BJ's eyes plead, "It's critical and urgent that I find a good-paying job."

His blue eyes narrow. "May I inquire as to why you're so desperate?"

"I don't like to go into all the details, but I have two young daughters to raise alone."

"I see." He glances back at the application. "It says here that you reside at the Studio 8 Extended Stay Motel."

"Yes, they've been very helpful. The owner's wife and teenage daughter have been helping me by watching my girls while I'm looking for work."

After a short pause, "I'm still not sure. I know the boss wouldn't take too kindly to a lady dockhand." Brady shakes his head.

"As long as I do my job and do it well, he shouldn't care which gender I am," she asserts, trying to sound convincing and confident.

Wise eyes view the face before him, determination etched in the set of her jaw and the diamond-hard clarity of glistening blue, pleading eyes. Their eyes meet, his soften as he responds frankly, "You don't know RJ Fenton."

Silence falls between them. The dock manager fidgets with the application. Abruptly, he is on his feet. His sudden movement startles BJ. When he glances at her, he witnesses fear flash in her eyes, as if she feared he would yell at her, or worse... "I'm sorry, Mrs..." he begins, she bristles. "BJ," he corrects, then continues, "I didn't mean to startle you. I'll tell you what. Let's say we have a little test?"

"OK," she answers slowly. "What kind of test?"

"Why don't we go out to the docks, and if you can prove to me that you can lift some of those boxes, we'll give you a try." BJ's face brightens with excitement. "Hold on now, don't go getting too excited. RJ may override my decision, even if you do pass; his word is final. After all, he owns the company."

Her spirits sink marginally; then, giving herself a mental shake, silently affirms, "Fine. *I'll show Mr. Chauvinist RJ Fenton that I can, and will do my job as well as any man.*"

Out on the docks, the men are busy unloading a truck. A few heads turn sharply at the appearance of their boss and a woman. One man, heavy set with full black beard and milk chocolate complexion, stands up from his crouched position by a box. His deep, brusque voice annoys BJ with what he says, "Well, well, what have we here, Brady? A little entertainment for the crew?"

"That'll be enough, Butch," the Brady glowers.

Another man, tall, good-looking, with coffee brown hair, and sparkling green eyes, joins them. Smiling politely, he greets, "Good day, Miss. Ignore my buddy here; he has what most men are said to have... a one-track mind, and no manners. I'm Jake Benson. You are?" He holds out his hand to shake, but is interrupted before she can extend her hand in return or utter a word.

"This," he announces gruffly and loudly to the crew, "is BJ McCallister. She is applying for the position we have open."

"Huh? You've got to be kidding," the boisterous dockhand laughs.

"Butch!" Brady cuts him off sternly. "I've agreed to have her perform a test of her strength. If she passes, I said we'd give her a try."

"The Boss ain't gonna like it," one of the younger men off to the side pipes up.

"He won't have to know about it. She'll never be able to lift these boxes. She'll be long gone before he ever finds out," the abrasive employee chuckles.

"Oh, I wouldn't be so sure about that, my friend," Jake smiles at the man, then, back at BJ. "By the look in her eyes, I believe she can do anything she sets her mind to," glancing back at his pompous pal, "Even take you."

"Ha!" the brusque man laughs. "You think so? Fine, let the test of her strength be arm wrestling me," he announces, sounding totally macho.

"Wait just a darn minute here," Brady bursts in. "Her job will be handling boxes... Not Men!"

"It's OK with me, Sir," she whispers to the older man at her side.

"Where are my manners? I never told you my name. Just call me Brady. What do you mean by 'it's OK with you'? He's beaten almost everyone who tried."

"Well, if I intend to work here, I need to prove myself to them," she glances at all the men now standing, watching. "If I don't accept, I'll only be the weak female they already believe me to be. Besides, I'll still do your test for employment purposes."

"Are you sure about this?" he whispers.

"I'm positive." BJ wishes she felt as confident as she sounds.

"Well, Butch," the manager announces. "The lady accepts your challenge, BUT," he says, looking at everyone, "the determining factor for work trial will still be lifting boxes. So even if she loses to you..."

"She will," is Butch's barely audible interruption.

"Even if she does," he goes on, "it will not affect whether she gets the job. Is that clear?" He glances around again, then intently at Butch.

"Yeah, yeah," they all mumble in unison.

Two chairs and a small, sturdy table are pulled onto the dock from the break room so they all can watch.

Butch seats himself with the smug look of an assured winner.

Looking at all the smiling faces taking bets, BJ overhears a couple of the guys say they'll take the long shot at 10-to-1 odds. Jake and Brady stand off to the side, refraining from betting.

Brady shakes his head and gives this brave woman an encouraging smile, whispering, "I sure hope you know what you're doing. Good luck."

Jake smiles confidently. "You've got this," he states with a wink.

Cheryl appears at the sound of all the commotion. She whispers in BJ's ear, "Give him heck, honey! He deserves it!" She smiles shyly and steps aside.

One of the other men, along with the boss, are acting as referees. The competitors clasp hands to comfortably secure their grips. The ref holds their doubled-up fists upright and centered.

"Are you both ready?" Brady surveys the two opponents, awaiting their nods of agreement. "Go!" He shouts as he releases them.

Butch gets the upper hand, and his face glows instantly with smugness as he glares at the little lady across from him. BJ stares her opponent square in the eyes and smiles sweetly, and begins forcing his hand the other way, past the starting point. Butch's face changes to one of terror as his hand creeps closer and closer to the table. He glances from his hand to the sweet smile still adorning BJ's face.

The noise of the cheering crowd around them washes over him until the sound becomes muffled, like a dense fog enveloping him.

When the back of his hand hits the tabletop, the breath he's been holding bursts violently from his lungs. "Holy..." he exclaims. Eyes, dark as strong black coffee, meet and lock with the shimmering blues of the winner.

The dock crew falls silent, unsure how Big Butch is gonna take defeat by a woman. A smile cracks from under his bushy black beard, and everyone starts hooting and hollering.

Cheryl lets out a yelp, then immediately pulls her shy self together and lowers her eyes, peeking from behind her lashes to sneak a glance at Jake to see if he saw. An amused expression sits on his face as he regards her just before returning his attention to the two contenders shaking hands.

"I would never have believed it if I hadn't seen it with my own eyes," Brady announces with evident astonishment.

Bets are being paid up by the confused yet excited men. It seems everybody is jabbering at once, until Butch puts a hand up high, and silence comes over the gathering.

Once no one is talking, he states, "I salute you, ma'am. I thought a stiff wind would blow you down when I saw you walk out here, now I'm sure you'd probably blow it right back where it came from."

A collective laugh follows from the group.

"Brady," he continues, "as far as I'm concerned, Ms. McCallister has the job, and as far as Boss Man is concerned?... Let's just say that up 'til now, he and Jake are the only two who've ever beaten me. Let him try to get rid of her. I've no doubt she can knock some sense into him...in more ways than one," Butch smiles and winks.

Again, laughter erupts. After all the congratulations, welcome aboard comments and handshakes are dispensed with, he turns to BJ and says, "I have a couple questions for you."

"Of course. What?"

"Where'd you learn to arm wrestle like that, and where do you hide all that strength?" he asks, chuckling.

The moments ago joy evaporates from BJ's features as dark memories of where she learned wash over her as memory flashes before her mind's eye... *"You want groceries? You know the only way to get 'em is to arm wrestle me. Same stakes as always. You win, you get money for food. You lose, I get you, my way, here and now." Those were always her husband's conditions. Many times, she would forego his terms and make do with whatever scraps she had on hand. Sometimes she risked waiting for him to be drunk asleep and sneak most of the change he would empty from his pockets when he went to bed, always leaving some so it wasn't obvious. On rare occasions, she would risk taking one or two dollar bills if he had enough that he wouldn't realize any were missing. She would save up until she had enough to buy some decent food, then she put Chumani in the rickety stroller and walked to the store while Matthew was at work. She would hide the groceries when she got them home so he wouldn't find out.*

Dragging herself back to the here and now, she forces a smile, "I grew up on a farm. My late husband *taught* me to be strong by arm wrestling." She tries not to let the anger and bitterness sound in her reply.

"Oh, I'm sorry for your loss." He feels bad that he's brought up thoughts of her deceased spouse. It appears as though the memory still hurts.

"Don't be," she attempts to brush off the negative memories. She doesn't want anyone to know what her 'beloved' husband put her through. "As for hiding my strength?" She glances around at those still nearby. Donning a dazzling smile, she asks, "Didn't your mamas teach you not to judge a book by its cover?"

"You can say that again," Butch replies, shaking his head.

BJ smiles sweetly at the blowhard. "Well," she inquires, batting her lashes jokingly, "was that entertaining enough for you?"

Exuberant laughter erupts. "Best entertainment ever! Welcome aboard, Ms. McCallister. I think you'll be a refreshing change to the crew." He shakes her hand once more and goes back to work.

Jake stands quietly nearby, smiling.

"Why didn't you bet?"

"I don't find it fair to bet on something I already know the outcome of," he discloses.

"But how could you know the outcome?" she asks

"As I said earlier, the look in your eyes said it all. Now I better get back to work before our new employee thinks we don't do anything around here. Good day to you, Ms. McCallister."

"BJ, please," she requests earnestly.

"Welcome, BJ," he corrects, "Brady..." he nods his parting. "Ms. Peters..." he smiles at Cheryl, and her eyes fall demurely as she returns to her desk.

"Well, ma'am, you've got yourself a job, and you've already won over the gang. Let's hope when the boss gets back in a few weeks, and catches wind of your presence, that he accepts you as readily as the rest of us." Then, getting back to the business side of the situation, he heads back toward his office, motioning for her to follow. "We punch in at 7:00 AM and out at 4:00. We take an hour lunch, 11:30 to 12:30."

"Thank you so much for this chance, Mr. O'Malley. Now I need to find an inexpensive, reliable full-time sitter, and I'll be set."

"Brady," he corrects, then is silent a moment before looking back at BJ, saying thoughtfully, "I think I might be able to help you out with that, too." He pauses, "My missus used to run a day care center at our home after our kids grew up and moved away. She gave it up a couple years ago, but last week she said how much she misses having little cherubs around. Would you be interested?"

"I don't want to push her into something if she might have only been reminiscing, but if she really wants to..."

"I'll call her right now and ask. I'm sure she'll think it's a wonderful idea."

Brady gets his wife on the line, and explains the situation briefly, "Her name is Millie," he informs as he hands the phone to BJ to discuss the particulars.

"Hello, dear. Wha'a pleasant surprise this truly is. I just said last week that I need to find some wee cherubs ta care fer. I dearly miss having youngins 'round. Me husban' says ya have two garls. Wha' be their ages?"

BJ smiles at the sound of the Irish brogue, evident in the woman's folksy voice. "Chumani is 5, and Chenoa is 8 months."

"Oh, my. They are little tykes."

"I understand if they are too young for you," she hurries to assure the older woman in case their being so little would be too much at her age.

"Aye, nonsense, lass. I'm no' that old. I only meant that bein' on yar own an' all with two wee garls, an' havin' ta work 'tis understandably hard. When do ya start yar job?"

Not knowing the answer to that, she turns to Brady, "When would you like me to begin, Sir?"

Before he can respond, Millie, hearing the young lady call her husband Sir, pipes up, "Now don'a be callin' 'im, Sir. He'll be thinkin' he's sumthin special," she chuckles brightly.

"I mean, Brady." BJ smiles at the infectious good-naturedness of the woman on the phone.

"Being that today is Thursday, I think Monday would be best. That'll allow you a few more days to situate things for your little ones. You should take them to meet my missus so you're not plopping them off somewhere completely strange come Monday morning, and it'll give you time to rest up," he winks.

Millie hears what her husband says, and agreeing inquires, "Wha' are yar plans fer the next couple o'days, dear?"

"Nothing other than looking for work."

"Well, then, I think we need to figure out some fun thangs to do with yar garls. I'll be guessing yar new to the area, so I can show ya round town a bit. That'll give the wee cherubs a chance ta get ta know me with ya 'round fer reassurance. Wha' say?"

"Sounds like a good idea," she agrees.

Arrangements are made for BJ and the girls to go to Millie O'Malley's around ten the next morning.

"Thank you again, Brady, for giving me this opportunity. I won't let you down. I'll see you first thing Monday."

"You're welcome, lass. I believe you'll do as you say. Remember, one obstacle still remains on this course that we still have to hurdle, and that's the owner. On the upside, he's not due back for three weeks."

BJ's handshake with her new boss, firm as she assures him, "I have no intention of allowing myself to be intimidated by him or anyone, for that matter. I'll prove to him that I can handle the job. You just watch."

"Of that I have no doubt. Like Butch said, I've a feeling you'll have no trouble teaching the Mr. Fenton a thing or two in more ways than one. Have a good night."

"I will, Sir."

As BJ begins to leave his office, "Wait a moment." Brady reaches into his back pocket, pulls out his wallet, opens it, takes out two twenties, handing them to her, saying, "You take the youngins out for a good meal tonight to celebrate."

"Thank you for the kind gesture, but I can't take your money."

"Well, now if you don't take it, I'll be mighty aggrieved. Now you don't want to hurt an old man's feelings, do you? Go on now, take it," he extends the bills closer to her. "But if you tell the fellas on the crew, I'll deny it with my dying breath. Wouldn't want them thinking I've gone soft now, you understand."

BJ realizes that this is out of character for the man who faces the world with his gruff old codger exterior. Smiling politely, she accepts the money, then, without thought, gives the man a quick hug.

Flustered by the gesture, Brady halfheartedly brushes her off, saying, "Aw, now, be off with ya." His action is tempered with a shy smile and a wink as she leaves.

2

Cheryl is watching for BJ to come out. When she does emerge from the dock manager's office, the AA goes to her immediately. "I'm so happy you got the job, and I'm ecstatic that you put Butch in his place. I gotta tell you, I had one moment of doubt, but it disappeared almost instantly, and I knew you could take him. Tell me truthfully, did you ever think that you could beat him, and how did you do it?" She guides her into her cubicle, where they each take a seat.

"It's like you said, you had a moment of doubt. That's all it takes. Due to his confidence that he could take me, and at the start, he had the advantage, but his fatal mistake occurred when he looked up and saw the confident smile on my face. That was his undoing, because in that instant, he had a moment of doubt in himself, and I easily capitalized on it by continuing to smile confidently. The more I smiled, the more he doubted his own abilities. Belief is a very powerful attribute. If you believe you can't...you can't, but if you believe you can...you can!"

"Wow, that's pretty profound, and you proved it."

"Enough about all that. A 'benefactor', to remain unnamed, gave me a monetary gift to take my girls out for dinner tonight to celebrate getting my new job. Since I have no idea where to go, and have no friends, I'm wondering if you might have a recommendation for someplace good and if you will join us?"

"It would be my pleasure to suggest somewhere, and I am honored to be asked to celebrate with you. On one condition."

"What's that?"

"That you allow me the honor of being your first true friend here."

"You got it. It's a deal."

"I'm off work at four. I'll run home, clean up, and come by and pick you up, say around 6? Is that too late?"

"No, that's perfect. We're staying at..."

"I know where you are... I already input all your employee information." They chuckle.

Cheryl arrives at Studio 8 Extended Stay, a white two-story all-efficiency motel, shortly before six.

"Hi, come on in," BJ welcomes. "This is Chumani. Say hello to Ms. Cheryl."

"Hi, Ms. Cheryl. Mommy says you're very nice. Thank you for helping her get her job."

She is a bit surprised that both adorable girls have pale blonde hair in sharp contrast to BJ's rich, deep brown hair. However, they look just like their mother with their sparkling blue eyes.

"It's a pleasure to meet you, and you're welcome, but your mamma got the job all on her own because she deserves it."

BJ finishes changing her younger daughter and picks her up, introducing her, "This is Chenoa."

"Hello, Chenoa." She touches the baby's soft cheek, bringing a smile to the infant's pudgy face. "Such beautiful names you girls have." She inquires, "They sound Native American. What are their meanings?"

"Yes, they are. I like unique nature-based names. Chenoa means white dove, and Chumani means dew drop."

"Lovely, and what does BJ stand for?"

After a brief hesitation, "I generally don't tell anyone, but... I guess if we're to be best friends and..." she regards her new friend sternly, "...you promise never to tell a soul."

Cheryl uses her index finger to cross her heart, then locks her lips to indicate her promise.

"Breezy Jo."

"That's a beautiful name!"

While BJ finishes packing the diaper bag, she says, "I'm thinking we should take my car since the girls' car seats are already in it, and you can either ride with us, or if you'd rather not, we can follow you."

"I'd love to ride with you. Is that OK with you, Chumani?"

"Yup. I'll grab the diaper bag, Mommy."

"Careful, it's heavy. I appreciate you being my big helper." BJ gathers up last-minute items, makes sure everything is turned off, grabs her keys, and heads toward the door.

"Anything I can help carry?" Cheryl inquires.

"Um... sure." She hands Chenoa to her new friend, "I'm so used to doing everything on my own. Thank you."

"No problem. Thank you for entrusting me with this precious bundle." She nuzzles the infant in her arms, bringing forth a giggle from the baby.

They load up, and Cheryl provides directions to one of her favorite little restaurants across town. As they drive through the mid-sized town, BJ glances around at what it has to offer, wondering, "Is this to be the end of our homeless lifestyle? Are we finally going to be able to settle down and stay put? Don't get ahead of yourself, girl. You haven't even begun work yet, and you still have to pass muster with the chauvinist boss man?" She continues to assess her surroundings. Driving down the main street of what she believes is the original old downtown, with its quaint old colonial and Old West mixture of structure styles, with many of the sidewalks still constructed of wood, which is obvious were built in a bygone era. She is comforted by the old-time feel, which she is quite sure is preserved by restrictions on the types of businesses and homes allowed to be built in the vicinity. However, she remembers she also saw more modern and big-box-type stores on the outskirts. *I think we just might be able to be happy here.*

They arrive at the restaurant, a family-style establishment with the promise of great food, nice people, and a child-friendly atmosphere. The girls are given crayons and a placemat/menu to color while they wait for their meals. BJ is pleased to discover a few vegetarian and even a couple vegan options on the menu.

BJ orders all plant-based items, and Cheryl decides to follow suit since she has been considering altering her eating habits to plant-based. "I'll have what she's having. It sounds delicious."

A discussion about plant-based lifestyle and food choices ensues as they wait for their entrées. The conversation continues into general small talk during their meal as they consume the mouth-watering Bef veggie burgers, with both vegan thousand island dressing and mayo, ketchup, dill pickles, vegan cheez, lettuce and caramelized sweet onions.

Chumani overhears Miss Cheryl tell Mommy that she hasn't tried many plant-based foods but is interested in changing her diet. "Miss Cheryl, do you want to try one of my chickun nuggets?"

"That's very kind of you. I want to be sure you have enough to eat so I'll try half of one," she takes and tastes. "That is delicious. Thank you for sharing, Chumani."

Once everyone is finished eating, Cheryl holds Chenoa while BJ plays arcade games with Chumani. Returning to their table for dessert, she realizes it is getting late when her youngest begins to become fussy, so they finish quickly, gather up their belongings and head home.

Back at the motel, Cheryl helps BJ bring everything in, then assists readying the girls for bed.

"Can you read us a story tonight?" Chumani asks.

"Of course, I can. If it's all right with your mommy."

BJ nods her approval, then sits on the dinette chair holding Chenoa with her bottle while Cheryl sits on the edge of the bed next to Chumani and reads. Chenoa falls asleep, so BJ places her in her bunting bag, which is a baby sleeping bag, in the bassinet-sized pop-up play pen she picked up in one of the towns they spent several days in during their travels.

When the story is finished, Chumani thanks and hugs her, then hugs and kisses her Mommy good night, snuggles down into her sleeping bag next to her baby sister's pop-up, rolls over, then drifts off to sleep.

The ladies sit talking long into the night. When they finally realize how late it is, Cheryl heads home since she needs to be at work in a few short hours.

BJ apologizes, "I'm sorry for losing track of the time. It's so late."

"No worries. "I have enjoyed spending time with you and getting to know each other."

They exchange hugs, honoring their new friendship.

"Good night. Drive safely."

Morning comes too soon for BJ as the girls wake at their usual 6:30. Once their morning routine is completed, she gets the trio ready to go meet Millie O'Malley.

Chumani chats excitedly on the drive over. As BJ pulls into the driveway, Chumani is practically bouncing in her car seat. "Is this it, Mommy?"

"I think it is," BJ replies as she takes in the small, country cottage-style house with a raised covered porch and moss-embossed stone chimney on one side. The mossy stone walkway leading to the porch is surrounded by a plethora of flowers you'd find in a fine English garden. The myriad of colors is glorious. "It's so pretty," Chumani whispers in awe.

"Yes, it is, baby girl."

Millie spies the car as soon as it pulls in the driveway. She scurries out to greet her guests in her usual exuberant manner. "Hello, lass, you must be the infamous BJ McCallister," the woman enthuses. "An' these must be yar wee darlin's."

Millie seems the stereotypical Irish grandmotherly-type woman. She is much shorter at only about 5'5". She is of stout, sturdy Irish stock to be sure, with short curly salt and pepper hair almost the same color as her husband's. Chumani gets out of her car seat and the car on her own, and comes around to the other side of the car as BJ is removing Chenoa from her car seat. "Which lass might you be?" The woman asks.

Chumani quizzically eyes the woman, then asks, "Mommy, what's a lass? Am I one?"

The older woman laughs heartily, "Aye, deary. Yar a lass. A lass is another word for garl."

Seeing the quizzical look deepen on Chumani's young features, she says, "Yes, baby girl, you're a lass, which, as Mrs. O'Malley said, is another word for girl," she supplies the pronunciation correction for her daughter, hoping not to offend Millie before they even become acquainted.

"Yes, tha's exac'ly wha' I said, Deary," the woman says while belly-laughing again.

Chumani tells her mother, "She talks funny."

Before BJ can respond, Millie bends lower to the child's level, "Righ' ya are. I do talk a might bit funny, but yal get used to it soon'nuff," then gives a gentle tweak to Chumani's cute little nose. Straightening up, she turns her attention to BJ, who now stands holding the baby. "So, if yar Chumani," she says, "then this mus' be Chenoa," she points to the youngest, "Hello, lass." She gently rubs the baby's head. "Come now, let's go inside fer a wee while." Millie leads the way to the front door. Upon entering the house, they pass through the small parlor, then enter and sit in the informal living area.

Chumani wanders around the room looking at things. "Chumani, please remember, this is a 'hold your elbows' kind of room. OK?"

"Yes, Mommy."

BJ places a 45" x 72" handmade quilted blanket on the floor, and lays Chenoa on it with a few toys pulled from the diaper bag she brought in. The women talk for quite some time about a myriad of topics to become better acquainted, while allowing the girls to play and get comfortable with the surroundings.

Millie glances at the clock on the fireplace mantel. "Oh, my where has the time gone?" she calls to Chumani, who is sitting at a table coloring. "Lass, migh'cha be a wee bit hungrah?"

BJ efficiently translates "Would you like some lunch, sweetie?"

"Yes, I'm hungry."

"Wha' say we go out an' 'ave a bit of lunch somewhere? My treat," her conclusion firm.

"That's not necessary; we'll be fine with something simple like a PB&J," BJ assures the kindly woman.

"Aye, and while I'm sure ya kin, I'm sure ya've had more than yar fill of that now, haven'cha?" It is a rhetorical question, and with that, she is up and begins gathering up Chenoa as she continues, "Let's us be going now. I'll drive."

"It would be easier to take my car because of the girls' car seats."

"No' ta worry," Millie informs, "I use ta run a day care an' still have the car seats I used. I've already latched 'em in the back seat." She smiles. So, they load up and are off.

After lunch at a local diner, they spend the afternoon doing a bit of sightseeing, playing in a nearby park, just letting the girls become more familiar with their caregiver so they'll feel more at ease with her when she begins caring for them in two days.

Being in this woman's presence today creates a sense of how she imagines it would be to spend time with her grandma if she had one. The best thing is that Chumani and Chenoa seem to be extremely comfortable with her as well, which bodes well for her taking care of them.

BJ's spirit soars with thoughts that things appear to be working out well, as she always believed they would one day. She's also overcome with a calmness, unlike anything she's ever experienced. *"Yes, I think I like it here."*

3

"You look like you've had a rough night," Cheryl states.

The two have already become good friends in the three weeks since Brady hired BJ.

"Yeah, right after I started here, I also got a job waiting tables at Buddy's Lounge. I work there Wednesday, Friday, Saturday, and Sunday evenings, making Thursday and Monday mornings a bit tough." BJ yawns before taking a long draft of her hot coffee.

"I don't know how you do it. You're here five days a week, the bar four nights, and take care of two kids? You're amaz..."

"Enough," BJ cuts off her friend. "I'm nothing special. I'm not doing anything any other single mother wouldn't do." She smiles to soften her abruptness as she turns to walk away, "Sorry, I didn't mean to snap at you. Gotta go to work. See you at lunch?"

"Of course, no worries. See you, then." Cheryl returns to her tasks.

"Hi, Jake. How's it going?" BJ's blitheness is refreshing as she emerges onto the dock.

"Not bad. How are things with you? Find a place to live yet?"

"Nope. I haven't had time to look. Now that I'm working two jobs, I try to spend the rest of my time with my girls."

"I understand that." With that, the first truck of the day arrives.

Just after lunch, Brady is in his office when Cheryl opens his door, speaking quietly, "Brady. The Boss's mother just sent me a text saying RJ's on his way here!"

"Correction," a deep voice booms from behind her, startling her so that she yelps and jumps further into the room. "I'm already here," he informs them.

She waits for the large man to fully enter, carefully slipping past him, trying to sneak out when he speaks. "Cheryl," his tone and expression stern, "I don't want the verbal alarm sounded on the dock. If employees are forewarned, it does not make for a true inspection of performance." He gives her a warning look, then smiles, "Do I make myself clear?"

"Yes, Sir, Mr. Fenton. Perfectly clear," she stutters, physically shaking.

As she turns to go, RJ's tone, now softer. "And Cheryl, my bark is much worse than my bite. I apologize, but I am serious." His eyebrows raise in question of her acceptance.

"Yes, Sir." She hastily retreats. Panic-stricken over the forthcoming discovery of a woman on the docks, she pours herself a cup of coffee, then sits at her desk trying to calm her nerves, thinking about poor BJ. In the mood the boss seems to be in, she wonders if there will be any survivors of the coming storm.

Brady and RJ emerge onto the loading dock about a half hour later. The crew is bustling around unloading a semi-trailer and putting the cartons on pallets according to specifications received with each shipment.

"Hey. Who stacked this pallet?" BJ's voice rings out. "It's got one too many layers."

Brady's eyes shoot to RJ's face in time to witness the myriad of expressions flash across his features. From puzzlement to shock to red-hot anger. "Now, Boss, I can explain..." Brady rushes in response to the look RJ shoots at him like a bullet from a gun at close range. "I intended to tell you, but you haven't given me a chance t..."

"Who in the heck...?" RJ bursts out.

"Nice to have you back, Boss," Butch breaks in, reaching out to shake the boss's hand.

"Have a good trip?" Jake inquires smoothly, smiling.

Jake and Butch have seen the developing situation and swiftly come to Brady's rescue. Accepting Butch's hand in greeting, RJ scowls at the two men. "Good to be back...I think!" he glares at Brady. "Yes, I had a good trip." His features soften as he continues, "Thanks for cutting me short, guys. I about lost control. Would someone mind explaining to me why a woman is working on My loading dock?" His voice is forceful, but he keeps the volume down for their ears only.

"I...I... hired a new hand who is a real go-getter."

"A woman? You hired a woman?" RJ spits incredulously, the intensity of his voice rising slightly.

"Now, hold on a minute," Butch pipes up, seeing Brady squirming under the furious look from their boss. "She ain't *just* a woman. Why, that's what I thought... we all thought, but I'll be the first to tell you she's somethin' special. That *woman* beat me arm wrestling!" He announces, sounding almost proud to have lost to her.

"Yeah, right!" RJ scoffs in disbelief.

"Every one of us witnessed it right here on the dock. Ask Cheryl. You know she'd never lie to you. Not that I ever have in our 39 years."

Jake and RJ's parents have been friends since before the boys were born, only two weeks apart. They've literally been best buddies since birth.

"Fine. If you say so, but I don't believe any woman could..." He pauses, then continues, "...unless she's..." He stops.

"Oh, I doubt that very seriously," chuckling, he gives RJ a wry smile.

Their lifelong friendship is more brotherly than mere friends, and though Jake works on the docks like any other dockhand, he is well-versed in every aspect of the company. RJ is the owner who took over at only nineteen when his father died unexpectedly. Brady worked for RJ's father for as long as anyone can remember, and there are no intentions of putting him out to pasture, but when the day comes for him to step down, Jake is ready to take over without a hitch.

During working hours, the two manage to maintain matters in a business manner for the most part, but they are so connected with each other, they can read each other's expressions. "Seems she's already got you as an ally, but I still don't like it. A woman on the docks?"

"Would you like to meet her, Boss?" Brady asks hesitantly.

"I suppose now's as good a time as any. But I'll tell you all right now, she gets *no* special treatment. If she wants to work like a man, she'll be treated accordingly," the boss informs the three men with a warning look.

Jake smiles at his friend, saying, "Sure, Boss, but don't forget, you have to practice what you preach, and you haven't met her yet."

RJ suspiciously eyes his friend, wondering if his interest changed from the woman he's been pursuing silently for quite some time.

"I'm sure that won't be a problem," RJ states.

In unison, Butch and Jake cough to cover their laughter. Brady clears his throat to hide his as he calls out above the din of the dock, "BJ? Can you come over here, please?"

A conversation taking place near the door leading to the office area catches BJ's attention and figures the never-before-seen man must be 'The Boss'. She tries to stay out of his line of vision and is doing her best to squash the feelings of dread and fear of being fired by this chauvinist that begin to wash over her at the sight of him. With her back to the foursome, she draws in a long, deep, steadying breath, straightens, closing her eyes, she visualizes her daughters to bolster her steadfast determination to do whatever she must to prove herself worthy of this job. She'll do anything for her babies. At least anything legitimate and legal. Securely ensconced in her armor of tenacity, she strides over to where the men stand. As she approaches, Jake and Butch turn to return to work, both give her reassuring smiles, winks, and thumbs up. As they cross paths, Jake states reassuringly, "No worries. All bark, no bite. Simply be the *you* we all know you are."

"You'll have him wrapped 'round your little finger in no time," Butch assures her with a bright grin.

RJ eyes her approach with a guarded expression. Dressed in blue jeans, their snug fit showing with each step. A baseball cap covers her hair and shades her face. The T-shirt she's wearing reveals her slender figure and bears witness that she is, in fact, female.

He is of the opinion she can't be much of a 'lady' if she beat Butch and gained acceptance of the crew, yet seeing her slight athletic build causes him question her ability to have, in actuality, won the match. "Is this some kind of joke? Are you all trying to prank me?" he asks the dock manager he's known all his life, under his breath as she draws near, "She looks as if she'd blow away in the slightest breeze," he mumbles.

Brady chuckles. "That's exactly what Butch thought and said," he informs.

BJ performs a visual assessment of her new boss as she approaches. She's taken by the man's towering height, 6'4" at least. Sturdy yet almost slender build. Thick, wavy chestnut brown hair. Amber eyes, hard and cold at the sight of her.

"BJ McCallister," Brady makes the introductions, "This is RJ Fenton, affectionately referred to as Boss.

"Boss, meet BJ McCallister, our newest dockhand," he states, sounding proud.

"Ms. McCallister."

She is greeted by his warm, resonant voice, contradictory to the cool, businesslike manner with which he extends his hand.

She accepts the gesture, knowing now is the time to make the right impression. Making appropriate confident eye contact proves an unnerving decision; she discovers this might be a bit more difficult than she thought it would be. In his eyes, she experiences his obvious disdain toward her. She makes sure her handshake is firm, which causes a cynical look to cross his handsome features. Smiling her sweetest ladylike smile, sparks something akin to surprise, flash in his eyes momentarily. She states charmingly, "Just BJ."

Ending the gesture of greeting, he quizzes, "What does BJ stand for?"

She again graces him with a charming smile, questioning in return. "What does RJ stand for?"

A slight head-tilted, squinting expression crosses his face, "Touché," he nods, understanding she has her reasons, as does he, for using initials rather than given name.

"I'm sure you've been told, but I want to make it perfectly clear and straight from the horse's mouth that I do not approve of a woman working on my docks. Let it also be clear to you, as I have already made it abundantly clear to these gentlemen," he glances at the trio that appear to have found 'busy work' nearby so they can keep abreast of the conversation, "If you choose to tackle a man's job, you will be treated as such. You will receive no preferential treatment. Nor will any variance of privileges be afforded you," he states as a matter of fact.

"I wouldn't have it any other way, Sir," she replies, with strong emphasis on the Sir.

The corner of RJ's mouth quirks, and his amber eyes sparkle fleetingly. His rigid expression returns. "Back to work, all of you!" he barks out, trying to sound authoritative.

The other three men smile, responding knowingly with, "Yes, Boss," followed by smirks and chuckles.

BJ gives her new boss a mock salute, replying stiffly, "Yes, Sir," then clicks her heels and does an about-face.

The observant trio and a few others with eyes on the situation burst out laughing. The warning look from the boss subdues them into quiet chuckles, as they all return to the tasks at hand. Jake turns to Brady before walking away, saying in stage whisper fashion, "She's got him pegged!"

The next couple days go well. RJ can't find fault with BJ's abilities. On Thursday, RJ overhears Brady and Butch talking and learns that BJ also holds a night job as a cocktail server. RJ's curiosity gets the better of him. Knowing the best and safest source of information would be gleaned from Cheryl, and that she is just intimidated enough by him to keep his inquisitions to herself, he approaches her. "How are you doing, Cheryl?" he inquires almost cheerfully, entering her office, but when the secretary winces and closes her eyes, he asks concerned, "You all right? You look like you had a rough night."

"Rough is too mild a term," she grimaces.

"What happened?" He tries to hide the amusement in his voice.

"I agreed to go with the crew to Buddy's Lounge last night; it's where BJ works a few nights a week, and she told us about this band that is playing there this month. So, Butch, Jake, a few others, and I went to check it out last night," she pauses a moment, blushing, then finishes, "I'm not much of a drinker. I'm afraid I made quite a fool of myself." Her eyes drop to avoid the smirk on the boss's face.

"In the presence of Jake, you mean?" he says, trying to suppress the laugh threatening to choke him. She shoots her boss an angry look.

"I'm sorry, Cheryl, but if you two would ever stop pussyfooting around, you might just find each other." Deciding it might be best to leave before he says too much and realizing he's gotten the information he wants without having to ask for it, RJ departs, bidding her good day.

On his way to his office, he passes his buddy, "Morning, Jake," his greeting cheerful.

"What's so good about it?" comes the grunted response.

RJ shakes his head as he walks on, his smile broadening, thinking to himself that it seems as though Cheryl isn't the only one who had a bit too much to drink last night.

4

The weekend comes and goes. Monday rolls around right on schedule. RJ finds himself keeping a close eye on BJ McCallister. He isn't very convincing in his attempts to reason with himself that his intense scrutiny of her is because he doesn't trust she is pulling her weight. Learning more about this woman who evidently fooled everyone into believing she is tough enough for this job for the long haul becomes a mission. His mind wanders back to the tidbit of information concerning her cocktail serving job. Having been to Buddy's a few times he's seen some of the servers are very flirtatious, just shy of trampy. Most of the others? They're full-blown tramps.

By Wednesday, RJ's curiosity gets the best of him, and he surprises himself by strolling into Buddy's right about ten o'clock.

The lounge is jumping, the colorful lighting flashing and strobing, the music blasting, the dance floor crowded. Not his scene, but his compelling desire to learn more about this woman who so readily became accepted by his all-male crew urges him on.

RJ locates an empty seat at a table where some other men are seated. They nod their acceptance of his arrival. He sits scanning the room. A waitress wearing a name tag proclaiming her to be Josie appears and takes his order for a draft beer. "Excuse me. Is Ms. McCallister working this evening?" He inquires, having to shout.

"You mean BJ? Sure, honey, she's..." the server scans the room quickly, "...Umm, she's right over there. Want me to send her over to you?"

"No! No, thank you."

Josie squints at him, trying to decipher the look on his face in an attempt to decide if he's friend or foe, then heads off to grab his drink.

When the waitress returns with his beer, she follows his gaze to where BJ is serving a table of rough, rowdy men. A large, loud, grubby man reaches under the buttocks length cocktail uniform and grabs BJ's behind. She calmly reaches back, takes hold of the man's hand by the thumb, forcing it back in the direction of his forearm. Smiling sweetly, she leans down toward his ear. His expression, that of shock at the strength she is applying. Still smiling, she speaks most politely, very close to his face, "If you care to keep all your bones in one piece, keep them to yourself. Thank you." She releases his hand and walks away, back turned triumphantly on the laughs sounding from the man's friends.

From RJ's point of view, he can only see her take hold of the guy's hand, smile that sweet, inviting smile, lean close and speak to him. The look of shock and pain on the patron's face is obscured from RJ's view.

Peculiar gut tensing sensations grip RJ, as he takes the mug Josie hands him, downs it and hands it back. The sound of his heartbeat angrily pounding in his ears commands the need for something stronger. "I'll have another, along with a double shot of whiskey," he orders above the noise of the crowd.

The server smiles, mumbles something, and goes to pick up his drinks, but she orders two doubles. Being a cocktail waitress for as many years as she has been, she's come to recognize the signs of a man who feels the need to 'have a few'.

As before, when Josie returns, RJ's attention is riveted on BJ, oblivious to everything else.

He tries to figure out what is wrong with him. His thoughts ramble in his head, *"So what if she is being nice to a customer? That's her job. She has great legs! Long, slender. That uniform surely doesn't leave much to the imagination, so short and..."* Seeing her turn toward him, he continues with his musings, *"so much cleavage visible... Damn,"* he scoffs. *"What are you thinking? She's a woman. Something you don't want anything to do with!*

Besides, she's an employee. A butch dock hand at that. So how does she fit in so well with the crew during the day, then fit in here at night looking so damn hot? Stop it!" he scolds himself in a whisper, *"You're here to... to what exactly? Why did I come here?"*

"Did you say something to me, honey?" Josie sets the first double down on the table.

"No," he picks up the glass, tosses back the warm soothing amber liquid, and continues... "Talking to myself. I'll have..."

"Another Double," Josie finishes for him, smiling as she sets the second glass in front of him, removing the empty.

"What...? How'd...?" he sputters, looking at her still smiling face.

"Chalk it up to many years of experience in reading expressions," Josie informs as the man downs the second double in the same quick fashion.

"I know... Keep 'em coming." Josie takes the second empty and walks away, shaking her head, chuckling. "That man fell hard, and he doesn't even realize it," she muses to herself while making her rounds.

BJ is bustling. The crowd is wild tonight. Word of the new band spread fast, and they are drawing larger crowds every night. She is so busy she hasn't noticed the presence of her day boss, so when, an hour and a few doubles later, he reaches out and grabs her by the wrist as she walks past, she gasps in surprise. He pulls hard on her arm until she is forced to bend nearer to him. He hisses on whiskey-saturated breath, "Dyke by day, and tramp by night, eh?"

BJ jerks her hand away and, without a second's thought, uses it to firmly slap the contemptuous man's left cheek. The band has just ended a song, and the sharp cracking sound of flesh meeting flesh seems to ring out over the crowd noise. The look that crosses his features is a mixture of surprise and pain. Some of the people nearby chuckle and mumble curiosities. The band strikes up another number, and the crowd goes about its business, having a good time.

BJ's eyes are blue flames, throwing sparks at her boss. She lifts her chin, trying to fight the regret threatening to overcome her. She walks away defiantly.

Josie appears instantly in her stead, holding out his bill to him. "How'd you...?" He stops short. "Right, *years of experience*, got it." He pays what is due plus a generous tip and stands to leave.

"See you again soon." Josie nods, smiling knowingly- as they part, he to leave, and she to return to other patrons.

"You OK, Hun?" Josie asks BJ as she enters the back room, where BJ went to collect herself after the incident.

"Josie, I think I just made one of the biggest mistakes of my life!" BJ replies sorrowfully.

"Don't worry about it, Hun. He's had a few double Jacks along with a couple beers. Whatever he said or did, I'm sure he didn't mean it. Jealousy and whiskey can make a man say horrible things he'll regret in the morning," Josie consoles.

"You don't understand! He's my..." she stops mid-sentence. "What did you say?" she asks, not trusting her hearing.

"I said he'd regret it in the..."

"Before that. What, and Whiskey?"

"Jealousy, Hun. When he saw Big John put his hand on your der-riere, he started downing double shots and watching your every move," Josie chuckles.

"You don't understand," BJ states again, not understanding Josie's appraisal of the situation. "He's my Day Boss! The owner! I just kissed my job goodbye!" BJ is near tears. "I don't understand why I reacted that way. I've had things much worse said to me and walked away smil-ing. Why did I slap *him*? He didn't like me to begin with. Now...?" she lets the scenario hang.

"That's where you're wrong, sweetie," the older blonde waitress in-forms the younger, confused BJ, "Don't worry about it. I guarantee you'll still have your job. I've a feeling things are going to get better between you two."

"I seriously doubt that after..." BJ shakes her head tiredly.

"Trust me," Josie advises.

RJ, stunned by the slap, admonishes himself. *"Why did I drink so much? I've never been the drink 'til I'm drunk kind of guy."* His internal monologue rages while he calls a cab to take him home. He'll come collect his truck tomorrow. He must apologize to BJ for his uncharacteristic loss of control.

A short while later, BJ arrives at the motel room she and her daughters currently call home. She lets herself into a sight she can't believe. The motel owner's 17-year-old daughter, Kristen, does the caretaking of BJ's girls the nights she works at the lounge. Kristen is sitting on the floor between the two girls, where they sleep, lying side by side on the floor in their sleeping bags. A pan of cold water in front of her, and cold, wet wash clothes on both little foreheads.

Looking up at the searching expression on BJ's tired face, she explains, "They both came down with something. They have fevers of 102° and 103°. Mom called my old pediatrician, and he said it's most likely the viral flu that's going around. He told her to have us keep cold cloths on their foreheads and backs of their necks. He also said to put them in a tub of tepid water every hour and a half to two hours. Dad went and got the prescription the Dr. ordered. Here." Kristen stands and gets the bottle. "The instructions are on it for each of them."

BJ sighs, "Thank you, Kristen. Please tell your parents thank you for everything; tell them I'll repay them for the medicine."

BJ closes the door behind Kristen's departing figure. Dead tired from experiencing a tough night at work, she shoves that out of her mind as all thoughts now focus on her girls. Knowing a long night and day stretches ahead of her, she starts a pot of coffee to help ward off the sleepiness, then begins the routine of cold cloths, tepid baths, medicine, and comfort for her little angels.

Last night, after arriving home and discovering the poor health of her daughters, BJ left a message on Cheryl's office voicemail to call off work, while pushing aside any thoughts of what RJ Fenton will think is the real reason for her calling off. That is, if he hasn't already decided to fire her.

BJ now lets her thoughts wander a bit. *"If RJ does fire me, I can fight it because he doesn't have grounds for termination. But what good would that do? Even if I won and got my job back, he'd be watching like a hawk for any little slip-up to fire me again. No, I won't fight it. I can always find another job, and besides, I at least still have the job at Buddy's, so I won't be totally broke. Why does the thought of not working at Fenton bother me so much?"* She chalks it up to exhaustion, and the knowledge she's become friends with the crew, and Cheryl, and that she'd miss them. *"And RJ,"* a little voice whispers at the back of her mind. *"Why would I miss him?"* she asks herself. *"Because you think he's a hunk and you kinda like him. I do not! Now I know I'm exhausted! Or have gone crazy. Not only am I talking to myself, I'm answering!"*

BJ's stomach chooses this moment to speak loudly, letting it be known that it is already supper time, and that it would appreciate being fed.

First, she checks on her daughters, who are resting a little better. Their temperatures are down to 100° and 101°, bringing hope that they're on the mend.

BJ stands, stretches, and peeks in the box of food, deciding she is too exhausted to cook anything and nothing even sounds good. She opts to catch a catnap while the girls seem to be resting peacefully.

As she sits on the edge of the bed, poised to lie down and curl up, first Chumani, then Chenoa begin to cry. With a sigh of resignation that the catnap isn't to be, she goes to her girls and checks their temperatures to find they are back up. Two and a half hours later, they're finally calmed down. She now sits between them as Kristen had been the night before, performing the cold cloth routine while she hums soothingly. Her body begins swaying, the room swirls around her, the girls' flushed faces blur before her eyes; all sound recedes, she is spinning downward in a whirlpool of deepening darkness, until she is startled by a touch on her back, and a deep, unknown yet somehow familiar-sounding voice seeps past her ears and reaches her brain.

5

BJ jumps, turns, and finds herself looking into sparkling amber eyes. RJ's eyes. Initially, she is engulfed by panic, then, deciding she is only dreaming, she relaxes.

With a sudden, graceful, smooth movement, she finds herself being swooped up. Realizing this is too real to be a dream, her eyes fly open.

"What? What are you doing? Put me down this instant!" BJ demands, confused by the jumble of anger entwined with excitement at the sight of him, while also encountering the warm strength of his grasp, easily lifting her and carrying her across the room.

"As you wish." He drops BJ on the bed. "Thank you, Kristen. I'll take care of it from here," he smiles at the young girl, who winks at BJ, then leaves, closing the door behind her.

"You'll take care of what, from here?" BJ squawks. RJ shoots a quick look at the little ones sleeping, then at her, "Shh! You'll wake them."

"Don't you Shoosh me!" BJ grits at him. "Who do you think you are coming in here like this? You..."

Cutting off her tirade, "I am your relief."

"Relief, Hell!" is met with hushed demands.

"Shut up! Take off that uniform..."

"What???" She interrupts, her jaw dropping in disbelief.

"...and go take a hot shower, then go to bed," he continues, as though she hadn't said anything.

"What makes you think you can come here, where I live and tell me what to do?"

"I'm the boss, remember?" he smirks.

"At work? Yes! Here? No!" she shouts in a whisper.

"If you want to keep your job, I suggest you do as you've been told," he smiles wryly.

"You can't..."

"I can do anything I want to. I own the company. Remember?"

BJ hangs her head slightly, defeated. Hadn't she already argued this all out with herself?

"Hey." BJ glowers at the handsome man before her, looking somewhat like a sad puppy. "I'm..." he pauses, "I'm here for a couple of different reasons, which we'll discuss later. Right now, you look like you're at death's door. I..."

Seeing that he is struggling to hide something that resembles concern, BJ turns away quickly. She schools her features, then turns to face him, and snaps, "Fine", gets up, and goes into the bathroom.

She admits to herself that a nice hot shower does sound good. She pulls her hair up in a claw clip to keep it dry, then succumbs to the luxurious feel of the hot water.

Getting out, she realizes she neglected to bring in any clean clothes. After drying off and trying to determine what she should do, *"Damn the man,"* she curses; wraps a towel tightly around herself, steels her nerves, thinking, *"Well, he said the first day I met him that if I intend to do a man's job, I will be treated as such. A man wouldn't think twice about walking out wrapped in just a towel."* She heaves a heavy, steadying breath, then whispers to herself, *"Here goes nothing."* She opens the door and gasps as she is greeted by her light blue satin robe hanging from RJ's index finger over his shoulder, with his back turned to her.

"I thought you might need this," his voice sounds cool and calm to his own ears when actually his nerves are all a jangle. His mind wonders what sight stands so close behind him. *"Damn it, man, get hold of yourself,"* he silently scolds his wandering imagination.

BJ takes the robe carefully, wondering at the feelings vying for position in her thoughts. She should be thankful that he is being thoughtfully considerate by providing the garment, and turning his back, saving her the embarrassment of walking out in the skimpy hotel towel. Yet something akin to disappointment washes over her at not having had the satisfaction of shocking him with her indifference to his presence. But is she indifferent? BJ steps back into the bathroom, closing the door behind her, then emerges in silence a few moments later, donning the garment. She notes the girls are still sleeping. There is fresh ice in the pan of water on the floor near them, which RJ must have gotten while she showered. He is sitting at the small dinette table. BJ is gathering her clothes to change when there is a knock at the door. "Who...?"

"The pizza delivery, I imagine," RJ supplies the answer before she can complete the question.

"Pizza?"

RJ goes to the door, pays. He tips the young man generously. "Wasn't that a bit much for a tip?" BJ asks before realizing it's none of her business. Biting her lip, she begins, "Sorry. None of my..."

"I told them if they got it here in twenty minutes instead of thirty, a big tip would be waiting," he answers, cutting off her apology.

"Oh," is all she can say.

BJ slips into the bathroom and dresses. She emerges to find plates, flatware, and glasses on the table. RJ pulls ice out of the small fridge and puts some in the glasses, then fills them with the pop he ordered with the pizza. RJ goes to the pizza box he set on the counter of the tiny efficiency kitchen. From it, he places two slices on each plate, then carries a plate and a glass of pop over to BJ, where she stands by the dinette table. "Sit. Eat," he instructs. Then, after retrieving his plate and glass, seats himself next to her, saying, "May I?"

She nods. What could she say? He is already sitting. "Why did...?" she begins, only to have him once again cut her off and answer before she can ask the whole question.

"I figured if you haven't taken the time to change out of your uniform, chances are you haven't taken time to eat anything either." Realizing that sounds more concerned than he wants to, he adds a bit coolly, "We don't need you getting sick, too, and need to take off any more time."

"Oh." Again, the twinge of disappointment is brushed aside. They eat in silence, though it's not strained.

Relaxed from her shower and full of pizza and pop, BJ's eyes become heavy and begin to flutter closed. Seeing her struggle to keep them open, RJ swiftly begins to clear everything away.

"Thank you for..." Again, he cuts her off.

"Go to bed," he states flatly. The flash in her sleepy eyes hurries him to add, "I'll clean this up and keep an eye on the girls. When do they need their next dose of this?" He holds up their medicine bottle.

"At midnight, but..."

"Fine. If I turn the TV on quietly, will it bother any of you?"

"No, but..."

"Fine. Goodnight, BJ." He turns to the sink and begins washing their glasses and forks.

"Of all the nerve..." BJ muses. *"Who does he think he is?... The boss. Well,"* she thinks as she lays her head on the pillow, *"I am tired, and besides, I doubt I could make him leave anyway."* With that thought barely complete, she falls asleep.

"Mommy?... Mommy?" Chumani calls out.

"Shhh. It's all right," RJ soothes.

Shock spreads across the five-and-a-half-year-old's face. "You're not my Mommy," she demands, half scared, half angry.

RJ chuckles at the announcement. At least she is well enough and smart enough to know that.

"Don't laugh at me! Where's my mommy?" She sits up, staring at him, now fully angry.

In a hushed voice, he replies, "Well, you're your mother's daughter, all right. Your mommy is sleeping right over there on the bed." RJ points to BJ, all snuggled up. Relief overcomes the child's features. "You and your little sister have been very sick. Mommy's been taking care of you both, and she got really tired, so I told her to take a nap, and I will take care of you two." Looking at his watch, he continues, "Good thing you woke up. It's time to take your medicine. Picking up the bottle and medicine spoon, he says, "I bet you're Chumani."

"Did Mommy tell you that?"

"Nope. This bottle did."

"Bottles can't talk," she giggles.

"In a way, they can. Look here," he points at the label. "This writing says that Chumani gets to take one and a half teaspoons of this pretty pink stuff, and Chenoa only gets to take three-quarters of a teaspoon. So, the bigger girl gets more good stuff. Since you're bigger than her," he points to the still sleeping baby, "you must be Chumani. Right?"

You're pretty smart, but you still haven't told me who you are."

"You're right. I'm sorry. My name is RJ."

"Ohhh, you're Mommy's day boss, Mr. Fenton."

"You're pretty smart too," RJ states sincerely.

"You don't seem as bad as Mommy makes you sound, but I think she likes you even though she pretends not to."

From the mouths of babes, RJ thinks as a strange warmth enters his chest. *"I'm just getting tired,"* he tries to explain away the sensation.

"Mommy said if I ever met you, that I have to call you Mr. Fenton, and not any of the things she calls you 'cause I'm too little."

RJ wonders exactly what this little one's mommy calls him that she can't repeat.

"Mr. is for old people, but you're not old. Can I call you something else? Can I call you Uncle? I don't have any Uncles."

RJ thinks a moment, then decides it can't hurt, "Sure, sweetie, you can call me Uncle RJ, but tell me, what does Mommy call me?"

"I'm not 'posed to say those words," she adds, "She doesn't really mean them. She only says 'em when she's mad, then she says sorry for being bad."

"Oh, I see. That's good to know." RJ pours the medicine and gives it to her.

"What does RJ stand for?" Chumani asks.

"I don't tell people my real name," he responds.

"Mommy doesn't either."

"I tell you what," he begins in a conspiratorial whisper, "How about you and I make a secret deal? I'll tell you what RJ stands for if you'll tell me what BJ stands for, and we won't tell anyone else. It will be our special secret. Deal?"

Chumani thinks about that, "OK. You first."

"My name is Rainier Julian."

"Hmm. I like that. Mommy's name is Breezy Jo," she informs him proudly. "I like it, but Mommy says people treat her different if they know it."

"That's a very nice name. I think it's beautiful." However, he thinks, sometimes she is more like a gale force wind.

"You know what? We'd better get you back to sleep so you can get better faster. OK?"

"OK."

RJ settles the little angel back down on her makeshift bed on the floor.

"Are you going to stay all night, Uncle RJ?"

"Yes, Honey. You get some sleep now," RJ whispers.

"Cool. Good night, Uncle RJ. See you in the morning."

RJ gives the honest little girl a kiss on the forehead.

"Good night, sweetheart."

Strange is the sting of tears in his eyes. *"I'm getting sleepy, and my eyes are tired,"* he reasons. A few minutes later, baby Chenoa wakes crying. RJ picks her up, cuddles her, gives her a dose of medicine, changes her diaper, then stands rocking and humming softly until she falls back to sleep.

Seeing them all settled makes RJ even more drowsy. He is uncomfortable from being dressed in the same clothes all day in the summer heat they've been experiencing, so he decides to take a quick shower. RJ emerges from the bathroom wearing only his boxer briefs. After checking on the girls again, he sits watching TV for a couple hours, keeping tabs on them until finally the empty half of the king-sized bed calls so invitingly, he can no longer resist stretching out. *"Only for a few minutes,"* he assures himself, *"then I'll get up and sleep in the chair."*

BJ is having the most wonderful dream of lying in a bed, snuggling up against a hard, muscular chest covered with warm, smooth skin. So sumptuous is the sensation, she nuzzles deeper into the covers, not wanting to emerge from this luxurious dream. Trying to picture the face that should go with the body that her mind conjures up, reveals shiny chestnut hair, thick and wavy, atop a head with molded bronze features. A lazy smile plays across the face, making the amber eyes dance invitingly. Something moves against her, jolting her back toward reality. Caught somewhere between dreamland and real world, her mind races with possibilities.

"Mmm," comes a low moan close to her ear. There is no way that sound is coming from either of her daughters. The memory of last night comes flooding back.

"Mmm." The sound comes again, and the warmth of the body clinging to her moves closer, if that is even possible.

BJ can't decide if she is angry and should scream the man awake and ask how he dared invite himself into her bed, or if she is enjoying the situation so much that she should remain still, and continue enjoying the delicious feeling, while it lasts. *"Pretend you're still asleep,"* she tells herself. *"Then, after he wakes up, you can be angry."*

6

Her body stiffens against him in surprise at the situation she's found herself in, then relaxes with the obvious decision to let it ride temporarily, of course, for he is sure, once she is 'awake', she'll be all spitfire again. RJ smiles, wondering why he isn't upset for allowing himself to get in this predicament. The fact that he is comfortably enjoying the feel of this woman so close is even more disturbing, but he decides he'll analyze his actions later. Right now, all he wants is to hold on to this comfort.

"Ma-ma, Ma-ma," the sweet little voice cuts through the cocoon in which BJ is enveloped. In haste, BJ gets up, hating the hollow feeling at having to leave those strong arms.

"Mama's right here, sweetie." She picks up her baby. Remembering she should be angry, she stands holding and comforting Chenoa, as she turns toward the man on her bed, "What do you think you're doing in my bed?" she spits out through gritted teeth.

Rising to the challenge, RJ slides off the bed and pulls on his pants, saying, "I got tired, so I took a shower, and lay down on the bed to relax my back for a moment. I honestly intended to get back up and sleep in the chair." Turning to face her now that he is safely covered and securely contained, he continues. "I guess I was more tired than I thought. I apologize. I should never have sat..." he scans at the rumpled bedding, "there, in the first place."

BJ isn't sure what it is in his tone of voice. He sounds as upset as she is trying to pretend to be, and should be, "Apology accepted" is all she can say past the lump in her throat brought on by her glimpse of his muscled shoulders and back atop boxer-brief–clad tight buttocks. She swallows hard and turns her eyes away.

"They both had their midnight dose of medicine. Their temperatures seem to be down. I think their fevers finally broke." His tone full of tender concern. Not at all like what she thought of this man. At least not what she wants to think. "I suppose I should be going now that you've gotten a good night's sleep and the girls appear to be on the mend." He pauses, looking at BJ from under his lashes, then picks up his shirt. Looking at it with deep interest, he says in a low voice, "About the other night at the lounge. I... um... well, I had a few too many. I rarely drink, let alone...I didn't mean what I said. I... I don't actually think that of you. I...I'm not good at apologies, yet this is my second one to you already this morning," he almost laughs.

Seeing this man, normally so self-assured and confident, now so ill at ease, she responds, "Apology accepted... again." She smiles. "I owe you an apology. I don't usually react that way. It was a crazy crowd that night, and... you caught me off guard... and..." She tries to reason away her reaction, knowing it had nothing to do with anything or anyone other than him. "I apologize."

"No need. I deserved that, and more. I must admit," he says, chuckling, "You do seem to have more strength than your size belies. I was skeptical when I heard about the arm wrestling, but after that slap? I'm inclined to think it just might be possible," he finishes as a broad smile stretches across his face.

"Yeah, you'd rather believe I've won their approval in some *other* way!" Her temper flares.

"Hey, I didn't say that. Calm down, I apologized."

BJ stands looking at him, gritting her teeth, when she realizes she is staring at his muscular bare chest. Her eyes move slowly up to his face, where his features dance with amusement, which swiftly vanishes. They both stand silent.

"Mommy?" Chumani's small voice breaks the silence. "Morning, Uncle RJ," Chumani now bubbles at the sight of the friendly man from the night before.

BJ, totally taken by surprise by her daughter's greeting, spins around; "What did you say?" her tone shrill.

Smiling first at the man, Chumani then sheepishly glances at her mother, lifts her head proudly, and replies, "I said, morning, Uncle RJ."

Angry eyes are turned on RJ. She doesn't want her daughters getting attached to this man, or any man for that matter.

RJ nearly laughs at BJ's expression, but sobers and fills her in, "When she woke up last night to take her medicine, she asked if she could call me that. I told her it's OK with me."

"Well, it's not OK with me!" BJ snaps, turns to Chumani, trying to stay calm, and explains, "*Mr. Fenton* is Mommy's boss, not my brother. You're to call him Mr. Fenton. Understood?"

"But that's yucky. 'Sides, I called Daddy's friends Uncle. Why can't I call your friend Uncle?" Chumani questions.

"We're not talking about Daddy or his friends. Besides, Mr. Fenton is not my friend," her mommy states resolutely.

"If he's not your friend, why did you let him sleep with you?"

BJ stares at Chumani, not knowing how to answer. She and her husband had explained that they were special friends, and they loved each other, so they liked to snuggle to show that love to one another. How, then, can she explain sleeping with a man whom she is neither friends with nor loves?

RJ, chuckling, says, "Explain that one, Mom. Why did you?"

She tries to satisfy her daughter's curiosity, "Mommy was very tired last night, and I fell asleep. I guess Mr. Fenton got sleepy, too. There is only one bed in the room, and we have no more blankets to use to sleep on the floor. So, he got in the other side of the bed and slept. We didn't sleep together; we only shared the bed," BJ tries to explain.

Chenoa makes it clear with a squeal that she wants breakfast, and BJ takes the opportunity to change the subject. "OK, sweetie. Time to eat. Do pancakes sound good to you, Chumani?"

"Sure! Do they sound good to you, Uncle RJ?"

RJ can't help himself. He bursts out laughing. Chumani joins in, and Chenoa squeals with joy. Seeing the anger flash across BJ's features, he says, still laughing, "I'm sorry."

"I don't see what's so funny!" BJ responds stiffly.

"It's... well, even after your explanation..." he quells his laughter, "Sorry."

BJ stares at her daughter. "Sorry, Mommy. Still don't know why I can't call him Uncle." Turning to face RJ, "You're staying for breakfast, aren't you, Mr. Fenton?" Chumani pleads.

"I better be going," he says to the child.

Chumani turns pleading eyes on her mother, "Please, Mommy?"

BJ sighs, smiles at her daughter, then sets Chenoa down, who proceeds to crawl to RJ, arms up stretched, saying, "Uppie, uppie."

"She wants you to pick her up, Unc...Mr. Fenton." Chumani translates for her sister.

RJ obliges.

"Pancakes for four, it is," BJ proclaims, half defeated, half amused and totally amazed at how naturally the strong man handles the small child in his arms and how fast her daughters have taken to him. A look of pleasure creases his masculine features. BJ's heart softens toward this man. *'He'll make a good father...Stop it!'* she admonishes herself. She goes about preparing breakfast as her mind prattles on. *"This is the man who doesn't believe you won the arm-wrestling contest, the one who made it clear you were to have no special privileges, and made it quite clear the other night exactly what he thinks of you!... Why, then, did he come here last night, feed you, stay up with your sick girls and sleep in your bed without trying anything? He must have a reason, but what?'*

RJ is sitting playing on the floor with the two little girls, who, he is pleased to see, seem to be feeling much better, when BJ announces, "Pancakes are ready."

RJ, with Chumani's help, already strapped Chenoa's booster seat to one of the dinette chairs. Hearing the food is ready, he scoops up Chenoa, places her in the seat, then buckles her in, and connects the tray. BJ places two silver dollar-sized pancakes on her baby plate and sets it on her tray. Chumani climbs into the other chair at the table where mommy places a plate for her daughter, which she proceeds to devour like a hungry lumberjack.

"She must be feeling better," she says as she hands a plate stacked with hotcakes to RJ, saying apologetically, "I'm sorry there isn't another chair for you to sit on."

"No problem. Motel rooms aren't suited for much furniture," he states the obvious. They both settle on the foot of the bed and fall silent as they all consume the hotcakes.

After a few minutes, BJ again apologizes, "Sorry, there isn't much else to go with these. Would you like a glass of milk?"

"This is fine. These are good, and yes, I would, but I'll get it," he responds as he rises. "Would you like some also?"

"Yes, please. Thank you."

Minutes later, everyone is finished eating, and BJ begins cleaning up the dishes. RJ sits on the floor watching cartoons with the girls. He gets up and walks over to where BJ stands at the little kitchenette sink, washing dishes.

"Now I really need to head out. Delicious breakfast. Thanks," he states.

"Thank you for the relief shift last night. I have to admit I was pretty done in. I'd been up 39 hours without sleep." She pauses, her hands still, as she peers at her boss's reflection in the mirror before them. "Mr. Fenton, why did you come here last night?" All of a sudden, she wonders if he came to tell her not to bother coming back to work.

Well, if that is why, he'll have a fight on his hands. Her tumultuous thoughts and emotions begin to rear their ugly heads once again.

Looking suddenly sheepish and a bit guilty, RJ replies, "Cheryl told me you called in, saying your kids were sick, and you wouldn't be in to work. I um... well, I figured you just didn't want to face me, and made up that excuse."

"GREAT!" BJ blurts, irritated, "Now you think I'm a liar too!"

"Correction... I *thought* you were. I wasn't in the right frame of mind."

She opens her mouth to spout off again.

RJ puts up a hand to halt her tirade. "Please let me finish," he pleads.

BJ's aggravation is complete: the man is irritating and vexing. She doesn't want to hear any more. Chenoa comes crawling toward her, crying at that moment, causing a welcome interruption. BJ picks up her baby girl. "If you'll excuse me, Mr. Fenton, I need to change her. Now that the girls are recovering, I'll be in to work after lunch. I wouldn't want you to think I'm using them as an excuse for being lazy *or* for not being able to face *you.*" She stomps over to the bed and begins the diaper-changing process.

"You won't be coming in to work this afternoon..." RJ begins.

"If you think for one second," BJ thunders at the 'Boss man' while she continues her motherly duty, "that you can fire me for slapping you, you've got another think coming! That comment you made could be termed 'sexual harassment', bud. I'll fight you tooth and nail. I'm a good worker, and you have no grounds to fire me, so you'd better be prepared to fight a losing battle, Mr. Fenton!" BJ's tirade comes to an end as she sets Chenoa on the floor and turns to come face to face with the amused expression on RJ's face. "What's so funny?" she demands.

Glancing down at Chumani, who is watching the grown-ups curiously, RJ asks her, "Is she always this grouchy?"

The little girl giggles. "You should see her when she's *really* mad."

"You mean she gets worse?" she nods. "Oh boy. I better be careful not to make her *really* angry, then, huh?" He speaks to the girl in a silly tone that makes her giggle, and makes her mother even more irritated.

He turns his attention back to BJ. "What I mean is, you should spend the rest of the day and weekend with your daughters, and return to work on Monday. The fact that their fevers have broken doesn't mean they're well, and sick children... need their Mommies..." he trails off. A strange, distant look comes over his features. One of pain and remembrance, then it is gone as swiftly as it appeared. RJ gives himself a mental shake. "Monday. Got it?" he states sternly, then turns to Chumani. His tone softens when he speaks to the girls, "You two rest, and get all better, OK?"

"Will you come visit us again, Unc..." Chumani inhales deeply and sighs, then continues, "...Mr. Fenton?"

"Mr. Fenton is an extremely busy man with a business to run and employees to check up on," BJ's words hold a bitter note.

"I'll be glad to stop by and visit you as often as I can. You two are sweet little girls. It will be my pleasure to come again." He shoots BJ a challenging look as he bends to kiss the little ones on their foreheads and says goodbye. Smiling, he lets himself out, leaving BJ standing there thinking, *"That man is too much!... Too much what?"* the little voice in her head questions. She'd always been told by her father that 'too' is a qualifying word. One must be able to fill in the blank, so to speak. Well, in this case, the answer is *"Too much to even want to try to deal with."*

7

"Good morning, little buddy," RJ greets his son when he climbs into bed with him early Saturday.

"Morning, Daddy." Riyon snuggles up with his father. After a few minutes, "Are you working today?"

"Nope! Are you?"

"You're silly, Daddy. I don't have a job."

"Good, because I'm hoping you and I can spend the whole weekend together."

"For real?" his son beams. "What are we going to do?"

"What would *you* like to do?"

"I want to show you how good I can swim and dive now. Misho is teaching me," Riyon says, beaming with pride.

RJ is happy for his son and is looking forward to seeing his progress, but a twinge of sadness washes over him as the thought strikes him that he should be the one teaching his child these things, not that he minds having him taught by his Misho, but he realizes he minds not being home enough to do it. In that moment, he makes a pact with himself that after the already scheduled four-week business trip, he plans to find a way to do less traveling and shorter trips, and make sure that he is home on weekends to be with his son, who is starting kindergarten in a few weeks at the private school RJ attended. What good is it to be the owner of a company if you can't set your schedule to accommodate the most important part of one's life? Family.

"That sounds great. Is there anything else you'd like to do or somewhere you'd like to go?"

Thinking a moment, he says, "As long as I get to be with you, it doesn't matter what we do."

Wow, he realizes the decision he just made moments ago is of profound importance. "OK, Buster. We'll think of something fun to do. But right now..." RJ grabs his son and begins tickling him.

Riyon squirms and squeals with delight, trying halfheartedly to escape while attempting to tickle his daddy too.

"Hey, who's making all the ruckus in here?" Emily asks out teasingly over the din of laughter.

"Help, Mémère, the tickle monster is getting me!" he pleads with his grandmother using the French title of her native language.

"Oh no! I'll save you!" Emily responds as she begins tickling her son, Rainier.

"Help, Pops," RJ calls out to his stepfather amidst all the laughing. Jason enters the room to check out the commotion. "Don't just stand there. It's two against one."

There's a moment of hesitation, not sure what to make of RJ's attempt to draw him into the family frolicking. Emily's son was already an adult when Jason married her. The deep connection and unending love this young man has for his deceased father remains, but that doesn't mean he hasn't accepted Jason as his stepfather, only that they haven't shared much of an interactive familial connection. This invitation to join in on the family playfulness is a bit out of character, but a welcome event.

With that, Jason goes to his stepson's aid, tickling his wife and grandson. Five minutes or so later, they all collapse, exhausted and gasping for air.

"OK, you hooligans, breakfast is waiting. Time to eat," Emily announces.

After helping clean up the kitchen breakfast mess, RJ and Riyon head out to the backyard to lounge poolside while they allow their morning meal to settle. They play catch with a beach ball, and father shows son how to throw a Frisbee. After sufficient time passes, RJ asks, "You still going to show me your swimming and diving skills?"

"Yeah, watch this." Riyon walks to the end of the diving platform, dives in, and swims to the shallow end of the pool.

"Wow! Riyon. That is amazing!"

The duo spends the rest of the day having a wonderful time hanging together, swimming, playing all sorts of games, and helping Emily prepare a fabulous dinner.

That evening, after reading a bedtime story and tucking his exhausted son into bed, he is lounging by the pool in the glow of the ambient lighting and the afterglow of a fantastic day, when Emily and Jason join him. They sit in silence for a long while, then, in a hushed tone, trying not to break the mood, RJ states, "This may be the most fun-filled day I can recall in... forever."

"Agreed," Jason and Emily say in near unison.

"Son?" RJ's mère begins, and continues when his eyes raise to her in response. "I don't mean to sound critical in any way, but may I ask what came over you today? It's not that you're at all a bad Father. You work hard to provide for your son, and spend as much time as you can with him, but today you seemed so much more joyful and relaxed, yet at the same time, I felt an unexplainable tension in you."

RJ sits thinking about the day, and what is bringing about this newfound need to spend time with his son, and yes, his desire to be more accepting of Jason as part of the family, as his stepfather. He doesn't want to share all the details of the past few days, but believes his Mère and Jason deserve some explanation.

"I met a single mother of two, living on their own in extremely difficult circumstances. Struggling, working two jobs to provide for her children, and still taking care of them no matter what. Even forgoing a couple of days of pay and risking losing her job, her children still came first. It made me realize how genuinely blessed I am to have the two of you to help me raise my son. How lucky I am not to ever have to worry about not having an income, let alone where my next dime will come from. Being my own boss, I have what most people would give anything to have: the ability to set my own hours and never worry about being able to afford to raise my child. I want to thank the two of you from the depths of my soul for being here for me and for Riyon. I couldn't have done it without *both* of you," his focus directed at Jason. "I don't know how people have the strength and fortitude to do it all alone, like that girl is." RJ closes his eyes and pinches the bridge of his nose to ward off the tears.

Emily can hear tears clogging her son's throat. Eyeing Jason, she communicates with a shake of her head, not to say anything about who this woman most likely is.

"Thank you for your gratitude, and you're welcome. We do what we do because we love you and Riyon. This woman you speak of does what she needs to do because she evidently loves her children, too. Don't worry, you have just as much strength, fortitude and stubbornness in you as she must have. If you had to do it on your own, you would. You've already proven that with all the adversity you've overcome in your life."

"Your mother's right. We all have our share of trials in life, just different ones. Don't judge yourself lacking. You're a strong man, a great father to your son, and a great son to your mother... and to me. I'm proud to call you son. Your father would be proud of you, also.

RJ looks at the pair of parents before him, tears welling in his eyes. "I love you both," he then gets to his feet. "I'm pretty wiped. I think I'll call it an early night so I can be rested up for another long day tomorrow. I'm taking Riyon go-cart racing, and whatever else we can come up with to do. You're both welcome to join us for a fun-filled day of adventures."

Emily and Jason rise too, "I think I'll pass on the go-cart racing, dear, keep us informed as the day progresses, what other activities you come up with, we may join you later."

RJ hugs his mother, then turns to Jason and, foregoing the usual handshake, gives his stepfather a hug as well. "Good night."

"Goodnight, son," Emily and Jason again, speak in unison.

After RJ is out of earshot, Jason states, "Interesting. It appears this BJ McCallister Millie talks about, somehow, made quite an impression on our son."

"Yes, indeed. She seems to have made quite an impression on a few people, from what Millie said, such as her winning over the crew so easily. Brady told her there seemed to be some 'sparks' flying on the dock the day RJ discovered a female working his docks and met her. He said he is pretty sure they weren't all sparks of anger either."

"Really? I think I want to meet this girl. She may be exactly what our son needs to spice up his life a bit, and 'bring him back from the dead'."

"If today is any indication, I think maybe she's already begun reviving him."

Emily stands looking around, taking a quick mental inventory of the blessings that surround them. Her gaze stops cold on the small un-used pool house standing there before her in their backyard, and in that moment, a thought strikes, and a plan begins to hatch.

"Jason, Dear,"

"Yes."

"I have an idea. One that could serve multiple purposes."

"When that look appears in your eyes and that tone in your voice, I'm never quite sure if your idea is one I should jump for joy over or run for the hills from," Jason chuckles, and Emily joins in.

"You stated you'd like the chance to meet this girl. What I'm think-ing will hopefully accomplish that, and a whole lot more."

"OK. I'm listening," Jason replies cautiously.

"When is the last time we used the pool house for anything other than the storage of junk?"

"So long ago, I can't remember that far back. Why?"

Emily turns sharply to face her husband, her smile beaming brightly. "From what Millie said of this young woman, she loves her daughters dearly and would love to provide them with a good life in a stable home, not have to continue living from suitcases in a motel. She doesn't sound like someone who would take kindly to the offer of charity, but if it doesn't seem like charity..." She raises and wiggles her eyebrows at her husband, then rivets her attention on the pool house again.

"What are you proposing?"

"We can clean out, remodel and redecorate the pool house and offer to 'rent' it to her and the girls for about the same or less than she's paying at the motel. Of course, I'll deposit the rent she pays into a savings account for her, and the girls that she won't know about for some years. That way she won't feel like she is taking charity, she and her lovely daughters will have a wonderful place to live, Millie can still babysit, Riyon will have full-time playmates, the house will finally become properly useful, and..." Emily pauses.

"And...?" Jason prods.

"And we can watch the sparks fly, and possibly fireworks ignite, between this BJ and our son. Of course, he can't know about this until after we have her living here. He would find a way to put a kibosh on the whole plan."

"Scheme, you mean?"

"Semantics, my dear."

"Though I may not completely approve of your matchmaking attempt, I do approve of your charitable idea for the girls. When do you propose to put his plan into action?"

"Immediately. Rainier will be leaving Monday morning to begin a cross-country trip visiting existing clients and schmoozing up a few prospective ones. He'll be starting on the East Coast and making his way back with stops in several cities. He'll be gone the whole month. The faster we start, the better chance we have of getting the darling trio in residence right here before his return," she explains, ending with a bright smile.

"I sure hope you know what you're doing. How do you plan to get the ball rolling on this?"

"By enlisting Millie's help, of course, and yours." Emily takes hold of her husband's arm, looking up at him with loving, smiling eyes. "You will help, won't you, Dear?" The two are still as in love to date, as twenty years ago when they married.

"I always do, Dear," he answers, hugging her. They link arms and go into the house. Emily heads straight for her phone.

"Millie? I've come up with a wonderful idea..."

BJ has been bringing the girls to Mrs. O'Malley's every morning since she started work at Fenton Warehouse, well, except the two days they'd been sick. Of course, she sent a text during the wee hours of the first morning to let Millie know and told her she would let her know when they'd be there next.

Mrs. O'Malley is wonderful, teaching Chumani the alphabet, how to count and how to print her name. BJ finds it kind of cute when she catches a bit of an Irish brogue in the sound of her daughter's young voice on occasion.

"BJ?" Millie speaks with a thoughtful tone to her Irish brogue.

"Yes, Mrs. O'Malley?"

"I've a lady friend, ya know, the one I go visit with the garls sumtimes. She's helpin' ta raise her gransun, remember? Righ', yes, well we ware talkin' an' she's a two-bedroom guest house at her place, and she's been thinkin' 'bout rentin' it out, but she's been apprehensive 'bout gettin' bad tenants. Well, we discussed the matter, and she'd like to rent it to you and the garls."

"For real?" BJ is first overjoyed, then deflated, "Oh, but a two-bedroom is more than I can afford. That's very nice, but..."

"Nonsense. She does'n need the muney, so she's willing to let you have it for what e'er you can comfortably afford. Plus, there's one little catch."

BJ knew it sounded too good to be true without some kind of catch. "What's the catch?" she inquires skeptically.

"Only that once in a while you, and yar garls join her, the mister and their gransun fer dinner."

She waits, expecting Mrs. O'Malley to go on. When she doesn't, "That's it? That's the condition?" she questions disbelievingly.

"Yes, ya see lass, they're all quite smitten with yar wee lasses."

"Well, I guess that wouldn't be too difficult. I would appreciate it if you can set up a meeting with her for me to take a look at the place and discuss it further."

"Well, Miss, sure I was ya'd be sayin that, so I hope ya don'a mind I already did that." The older lady's eyes twinkle in her smile. "I've her address right here fer ya." She hands BJ a piece of paper. "I figure I can take the garls fer a wee visit with Master Riyon this afternoon, and ya can come straight there after work ta have a look-see, and pick up yar babes."

BJ smiles and shakes her head, thinking how very much a blessing this woman is already. "How thoughtful of you, Millie. I'll call you when I'm on my way there to be sure plans haven't changed."

"Don'a worry. We'll be there spectin ya."

"Thank you, Millie...for everything." BJ hugs the shorter, sturdily built woman, then hugs and kisses both girls goodbye, and heads to work.

BJ arrives at the warehouse to find the first trailer parked in the dock, ready for unloading. Greetings are exchanged as the crew arrives, clocks in, and sets about their daily routine. Brady appears on the dock an hour later. He is talking to Jake and Butch. As BJ passes by toting a loaded pallet jack, she overhears Brady saying, "Boss left this morning. Figure he'll be gone 3 maybe 4 weeks or more. He's got quite a few prospects he's trying to seduce. We all know how he is when it comes to his conquests."

"Like a hungry dog with a meaty bone. No stopping him 'til he's gotten what he wants."

Disturbed at overhearing that, BJ quickens her pace and moves with haste out of earshot of the conversation. "*Why?*" her inner voice queries. BJ thinks about that as she begins moving boxes from the pallet to the appropriate client shelves to fill orders. *"Plain and simple, because it is wrong to eavesdrop."* She tells herself it is nothing to do with the twinge of...of what? *Hurt? Jealousy? No, Disgust! She tries to convince herself. It is disgusting that RJ is off traveling with the intention of 'seducing various prospects'! Disgust that these men stand there casually discussing the boss's escapades.* BJ goes about her day, doing her best not to think about the overheard conversation. *"Men!"*

8

R J sits in the boarding area of the airport, smartphone in hand, looking over his calendar of appointments for the next few weeks. His itinerary is well packed with a variety of appointments, from visiting current clients to assure them of his company's continued appreciation of their business, follow-up appointments to sign contracts for newly acquired accounts ready to utilize his company's services, to wooing new prospects with the intention of bringing them on board as new Fenton Warehouse accounts.

RJ loves all aspects of his business. He literally grew up in the business. When he was a young boy, he went to work with his father most every day he wasn't in school, vacation days, even weekends. He was very close to his father and loved spending time with him every chance he got. He even began traveling with his father on business trips when he was 15. His father would schedule the trips during school breaks so RJ could go along and learn the account relationship-building side of the business. He not only went on the trips with his father, but he also attended the meetings with all current and prospective accounts at the time. Most CEOs, COOs, etc. had been fine with the teenager's attendance and involvement. Some, however, had been much less than fine. There were a couple in particular that found his presence unconventional and somewhat inappropriate. His father explained that they better become accustomed to the idea of seeing and working with his son, as he wanted his son to be fully capable of handling all aspects of the business when the time came for him to take over the day-to-day operations. No one could ever have anticipated how very soon that day was to arrive. A scant three years later, his father passed away unexpectedly, leaving RJ to take over at a mere 18 years and 7 months of age. His grandfather, the first RJ Fenton, came back on board to assist RJ the first year to make the transition smoother, mainly for those who already had issues with RJ's youth. However, it didn't take long for all to realize that RJ Fenton III was more than capable of handling himself and the business superbly. His father taught him well. RJ often wondered at how the Universe seemed to have known the timing all along and seen to it that he was well prepared to step right in with nary a hitch.

"Flight 367 to Richmond, Virginia International, now boarding at gate 4B. Passengers in First Class and Business Class will board at this time..." a voice announces over the intercom, bringing RJ's attention back to the present. He stows his phone in its belt clip, collects his carry-on, which contains his laptop, a complete change of clothing, rechargeable shaver, and toothbrush. He learned at an early age that luggage often doesn't arrive at your destination when you do. This being his boarding group, he gets in line, boarding pass in hand.

The petite business suit-clad woman in front of him steps back, allowing someone to cross through the line, and bumps into RJ. "Oh my. I'm sorry," she says, apologizing. Her eyes take in the masculine specimen she comes into contact with.

"It's all good," he replies calmly.

The woman gives him a second, more blatant head-to-toe once-over, declaring, "Indeed, it is all good." Obviously flirtatious.

RJ does a rapid inventory of the woman before him. Petite, well-dressed, silky blonde hair, sparkling brown eyes, pearly whites gleaming from behind rich red full lips. The type of woman he generally found himself attracted to. He meets her eyes and notes her appreciation of his visual appraisal. Normally, he would flirt back, maybe even ask where she is heading, since they are boarding the same plane, there is a chance they have a mutual destination, which leaves open the possibility of getting together for a drink. Though in this moment, RJ finds himself comparing this woman to one nearly completely opposite. A woman at least 4 or 5 inches taller, svelte yet sinewy, with shoulder-length, rich brown hair kept controlled with a baseball cap and ponytail. With eyes that changed like a mood ring. He's seen them silver blue with nervous apprehension the day they met, fathomless, placid pools of cobalt the night he went to the motel, and found her beyond the depths of exhaustion, and flame blue the next morning when she was angry.

"Thanks," is his simple reply, then returns his attention to the now moving line, but not before noting the look of disappointment cross the woman's face.

Due to his height, RJ always tries to book a seat in the front row of business class, where there is a bit more room for his legs to stretch out. Once seated, he pulls out and sets up his laptop to begin preparing some documents he'll need for his first meeting tomorrow morning. "Sir, you'll have to stow your computer for takeoff," a nearby flight attendant informs him. When he looks up, "Oh, hello again. Mr. Fenton, isn't it?"

"Yes, ma'am."

"I didn't realize it was you. You already know that, and I trust you'll have it all squared away in time." She smiles cheerfully. "Carry on, Sir, carry on," she ends.

RJ logged so many miles over the past 23 years; he's come to know more than a few flight attendants. Heck, in his younger days, he even dated a few.

Shortly after takeoff, the attendants begin the beverage service. The one who remembered his name pauses at his seat, "Hmm. Let me see if I remember correctly... Jack and Coke, extra ice, hold the Jack, right?" she asks with a touch of pride for her recall.

Reading her name tag, he responds, "You are correct. Very good, Arlene."

Arlene's smile broadens as she pours his Coke. After she moves ahead a row, RJ spots the woman seated across the aisle, noting it is the one from line earlier.

"Seriously? Hold the Jack?" she asks, sounding astonished.

He holds up his little plastic cup in a salute and takes a swig.

"I pegged you as the hold-the-Coke kind of man, for sure," she drawls with a slight southern accent which he didn't hear in their earlier conversation.

"Guess you pegged me wrong," he responds before returning his attention to his laptop, effectively ignoring any further attempts of the woman to strike up a friendly conversation.

RJ wonders what is up with him today? Her features are striking; she appears to be a businesswoman, so she most likely possesses some level of intelligence, and she seems interested in him. What is wrong with him that he isn't even interested in a little harmless flirtatious banter? It doesn't take long for the little voice in his head to whisper... *"Your mind is a bit breezy... Breezy Jo, that is." But why is that particular female occupying any part of my thoughts?* His hands poised over the keyboard, preparing to continue his work, he draws a deep breath, closes his eyes to try to regain his business train of thought. Instead, images of one BJ McCallister, aka: Breezy Jo, fill his mind. BJ, the tough dock hand, the hot sexy cocktail server, the fiercely defensive spitfire, the exhausted ardently attentive mother, and BJ, the sleeping beauty. The next thought brings a smile to his mind, he's seen her first thing in the morning, fresh from bed after a good night's sleep, make-up free, tousled hair...but what would she look like after a long night of lovemaking? His loins begin to tighten. Shaking himself conscious, away from his wandering thoughts, he returns his concentration to his laptop.

Over the years, RJ found that his father and grandfather had been right about the concept of mixing a little pleasure with business. It seems to build stronger, longer-lasting relationships that transcend business-only ventures. In his grandfather's era, when clientele was mainly local, he began with formal cocktail parties, then branched out to backyard barbecues, a tradition his father continued, with business still being mostly local. However, RJ took the expanded nationwide, which makes that option less possible. So instead, he schedules other activities with his clients, local to them, such as tennis, racquetball, and basketball. From horseback riding and snow skiing to beach volleyball and jet skiing. One client even enjoys going canoeing. Today, the activity is to be a friendly tennis match.

"Hey, RJ. How are you doing, my man?" Conrad Industries, based in Richmond, Virginia, is one of Fenton's longest-standing clients on the East Coast. Drew Conrad is second-generation COO; Chief Owner Operator, as he calls himself. He is RJ's age, and they get along well.

"Doing fine, as always. How about yourself?"

"I'm doing great. I'm ready to whip your butt on the court," Drew announces affably.

"We'll see about that. Our usual wager? Loser buys lunch?"

"Sure."

RJ finds his thoughts wandering during the best-of-three match against his longtime associate and friend. He misses shots he'd normally score. He catches himself wondering if one BJ McCallister plays tennis, and how she'd look dressed in a tennis skirt exposing her long legs....

"Dude! Where are you?" his opponent hollers across the court.

"What? I'm right here," RJ replies.

"Yes, physically maybe, but your mind must be somewhere else since I just served, and you stood there like a lump on a log, not even flinching as the ball sailed right past you. That is match point. You lost. Where are we going for lunch, Space Cadet?" Drew approaches.

"Sorry. I guess I did space out for a minute there. Anywhere you'd like to eat."

"Anywhere? Now you legitimately have me concerned. Seriously, are you OK, my friend?"

"Yeah, it's nothing. Just someone on my mind. I'll be fine."

"Someone?"

"No... Something."

"You said some *one*."

"Sorry, I misspoke."

He lets it drop for the moment. "I'm going to hit the shower. How about we eat at La Bière Château?"

"Sounds good. I could use a beer. We'll meet there in about half an hour and take care of business."

"That will take all of about 15 minutes." They both chuckle.

"That will give us more time for the business of drinking," Drew concludes.

RJ arrives at La Bière Château a few minutes before his client, finds a table, and orders the first round of beers.

When Drew arrives and sits down, the waitress delivers their froth-topped mugs. "Wow, what service. Thank you. You read my mind, Darlin'," he speaks flirtatiously with the server.

"Not me, Sugar. It was your boyfriend here who knows you so well; he ordered for you," she shoots back teasingly. "Best be thanking him," she instructs as she saunters off, Drew's eyes glued to her derriere.

The brief exchange brings memories rushing back of a night thousands of miles from here, not so long ago.

"Earth to RJ. Hel-lo are you there?"

RJ gives himself a mental shake, picks up his beer, and chugs down the whole thing.

"Start talking. What gives?"

Choosing to ignore the obvious attempt of his friend to figure out where his mind keeps wandering, he states. "It's time for your five-year contract renewal."

"Yeah, no! That's not what I'm talking about, and you know it. What is up with you today? You keep getting lost in thought. You look dazed. Are you alright?"

"I said, I'm fine. Just someo... something on my mind."

"There you go again with trying to cover. Not happening this time, Bud. Who is she?"

9

R J flashes a look at Drew. "What do you mean, 'who is she?'?"

"I've known you for... how many years now? Granted, we aren't best friends as we live on opposite sides of the country, but...we are more than mere business associates. I've gotten to know you when you are in town, and we spend time together outside business, and this... the way you've been acting, and *not* acting, is not like you. First, you played like crap today, and didn't become even a little upset when you lost. Hell, you didn't even see the last serve of the game. It zipped right past you. You didn't join in on the flirting banter with the server, then downed your beer in one swig. So, 'Who is she?' means who is this woman that is totally distracting you, and putting you out of sorts."

RJ fills his lungs, then lets out a heavy sigh. He doesn't want to talk to business associates about his personal life, even if they are friendlier than business associates. Hell, he doesn't want to talk to anyone about personal stuff. "It's nothing."

"Bull." Drew senses RJ isn't comfortable with the idea of talking about personal issues with him, partly because they do business together. Picking up the folder of documents sitting on the table that contains the contract to be signed, he grabs a pen from his pocket, flips to the last page, signs, dates, closes the file, and slams it back down on the table. "There! Business is concluded. Start talking."

"What are you doing? We need to go over that document. There have been a few changes over the past five years you need to be aware of before signing," RJ begins to explain.

"Whatever, Dude. It's signed. At this moment, we're just friends. So, talk."

"But we're still business associates. You signing that maintains that fact."

Drew picks up the folder again, saying, "Well, I can fix that. I can tear this to shreds, and we'll be nothing more than friends." He holds it as if to begin ripping it in half.

RJ grabs it. "That won't be necessary," He states, laying it back on the table.

Drew takes a swig of his beer. "I'm serious man, I'm here for you. Sometimes it helps to spout off. I know it seems like 'a woman thing to do', but trust me, there have been times that I needed someone to let it all out to. Helps put things in perspective. Besides, the fact that I'm in business with you doesn't matter. Maybe it's helpful, since you could claim our conversation to be under some confidentiality clause or something. Plus, we live on opposite sides of the country, so it's not like I'm going to be running into anyone you know and telling them your personal stuff. Not that I would anyway, but..."

RJ thinks about it for a minute while finishing off his beer and signaling the server to bring another round.

"It's a new employee, Brady hired while I was on my last trip..." he begins. Once the floodgate is open, there is no holding back. He tells all about this fascinating woman, including the episodes at Buddy's Lounge and the motel.

Drew listens and scrutinizes RJ's body language carefully.

"...I haven't seen her since Friday morning when I left them at the motel," he concludes looking at Drew. "So, that's it in a nutshell," he concludes flippantly.

"That's a pretty darn big nutshell."

"Sorry." he realizes he went into way more details than he intended. "Didn't mean to bore you with so much info."

"Don't be sorry. I'm not bored," Drew chuckles. "Describe this woman to me."

"Why?"

"Just describe her."

"Tall, slender, yet slightly buff. Long, silky, thick brown hair, mood-changing bright blue eyes," he pauses, "Haven't seen her smile, but nice teeth, far as I can tell."

"Now you sound like you're describing a horse. Describe *Her*. What do you know about her?"

"She works for me, works at Buddy's lounge, and lives in a motel with two little girls. That's it."

The server comes and takes their lunch orders.

"Look, I'm no psychologist, but I think you're attracted to this woman. Even though you don't want to be, because you vowed to stay clear of all relationships. This woman is so different than any woman you've ever been interested in, or even known, for that matter, that she intrigues the hell out of you. I also think that you have a parental concern for the kids."

RJ thinks about everything Drew said knowing he makes some very good points, and tells him so. "You're right about a lot of things. Even though she is not my type, for some reason, I am attracted to her. She intrigues me. At Fenton, she comes across tough as nails. At Buddy's, she is so damn sexy and flirtatious. But when I walked into that motel room and saw her on her knees between her sick babies, deliriously exhausted, she looked so... so vulnerable, fragile. She was like a totally different woman. That image keeps replaying in my head and tearing at my heart. I find myself wondering what brought her to this situation. Why the hell is she living in a motel with her girls and working her ass off at two jobs? Why is she alone? Where's the father of her kids? Her family? But it's none of my damn business. I'm just the owner of the business she happens to be working for. I've got no reason to worry about them. I have my own kid, my own troubles, my own family, and a business to run." He shakes his head, mumbling a couple expletives under his breath as their food arrives. They become engaged in eating for a bit.

"So, what's this bewildering, enigmatic female's name?"

RJ laughs. "What's with the large descriptive words? Trying to impress me or someone nearby?"

They both laugh. "Not trying to impress anyone. However, you now have my brain absorbed with thoughts of your mystery woman, and I haven't even met her. Figure I should at least know the name of the woman taking up residence in my head, and occupying my thoughts."

"Welcome to my world," RJ says, still laughing, "BJ McCallister."

"BJ? Any idea what it stands for? Or is she secretive like you?"

"Yes, and yes. She is secretive, but I made a pact with her 5-year-old. I told her my name, and in exchange, she told me her mom's."

"You tricked a little girl into telling you her mother's secret? You ruthless swine! How dare you?" Drew boldly feigns his appalled dismay. The duo shares a chuckle.

"Now that I think about it, that was not only underhanded of me, but also not very smart. Because if she could be conned into telling me her mother's secret, what makes me think she'll keep mine?"

"Yeeea, not your smartest move, I wager. So?"

"So, what?"

"What's her name?"

"I promised I wouldn't tell."

"So, did the little girl, and she told you, a perfect stranger...well not so 'perfect', ha ha, but I'm your friend, you can tell me. I won't tell anyone."

"Yeah, right... Breezy Jo."

"O...K. So why doesn't she want anyone to know that? It's a beautiful name.

"I'm thinking that's exactly why. Doesn't sound strong and tough. Probably figures people would think it sounds more like a stripper's name."

"Got a point there, it kind of does. So, what do you plan to do about this situation?"

"Nothing. Forget about it, her, them. Just go on with my life."

"Yeah, I don't foresee that happening. Why don't you Google her and see what you can find out about her?"

"Wouldn't that be like an invasion of her privacy?"

"You're her boss. Your search is justified as you legally have the right to do a background check on your employees, especially a new employee. I do BGC on all my new employees. It's good business practice. You want to make sure she's not running from the law, right?"

"Actually, you have a point there. Living like she is could be a red flag. I probably *should* do a background check on her for business reasons."

Drew pulls his tablet out of his briefcase and turns it on. Once it connects to the available Wi-Fi at the restaurant, he hands it to RJ. "Look her up."

RJ sets about doing a Google and People Search on one BJ, aka Breezy Jo McCallister. Aside from the normal items such as past addresses, phone numbers, etc., that come up in the basic searches, a newspaper article appears, which contains her name. RJ opens the article, and the two begin to read it.

Bizarre twist in A Head-on collision which claims the lives of three

In a bizarre twist of fate, yesterday, a head-on collision claimed the lives of three members of one family in the two vehicles. Reports show that Matthew McCallister was driving drunk when he left his home yesterday afternoon after a domestic dispute with his wife, Breezy Jo. Eight months pregnant Mrs. McCallister had phoned her parents, Mr. and Mrs. Joseph Hobbs, for help because her husband was drunk, and his temper was flaring, verging on violent. Shortly after her call to her parents, Matthew left the residence to go to the market for more beer. Joseph and Kim Hobbs were on their way to pick up their daughter and 4-year-old granddaughter when a drunk driver swerved, hitting them head-on at speeds in excess of 60 miles an hour just 3 blocks from their destination. The drunk driver was

their son-in-law, Matthew McCallister. All three family members were pronounced dead at the scene.

RJ and Drew lean back in their seats, exhaling heavily. RJ runs both hands over his face as he attempts to wipe away the visions flashing through his mind. Visions of the horrific crash pictured in the article on the screen before him, as well as visions of an eight-months pregnant BJ, and little Chumani having to face and deal with the horror of that whole situation, and the gut-wrenching losses.

Drew speaks first. "Holy crap!"

"Wow! Holy crap is right. I can't even wrap my head around how horrible that would be, losing one, let alone three, family members under any circumstances, but the horrifying knowledge that it was her phone call that put her parents on that road, inadvertently in the path of that drunken moron!" RJ is finding it difficult to breathe as he empathically experiences an infinitesimal amount of the pain she must have experienced.

Drew clicks on the link at the end of the article, which leads to the obituaries of the three deceased. The obituaries make it clear that BJ is without other family.

"I guess that explains her being alone with no other relatives."

"Damn. I thought researching her would uncover some deep, dark secret of some scandalous past that would help put her out of your mind. Instead, her deep, dark secret is one of heart-wrenching circumstances. Sorry dude. Just trying to help a brother out," Drew tries to inject some levity into the moment.

"Thanks for your background check idea. From an employer's point of view, I think it's better that I have this information about her. It will keep things in perspective if she experiences bad days, especially around that time of year."

"However, from a personal point of view? I'm pretty sure this knowledge won't be helpful in putting her out of your thoughts. More likely it will make matters worse," Drew comments.

"I'll keep my distance. If I see a need, I'll do what I can without her knowing. Besides, it seems she's determined to stay strong and do this on her own. Plus, I don't need any entanglements. I've got enough on my plate."

"Well, I hate to run and leave you after reading that, but my wife asked me to stop at the store on my way home to pick up some things she needs for dinner, so I better be going. It's been great seeing you. Do me a favor. Keep me posted on things with you and Breezy. OK?"

"There is no 'Me, and Breezy' to keep you posted on," RJ retorts.

"I think it was Shakespeare who said, 'I think thou dost protest too much'. Maybe not yet, but..."

"Whatever. Take it easy, and give Heidi my regards. Next time I'm here, we'll all have to go out for a night on the town."

The two of them part ways in the parking lot.

RJ flies out the next morning after a long, restless night of half-sleeplessness and half nightmarish dream-filled sleep.

10

Lunch time rolls around and BJ meets up with Cheryl in the break room. "You remember Brady's wife, Millie, is caring for my girls for me?" BJ asks as they eat. Cheryl, mouth full, nods, and BJ continues. "Well, she has a lady friend who has a two-bedroom guest house, and she's offered to rent it to me for whatever I can afford."

Cheryl's expression of surprise accompanies "Really? How cool!"

"I'm going after work to meet the lady and look at the place. I don't even care if it's ramshackle; it would surely be better for my girls than living in a motel.

"Well, I doubt Mrs. O'Malley would recommend it if it weren't in nice condition."

"I know. You're probably right"

"Let me know. If you want, I can help you move and settled in."

"Thank you. I appreciate the offer. Though we don't have much to move, a couple suitcases of clothes, a couple boxes of toys, and a few dishes. That's it."

"I tell you what. Once you're settled in, I'll plan your housewarming party and I'll play hostess so you can enjoy the evening."

"Housewarming *party*? You mean you, Millie, the girls and I?"

"No, silly. A real party. I'm sure the crew will be excited for you, and they can all bring their female counterparts. That way you'll meet them, and hopefully make some new friends too," Cheryl enthuses. "As long as I still remain your Best Friend," she adds with mock sternness.

BJ smiles broadly. She hasn't seen quiet, shy Cheryl this excited about anything since the day of the arm-wrestling match. Though BJ does not desire to have a housewarming, she doesn't have the heart to douse Cheryl's enthusiasm over the idea. Besides, she's right, it might be nice to meet some 'women folk.'

"That will be nice, Cheryl, thank you, but let's not get ahead of ourselves. I haven't even spoken to them about it yet, let alone gotten it."

The crew finishes unloading the last trailer of the day and clocks out. BJ goes to the restroom to clean up. She removes the cap she wears daily to keep her hair well out of her way when she is working. She runs a brush through her sable mane to fluff it a bit and pulls her 'just in case' make-up bag from her purse and applies powder, blush, mascara and a dab of tinted lip balm. "That ought to do it," she says to her reflection. Although she is sure Millie told her friend that BJ works on the docks, she wants to make a good first impression, which to her simply means she doesn't want to look like one of the guys.

BJ uses her Bluetooth to place the call as she maneuvers through afternoon traffic. "Hi, Millie, this is BJ. Giving you a heads up that I'm on my way."

"Are ya needin' directions?"

"No, thank you. I looked up the address you gave me on my phone's GPS for the directions. I should be there in about 15 to 20 minutes. See you, then."

Millie switches back to the call she put on hold, telling her husband, "That was her. The plan is in motion."

"Are you ladies sure you know what you're doing?" Brady asks his wife of 35 years. Knowing full well, she is sure she and Mrs. Kemp were doing the right thing.

"Yes, ya just mind yarself." She hangs up and turns to Emily, "She's on her way."

Twenty minutes later, BJ arrives at the entrance of Kemp House. Driving up the long driveway, BJ takes in the impressive two-story wood-and-stone home with its elegant charm. There is a stone chimney jutting above the various peaks of rooflines, and a covered front porch. The yard is home to a variety of mature trees. There are colorful flower beds bordering flowering shrubs and hedges. A rather cheery, yet refined-looking home.

"Hi, Mommy!" Chumani calls out as she jumps up and down happily, unable to contain her joy at seeing her mother. She runs to her mother, almost launching into her arms.

"Hi, Sweetie," BJ greets as she exits the car, scooping up her daughter for a big squeeze hug and smooch.

Standing on the front porch, Millie is holding a squirming, squealing Chenoa, arms outstretched for her mamma hugs, too. Setting Chumani down, BJ approaches the porch, reaching for Chenoa as Millie descends the steps.

BJ takes note of the other 3 porch occupants. The tall, slender, immaculately dressed, silver-haired woman with high cheekbones must be Millie's 'lady friend'. The taller, svelte, silver-haired, olive-complected gentleman at her side, with his hand casually resting at the small of the woman's back, must be her husband. The small, brown-eyed, chestnut-haired boy standing at their feet would be the grandson Millie told her they are helping to raise.

"BJ McCallister, this is Emily an' Jason Kemp, and their gransun, Riyon Joseph," Millie makes the introductions, intentionally omitting the boy's last name.

BJ ascends the steps, shifting Chenoa on her hip to extend her hand to each. "Pleasure to meet you, Mr. and Mrs. Kemp."

"Likewise, Ms. McCallister, but please do call us Emily and Jason," the pleasant contralto voice requests in response.

"All right, as long as you call me BJ, please."

"Very well. Let's all go in the house out of the heat."

Once inside, Chumani goes with Riyon to his playroom to play while the adults talk.

"Your daughters are such lovely girls," Emily proclaims.

"Thank you." BJ is still holding Chenoa, who is patting her mommy's face with her chubby little hands.

"Well, shall we get to the matter at hand?" Emily begins.

"May I suggest we show her the guest house first to see if it's acceptable, and if she's even interested," Mr. Kemp interjects.

"Of course, that would make sense, Dear," Mrs. Kemp agrees.

BJ responds, "Trust me, judging from your lovely home," BJ indicates the room they are in, "I'm sure it will be more than acceptable. Besides, and please don't take this wrongly, it could be a shambles, and it still would be better for my girls than living in a motel."

"You're quite right," Mrs. Kemp affirms, then quickly continues, saying "No offense. It's not that the motel hasn't been more than adequate in serving its purpose for the time necessary, only that it's no longer necessary. "

"No offense taken," BJ assures Emily.

"Shall we?" Mr. Kemp leads the way.

"I'll bring along Riyon and Chumani," Millie states as she moves to retrieve them.

"When we began discussing the idea of you renting, we opened it to begin airing it out. It's still a bit musty, but..." Mr. Kemp begins, and Mrs. Kemp continues, "Yes, and we intend to have it all freshly painted and cleaned for you."

"Oh, that won't be necessary. It will be fine as it is, I'm sure," BJ interjects.

"Nonsense," both Kemps state in unison, leaving no leeway for rebuttal. Mrs. Kemp continues. "We only waited so you can pick out colors to go with your color scheme."

"I don't have a color scheme, since all we own are our clothes, toys and a few kitchen and bath supplies."

"Well, then," Mrs. Kemp enthuses, "this will be even more fun and exciting than I thought! You'll be able to start fresh with whatever color scheme your little heart desires. We'll go shopping, design, and decorate the whole place exactly as you want it," her tone becomes veritably effervescent.

"I'm serious, that won't be necessary," BJ assures them.

The excitement on his wife's face as well as the look of unease on BJ's is not missed by ever observant, Jason Kemp. "Now, BJ, you wouldn't want to deny an old lady the pleasure of three of her favorite pastimes, would you?" At BJ's quizzical expression Jason elaborates, "Decorating, shopping, and spending money."

The Kemps chuckle together.

"I assure you, my husband knows me well. I've run out of rooms to redecorate in the main house. I will absolutely love your fresh ideas of colors, themes, and such on this project.

"But we don't need..." BJ begins to protest.

"Put it this way, Dear. Emily is determined to paint, and decorate the guesthouse for you and your girls with or without your input. You might as well enjoy the experience and have a say in it since you'll be the ones living with the outcome," Jason explains.

"It's just the expense..." BJ once again begins to protest.

"Is none of your business," Mrs. Kemp's statement indisputable. Her face lights with a smile as she realizes the issue of money is the cause of BJ's resistance, as does Mr. Kemp.

"I assure you, BJ, not a penny from your pocket will be necessary, nor accepted, for this project." Mr. Kemp's *'Not up for debate'* expression is tempered by the twinkle in his fern green eyes.

"Shall we take a walk through?" Mrs. Kemp asks, entering first.

"After you," Mr. Kemp, ever the gentleman, holds the door for BJ to follow his wife.

Upon entering, BJ finds herself in an open concept great room. BJ takes in the lovely little home with its fireplace and open feel.

"Wow, this is wonderful," BJ states. "It is so open and airy. I love it." She takes in all the space, the fabulous view out the sliders that open onto a patio overlooking the glorious rock waterfall, pool, whirlpool spa and gardens. "Oh, my gosh. Breathtaking," she speaks in a hush.

"I'm glad you like it," Emily states, standing near, enjoying viewing the scene through the fresh eyes of one who is obviously unaccustomed to the lifestyle she herself takes for granted.

BJ sighs heavily, and Emily takes the opportunity to move on. "This way," she begins, stepping toward the hallway door to the right of the coat closet. In the hall is a floor-to-ceiling linen closet, followed by the bathroom. Not huge, but functional. Across the hall from the bathroom is the first larger of the two bedrooms. Without hesitation BJ is sure this will be best for the girls as it is spacious enough to double as a playroom. There is already a bunk bed in the alcove area.

"That was our son's when he was young. Occasionally, he and a buddy would 'camp out' in here when they were in high school," Mrs. Kemp explains. "I'm thinking with some cleaning, maybe a fresh coat of paint, and new mattresses that would be nice for Chumani, and also for when Chenoa is old enough to be out of the crib, which, by the way, we have that also." She gestures to the crib they set up already. "It was also our son's. We refurbished it for our grandson Riyon when he was born.

"Washing will be fine. I wouldn't want to cover the beautiful wood grain. Chenoa will love it. That's very kind of you to loan us these."

As they reemerge into the hall, Mr. Kemp directs BJ to the second bedroom, though a bit smaller, it's still decent-sized. They all return to the great room where Millie is with the children.

"Well, lass. Wha'da'ya think?

"It's all just perfect. More than I can imagine being able to afford."

"Miss Millie said we get bedrooms!" Chumani gushes with excitement. "Can I see mine?"

"Hold on, Sweetie," BJ tells her daughter, then turns to the Kemp's. "This is worth so much more than I can afford..." She begins.

Mrs. Kemp comes to her, looks BJ in the eye, takes both her hands in her own and says, "Dear, we have calculated out what you've been paying for the motel room, and what we'll be asking you for, and this will save you at least $300 per month."

"But I only pay..."

"No 'buts,' Dear. I'm sure it's obvious that we don't need the money." She makes an expansive hand gesture. "But you need the place. All that matters is if you like it."

"Like it? I love it!"

"That settles it," Mr. Kemp announces.

With glee and excitement bursting in her tone, "OK, then girls, let's go check out your new bedroom." BJ takes Chenoa from Millie, grabs Chumani's hand, and they scurry into the other room.

The trio emerges from the room a short time later.

"Dear, I'm sure you're probably tired, but would you be up to joining me to go to the paint store yet tonight to pick out colors so we can begin the painting immediately?"

"I'd love to, but I need to feed the girls," BJ reasons.

"No problem." Jason steps forward, reaching for Chenoa, and looking down at Chumani as he continues, "Misho, and Riyon would love to have the honor of being escorted by these two beautiful young ladies out to our favorite burger joint." He winks at Chumani.

"Wonderful idea, Darling." Emily hugs her husband, then turns to BJ. "Jason will take Riyon and the girls to dinner. You and I can grab a burger on the way, to eat in the car to speed up the excursion," Emily concludes. "That is, if this is all acceptable to you, Dear."

BJ stares blankly for a moment before Millie pipes up, "Aye, it sounds like a splendid plan to me, lass, an' I dare say the mister would be heartbroken if he be denied this date with these wee lovely lasses. I best be going now, or me mister will be throwing a hissy fit fer wondering where I've gone off ta." The jolly woman chuckles brightly.

"Oh, Millie, I'm so sorry to have kept you. I don't want you getting in trouble with your husband on my account," BJ expresses with deep concern.

"Me? In trouble? Ahk, I was joshin', ya know. I'm the one wears the pants in me house, lass." The others chuckle with her. "I'll be seein' these yungins bright an early in the morn." The good-natured woman hugs the wee three good night, then takes her leave.

"Let's head out to start our night on the town," Jason says to the children.

"Can we, Mommy?" Chumani asks her mother.

BJ's mind is reeling from thoughts and emotions over the past few hours. The ones currently vying for attention are excitement about their new place, and conflicting emotions over how comfortable Chumani, even Chenoa, seem to feel being with all these people they hardly know. She herself seems to feel comfortable with everyone they've been meeting. Well, almost everyone. She does not feel comfortable with RJ Fenton, but Cheryl, and the crew at work, the Kemp family, and, of course, the O'Malleys are all so friendly and welcoming. BJ's mood lifts as she says, "Well, we are plant-based, so Chumani can maybe have some fries, and if they have lettuce for the burgers, maybe some lettuce with mayo. Other than that, it sounds fine to me."

"Yay!" the two five-year-olds cheer.

"No worries, they have veggie burgers also, so I'll order her one of those," Mr. Kemp assures. Then everyone is off and on their way for the evening.

Later that night, back at the motel, BJ is putting the girls to bed. "
"Mommy?"

"What, Chumani?"

"Are we *really* going to live there?"

"Yes, Sweetie, we are."

"GOOD! 'Cause I really like the house, and I like Mémère and Misho too."

"Who?"

"That's what Riyon calls his grandma and grandpa. It's French for grandmother, and Native American for grampa. They said we can call them that, too. Is that OK?" she asks cautiously.

"Of course, it is, Sweetie."

"Good. Sometimes in my head, I pretend they're my grandma and grandpa, too."

BJ's heart swells achingly, and she fights the tears that spring in her eyes, knowing this is probably the closest her girls will ever come to having grandparents.

"OK, time to go to sleep. Goodnight, baby girl. I love you."

"Night, Mommy. I love you more."

"I love you bigger than the Universe," BJ tells her girls as she kisses her them good night.

11

BJ arrives at work the next morning after dropping the girls off to Millie and is greeted by Cheryl rushing out to the dock as soon as she spots BJ.

"Well, how did it go? Did you get the apartment?" The usually quiet Cheryl is almost giddy with excitement.

"It went well. It's a guest house in their backyard, next to the pool and spa." Due to the contagious enthusiasm exuding from Cheryl, BJ can no longer contain her joy over the idea that they are to live in such a spectacular place. The two begin dancing about on the dock like a couple of schoolgirls.

"It's so amazing. The lady and I went and picked out paint last night. They intend to paint and redecorate everything. They told me to plan my 'color scheme' for each room. I'll be going shopping with the lady soon to pick out other items. I don't think I've ever thought about a color scheme. I've never had reason to."

"That is awesome." Noticing Brady and Jake approaching over BJ's shoulder, "We'll talk colors and stuff at lunch," Cheryl says and gives BJ a quick hug and heads to her office.

BJ turns to find out what causes Cheryl to rush her departure. Spotting the two men approaching, she isn't sure if it is caused by the presence of the dock manager or Jake. More likely, Jake, though Cheryl wouldn't admit it.

"What brought on all the giddy girl dancing going on over here?" Jake inquires as he approaches, his gaze following Cheryl's retreating back.

"I wager it is due to the fact Ms. McCallister here is now the proud tenant of a guest house," Brady supplies, grinning broadly.

"Yes indeed," is BJ's head-held-high response.

"Congratulations! Where is it?"

Brady interrupts brusquely, not wanting that topic discussed before having a chance to speak to Jake in private about it. "You can chit-chat about that later."

Jake shoots Brady a quizzical look before turning to BJ, "We'll talk later. Again, congratulations."

"Thanks, Jake."

BJ heads off toward the dock, the men toward the office.

When Jake is sure BJ is out of earshot, he asks, "What is that about?"

"What is what about?" Brady tries to pretend he doesn't understand what Jake is referring to.

"Seems you didn't want her telling me where her new place is."

"That, yes, well..." The burly Irishman steers the younger man into his office and closes the door. "It seems some explanations are in order, far out of earshot of one BJ McCallister."

That evening, BJ tells the motel owners about the rental opportunity. They are ecstatically happy. They make her promise to keep in touch after the move, and Kristen agrees to continue babysitting the girls.

Wednesday is one of BJ's double days. She arrives at Buddy's Lounge fifteen minutes before her shift to find the place in full swing as usual for the middle of the week celebration of 'Hump Day'.

"Hey, Sugar," Josie greets. "How's it going?"

"Hey, Josie. It's going great. How are you?"

"Same ol' same ol'. Been waiting all week to hear how things went with your handsome hunk from the other night."

"He's not 'my' handsome hunk or 'my' anything!" BJ states adamantly, then realizes, and corrects, "Other than 'my' Boss."

"As in present tense? So, does that mean he didn't fire you?" the smiling coworker asks. "Like I said, he wouldn't," she adds with a smirk.

"No, he didn't fire me, but that is probably more because of what ended up happening the couple of days following that night, and he doesn't want people to think he's a nasty ogre."

Josie halts her shift prep activities momentarily, giving BJ her full attention. "What happened?" she asks with sincere concern.

"I arrived home that night to find both my girls very sick," she begins."

"Oh no! Sugar, I'm sorry. What was wrong? Are they OK now?"

"Yes, they're well. Long story short, they had exceedingly high fevers. I was awake the rest of the night, all the next day, and evening. Literally 39 hours; No sleep, no food. Just tending to them. Which of course meant I had to call in sick. That caused Mr. 'Full-of-himself' to think that I was lying, and didn't go in to work because of him!"

"Ah, yes, that would be something he'd conclude. So, then what happened?" Josie prodded her to fill in more details.

BJ sighs a bit, exasperated by the memory of it all. "He showed up at the motel, evidently bribed the owner's daughter to let him into my room, where he found me on the verge of passing out from exhaustion, proceeded to swoop in like some fairy tale 'knight' there to 'save the day'."

Josie struggles to contain her laughter. She smiles and asks, "And did he?"

Looking up from the pre-shift side work they've been doing while they talk. "Did he what?" she snaps, a slight blush creeping into her cheeks.

"Did he save the day?"

"Well, I'm sure he, and anyone hearing about it, will think he did. The fact of the matter is that I was doing fine without his or anyone's help. I am perfectly capable of caring for my children on my own," BJ's voice rises and becomes forceful, tinged with anger.

Josie can see the hurt in BJ's expression at the thought that anyone would, for even one second, think her incapable of caring for her kids, combined with the pride and determination that, come hell or high water, she will. Josie consoles, "No one doubts that you are capable of taking care of your kiddos, but even Wonder Woman gets a little help from time to time," the older woman teases with gentleness. "Besides, sometimes it's nice to allow others to help."

"Fine. Whatever." BJ doesn't mean to sound snotty. "Sorry, it just irked me to wake up to a man in my...space," she stops herself from saying *bed,* which would put Josie in major romance overload mode.

"He stayed the whole night?" she asks, not hiding the gleam in her eye.

"Yes, well, I guess I *was* extremely tired, and after he made me take a shower," Josie's eyebrows shoot up at that, "I literally passed out cold. He took care of the girls the rest of the night, gave them medicine, did the cold cloth routine, etc. Even changed Chenoa's diaper."

"Wow! Sounds like he has experience," Josie states with amazement, then adds, "Wait, is he married with children?"

BJ looks at her blankly before heading out to the floor. Thoughts begin rambling through her mind as she sets to work in the crowded, noisy bar. She didn't think he was married or had kids. The conversation she overheard about his 'Prospects' and 'Conquests' led her to believe him he's single, and more likely to be the tramp he accused her of being. Not that it matters to her. What her boss does is none of her concern.

BJ's cell phone rings about seven the next evening. She checks the caller ID, 'Mrs. Kemp'. Her instant internal negativity rears its ugly head, *'Oh no. Please don't let something be wrong that changed their mind about me renting.'* "Stop it! Cancel, cancel!" she scolds herself out loud in a hushed voice. Taking a deep, calming breath, she affirms, *'I trust all is well with this, and every situation.'*

"Hello, Mrs. Kemp."

"Emily, Dear."

"Yes, I'm sorry. Hello, Emily."

"Hello, BJ, Dear. I hope I'm not catching you at an inconvenient moment."

"No, not at all," BJ assures. "How are you?" she asks politely.

"I'm fine. How are you and the girls?" They exchange pleasantries.

"I'm calling because I'm wondering if you'd be available to go shopping tomorrow."

"I'm scheduled to work at Buddy's tomorrow night."

"Oh. Is there any way you can take the night off?"

"I can call, and find out if anyone wants to pick up an extra shift, though I truthfully can't afford to lose one myself."

"Trust me, Dear, in the long run it will be worth it. Besides, you deserve a night off."

"I suppose. I understand you'd like to have things done in a timely manner. I guess I can still have Kristen sit for the girls for the evening."

"Actually, Dear, I don't in any way mean to be controlling, but I've already spoken to Millie, and Brady, and he's agreed to let you off work tomorrow at lunch so we'll have the whole afternoon, and evening to 'shop 'til we drop'," she informs, "That way Millie will keep the girls for the evening, no charge."

"Oh. Well, then I guess you've got it all worked out, so the answer is yes, I can go shopping with you tomorrow."

"Great! I'll meet you at your motel around 12:30. We'll go together in my car. That way, Millie can take the girls there to put them to bed so we won't have to rush."

"O...K. I guess that will work."

"Wonderful! I'll see you tomorrow. Sleep well," Emily's excitement is audible.

"See you, then. Goodnight." BJ quickly calls Buddy's, and Josie answers. BJ explains, and Josie assures her she'll get the shift covered and fill Buddy in on the scoop.

1 2

Emily pulls into the parking lot of a large warehouse furniture store. "Shall we?" she asks brightly as they emerge from the cool car into the midday sun.

BJ draws a deep breath. "We shall." She smiles at the well-dressed woman, a vivid contrast to her own jeans and T-shirt.

Emily lays a gentle hand on BJ's arm as they are about to head in. "I want to make something clear before we begin." BJ pauses, giving her attention. "I don't want you looking at the price tags. Only furniture and decor. You concern yourself with what you like. Leave the rest to me." She raises an eyebrow in question of acceptance.

BJ wants to argue, but agrees to the terms, knowing in the end that although she and her girls will be using the furnishings, ultimately, they'll belong to the Kemps, and they obviously would want high-quality items.

Upon entering, BJ pauses in awe. She's never been in a furniture store, let alone one of this magnitude. They begin walking around, browsing. "I'm thinking," Emily begins, "that it might be a good idea to have a Hide-a-bed sofa for the living room. That way you'll have a place for family to sleep when they come visit."

BJ takes a deep breath and swallows hard, "That won't be necessary. There won't be anyone visiting." Seeing Emily's expression of puzzlement, she continues matter-of-factly, "We have no family."

Both perfectly arched eyebrows rise sharply, "None?"

"No ma'am."

"But... I don't mean to pry, but what about your parents? Siblings?

"I was an only child. My father wanted a son to carry on the family name. What he got was me. Mother wanted me to be a girlie girl. So, I was a bit of each for them both.

Without thinking, BJ rushes on with her tale. "One night when I was eight months pregnant with Chenoa, my husband was in yet another drunken rage. I called my parents to come pick up Chumani and me. In the meantime, my husband decided to take off to go buy more beer. As twisted as fate can be, my parents were hit by a drunk driver on their way to get us. They, and the drunk driver, were all killed. The drunk driver was my husband," BJ recounts the incident succinctly.

Emily's face goes pale. She clutches one hand to her chest as her legs melt beneath her. With her other hand, she takes hold of BJ's arm, bringing BJ along with her as she gracefully collapses on the sofa they are standing next to. Emily's eyes fill with tears. "Oh my," she breathes, barely audible. "I am so sorry."

"Are you OK?" BJ asks the visibly shaken Emily.

"Yes."

"It's me who is sorry. I should not have told you that. I've upset you. I sometimes forget how my bluntness can affect others."

"No, Dear. Don't be sorry for your directness. I asked." Emily regains some of her composure. "Are there no Grandparents? Aunts? Uncles? Cousins?" She questions with a hint of humor in an attempt to lighten the mood, almost afraid to ask.

"Nope. Both my parents were also only children, and all of my grandparents passed when I was a child."

"What of your in-laws?"

"Let's say the apple didn't fall far from the tree. They are both drunks, also. They want nothing to do with the girls or me."

"Deary me, child. Again, I am so sorry. Well, enough of this glum discussion. The best thing to shake off a gloomy mood is to shop! So, let's get to it." Emily's spirits brighten. She quickly stands, taking BJ by the hand and pulling her to her feet.

Something about that bit of insight into BJ's past brings about a change in their connection. The two giggle and laugh throughout the afternoon and evening, making silly comments about peculiar things they come across, and occasionally, people they catch doing strange things.

The two die-hard shoppers pause in their spree long enough to grab a bite to eat at dinner time. Over a light meal at a local diner, Emily imparts a few stories about her family.

"I was married before Jason. I fell madly in love at the young age of 16. He was 19. We were inseparable. Like a fairy tale, it was love at first sight, a match made in heaven."

"How did you meet?" BJ asks, intrigued.

"Our fathers were business associates, and both loved to mix business with pleasure. My father invited Rainier SR., and his family to our house for a summer barbecue. I saw Rainier Junior walk around the corner of the house, and..." Emily's eyes take on a faraway gaze as if she is traveling back to the moment, they ignite like sparklers on the 4th of July as she relives the moment she laid eyes on her first love.

BJ witnesses the youthful Emily shining beneath the facade of the mature woman before her. She is sure those green eyes twinkled this same way all those years ago.

Emily sighs and brings herself back to the present moment. "Yes, well. It didn't take long for all to know that ours was the true love poets write about. A few short months later, Rainier asked my father's permission for my hand before asking me to marry him. We married two months after my 17th birthday. I gave birth to our son, Rainier the third, eleven months later." Emily beams with pride. She falls quiet, eating a few bites of her meal.

"Was he your only child?" BJ asks.

"No, though he was an only child for ten years," Emily chuckles, "Then I popped one out every two years until all said and done, I had four daughters."

BJ's eyes widen. "Four?"

"Yes, ma'am. Amelia, Cornelia, Delia, and Ophelia. Though they go by the nicknames of Mel, Neli, Del and Ophie."

BJ is intrigued to find that this slender, well-kept, poised woman is the mother of five, and finds herself drawn to delve a bit. "How old are they now, and where are they living?"

"Let me think, my son is 39, the girls are 29, 27, 25, and 23. They all live locally. You'll meet them all soon. They'll all love you and your girls," she assures BJ.

BJ smiles to herself at the possibility of more friends her age. Mel is even the same age.

The two eat in silence for a few minutes before Emily continues to explain. "Anyway, so the story goes, my husband died while watching a sporting event on TV. We were all home. Our son was shooting baskets in the driveway with friends. The three older girls were playing in the living room. I was taking 3-year-old Ophie potty. Mel looked up from her playing when she heard the sports event crowd cheering wildly, expecting to see her daddy join in, instead she saw her father lifeless, pale as a ghost. She was only 9, but she knew something was terribly wrong, and screamed, 'Mommy!!! Daddy's not breathing!' "

"Oh my gosh." BJ's hands cover her dropped jaw and open-mouth expression. "That's terrible. I'm so sorry."

"Thank you. Apparently, an undetected blood clot broke loose, went straight to his heart, and stopped it. The upside, I suppose, is the doctors said he most likely felt nothing at all," Emily concludes. "Well, enough of the morose talk. What else should we talk about?"

"How long have you been married to Jason?"

"Jason was a business associate of my late husband who attended the funeral and offered to help in any way he could. He helped my father-in-law and son immensely, and spent quite a bit of time mentoring my son. Somewhere along the way, we became very close. Three years later, we married."

"Congratulations. You seem authentically happy together." A couple of minutes pass as they order dessert.

"I'm wondering about your grandson, if that isn't yet another sensitive subject," BJ queries. "He's your son's son, correct?"

"Yes. My son stepped up and became the man of the house after his father's death, and as I mentioned, also took on running the family business with the help of Jason and my father-in-law, who started the business in the first place; he passed it to Junior, who would have eventually passed it to our son; it just happened sooner, and abruptly. Anyway, my son grew up in a hurry, dove headlong into the business, and took no time for, as he put it, frivolous pastimes such as relationships. He rarely dated at all. Then, 6 years ago, he met a nice, much younger lady. They dated a few times. He wasn't any more serious about her than any others he dated. I assure you, he is always very cautious where protection is concerned, as he didn't want any entanglements. But as fate would have it, sometimes even what seems to be the best precautions sometimes fail. The girl became pregnant. She seemed pretty sure she didn't want a child, but Rainier said they would make it work somehow. Even though I knew he didn't love her, he said he'd do the right thing and marry her. She agreed. However, she stipulated they not marry until after the baby was born.

"Riyon was born on a warm, sunny early summer afternoon, and though my son didn't think he was ready for children, he was glowing with pride and unbridled love as he held his newborn son. We all left the hospital late that evening, but received a call early the next morning informing us that the mother disappeared."

"What? Disappeared how?" BJ asks, confused.

"That's exactly what we asked. They said in the middle of the night, she simply left. They checked hospital security-camera footage, and it showed her dressed in her street clothes calmly walking out the front door of the hospital. The police searched, we hired private investigators, but no one was able to track her down. It's as if she just vanished, never to be heard from again. It's believed she moved away and changed her identity. So, Rainier and Riyon moved in with us so I could help my son raise his son. My son is a very loving, devoted father to Riyon, but he works long days and travels occasionally for business. It makes it much easier with them living there." Then abruptly changing the subject, "I think we are sufficiently refueled, don't you? Shall we resume our spending spree?"

BJ arrives home from shopping with Mrs. Kemp late Friday night. Both Saturday and Sunday, she spends with her girls during the day, and works at Buddy's both nights as usual, and is back to Fenton's bright and early Monday morning.

The next few days fly by, so when BJ's cell rings Friday, between jobs, she isn't expecting Emily to be on the line. "Good evening, BJ. How are you, Dear?"

"I'm doing well. How are you?"

"Wonderful. I'm calling to tell you the house is ready for you to move in tomorrow."

"Seriously? Wow, that's great."

"I have a few things to do in the morning, and I want to be sure I'm here when you arrive," Emily fibs. "What time do you think you'll be here?"

"I'll have to pack up our things after our morning activities, so we probably won't arrive until after noon, maybe one o'clock."

"That's perfect. We'll plan for you to arrive around one."

Saturday morning, Cheryl takes the bus to the motel to help as offered. They pack up and load the back of the station wagon with everything they have in their motel room, then tidy up the room, and turn the key in to the front desk.

"We're sad to be losing the three of you, but we are so happy for you," the motel owner tells BJ.

"Cheryl is going to plan a housewarming party. You must come," BJ informs them.

"We'll be there for sure. Let us know when and where." They all exchange hugs, and the McCallister trio is off to the next chapter of their lives.

BJ calls the lounge to once again have her shift at Buddy's covered for that night so she can get the girls settled in for their first night in their new place. Buddy is a gruff sort of character most of the time, but he seems genuinely pleased that BJ is getting settled in a place, and doesn't seem to mind letting her have the night off.

BJ turns into the driveway and parks in the spot Mr. Kemp told her will be her parking place. Mrs. Kemp called early that morning to inform her that everything they purchased the other night arrived, is set up and ready. "We're so excited; we can hardly wait for your arrival."

BJ thinks it is a bit strange how this couple seems so polished and poised, yet they are so warm and friendly, welcoming the three of them in a way she always thought long-lost relatives would be.

"Well, baby girls," she says to her two cherubs, "We're here, at our new home."

"Yippee!" Chumani squeals, eliciting an accompanying screech from Chenoa. BJ and Cheryl unbuckle the girls, leaving their belongings in the car for now while they go check out the status of things. BJ leads the way.

As they round the corner of the front house to enter the gate to the rear area where their house is located, they are greeted with a chorus of cheers of "WELCOME to your NEW HOME."

There before them stands Emily, Jason, Brady, Millie, Jake and Riyon, all standing under a handmade banner that reads the same sentiment in bright, colorful poster paint.

The girls squeal with excitement, BJ's eyes well up with tears; she struggles to hold back, yet fails miserably. Mrs. Kemp takes Chenoa from her arms, Mrs. O'Malley takes Chumani's hand, and Cheryl throws her arms around BJ, laughing, and saying, "I sure hope those are tears of joy!"

"They are. It's just, I've never... no one has ever... I'm just so..." BJ stammers through the tears.

"Well, Lass, then it's about darn time ya did... and someone did... and ya are... Whatever was to be filled in the blanks." The group laughs. Everyone hugs BJ and the girls.

"Enough of the mushy stuff," Brady announces, "Time for them to step over the threshold of their new home."

Everyone steps aside. Chenoa is returned to BJ's arms, and Chumani takes her mommy's hand. They step toward the door, then stop. BJ surveys each of her girls and asks, "Are we ready?"

"YES!" Chumani yelps. She and BJ take one last big, deep breath and enter the house. "Wow, Mommy. It's so pretty!"

BJ is speechless. She gazes around at the well-appointed kitchen and living space, freshly painted in the almond beige she chose with a burnt orange accent wall in the living room. The deep neutral-toned double reclining loveseat, the end table, new ladder-backed bar stools at the counter, the wood holder by the fireplace, the new three-door refrigerator-freezer, the stove replaced, and an over-range microwave hood installed. All the carpet is removed, and mid-tone wood floors have been installed throughout. The cabinets have a fresh coat of matching semi-gloss paint, creating an easy clean surface and the illusion of more space. So much more has been updated than BJ thought or ever would have imagined. Chumani is tugging at her hand. "I want to go check out my new room!" she demands.

"Yes, Sweetie." BJ turns her attention to her daughter, and they walk to the girls' room.

"Mooommy," the little girl draws out the word in stage whisper fashion with awed wonder. "It's so pretty!"

BJ lets go of her hand, and Chumani slowly begins to wander around looking at everything. Chenoa, seeing all the toys that have been placed in the room, begins squirming to be put down, and BJ obliges, placing her near the freshly scrubbed and polished crib. The bunk beds have been repainted, a beautiful cream. There are stuffed bears and other animals all around the room, big plastic tubs with art supplies, dolls, an easel with a paper tablet on one side, and a magnetic whiteboard on the other with magnetic letters and numbers on it. Tears are again flowing down BJ's cheeks. The girls are engulfed in all the things little girls should have, and they are overjoyed.

Chumani, seeing her mommy's tears, comes to her, "Mommy, what's wrong? Don't cry."

BJ slumps to the floor. Chenoa crawls over, and BJ holds her little girls.

"Why are you sad, Mommy?"

"I'm not sad, Sweetie! Not at all. I'm so very happy. These are happy tears."

"Oh, OK," Chumani smiles, "What about your room? Can we go see it too?"

"Sure, we can."

They get up from the floor, then walk down the little hall, stepping into BJ's room. It is breathtaking. BJ stands in awe.

Emily insisted on a queen-size bed, though BJ said a twin would be fine for her alone. Emily reminded her that there might be nights the girls would want to snuggle up with her, then the older woman added in a conspiratorial whisper, "Who knows, you might one day have adult company to share it with."

Though BJ blushes at the fact that this woman she hardly knows is comfortable speaking of things BJ hadn't even discussed with her mother, she distinctly assures her, "That's not gonna happen. I want nothing to do with any man. My girls are my life, and there is no room and no need for a man in my life."

Emily let the subject drop, though she had other ideas...

13

"It's all so amazing," BJ states, taking in her newly redecorated room, her voice rich with emotion.

The other adults have come to hear what she thinks.

"We're glad you like it," Emily responds.

"You deserve to have a nice place to raise your girls," Jason informs her.

Raise your girls sounds long-term, permanent. That thought strikes fear in BJ while it also fills her heart with joy.

In the past few months, everything has been in such upheaval that she didn't think their lives would ever be normal or balanced, not that it ever had been much of either, but since the accident, it has all been so much worse than she could have ever imagined.

Jason announces, "There will be plenty of time for you to discover and enjoy, but right now, I think we need to have a toast. Shall we?" He indicates they return to the living area. There is sparkling cider chilling in the fridge, which he now opens and pours for everyone in the champagne glasses he brought over. Even Chumani and Riyon receive some. Glasses are raised as he proclaims, "To BJ, Chumani and Chenoa, and their new Home Sweet Home!"

"Here! Here!" comes the chorused response, then all drink.

The group mingles, looking around at how beautiful everything turned out for a little over an hour before they begin preparing to head home.

Cheryl took the bus that morning, as she often does, because her car isn't the greatest, and she tries to conserve it for getting to work. Now she is standing off to one side, looking on her phone for the next scheduled pickup in the area that would get her home. Jake comes up behind her. "What are you doing? Hiding?" he asks with a grin in his tone.

Cheryl is startled, both at the question and the nearness of his voice. Her immediate tensing doesn't go unnoticed by Jake, and he steps to her side and away a bit. "Sorry. I didn't mean to scare you," he apologizes.

"I, I wasn't 'scared', just startled. I didn't realize you... I mean, anyone was near," she stammers.

"So, what are you looking at that held your attention so that you didn't hear me?"

"I'm checking the bus schedule."

"You leaving town?" he asks teasingly.

Feeling momentarily confused, she then realizes he is referring to the Greyhound-type bus, she clarifies.

"No. I took the city transit bus to the motel to help BJ earlier, so I'm checking for the next available return from near here."

"Where's your car?"

"It's not running very well lately, so I try to only use it for work," she explains.

"What seems to be wrong with it?"

She shrugs. "BJ's the kind of woman who might have a clue. However, I know nothing about cars."

"I tell you what. I'll give you a lift home and take a look at it. Maybe I can figure out what's wrong." Then, seeing the panic wash over her features, "I promise I won't bite...unless you ask nicely."

His wink and wicked grin cause her to blush six shades of red before stammering, "Oh, that won't be necessary, I mean, thank you for the offer, but I wouldn't want to bother you. I'm sure you have much better things to do."

He cocks his head to the side, rubs his chin with forefinger and thumb as if in deep thought. "Hmmm, nope. Pretty sure I have nothing better to do than rescue a damsel in distress."

Cheryl giggles. "That would imply that you are a knight in shining armor. I don't see your armor. Besides, I'm not a damsel in distress."

Jake looks intently at this coquettish, coy woman who intrigues him so. "I think it is you who wears the armor." She demurely lowers her eyes. "Unless you have someone else lined up to check your car, for free, please allow me the honor of driving you home, and doing so, mi-lady," he ends with a gesticulated flourish and bowing of his head.

Cheryl can't hold back the giggle that escapes her. "If you're sure it's not a bother..."

He likes the lighthearted expression that lights her face, and the sweet sound of her shy giggle. "I assure you, nothing would please me more."

The exchange taking place between Cheryl and Jake envelops BJ with joy that her friend seems a bit relaxed. They approach BJ. "We're going take our leave, so you lovely ladies," he gestures to BJ and the girls, "can enjoy your first night in your new home."

"We?" The quizzical raised eyebrow expression is directed at her co-worker and friend.

"Um. Yes, as you know, I came on the bus, and I was checking for the next scheduled return bus, but Jake kindly offered to give me a lift home." She again lowers her eyes demurely.

"Ahh. How very nice of you, Jake."

"'Tis a Knight's honorable duty to rescue a damsel in distress," he replies, continuing the lighthearted banter that moments ago brought Cheryl out of her shyness. His hope is to keep her in that headspace a while longer until she is better able to relax in his presence.

"That it 'tis kind, sir." Catching on quickly to the playful tone that she assumes is the cause of Cheryl's uncharacteristically relaxed state in close proximity to this man, BJ finds herself utilizing a bit of the brogue she sometimes picks up from being around Millie. "And a very noble Knight ya be for seeing safely home this gentle lass,"

Millie, hearing the accent of her native tongue coming from nearby, "I didn'a know twas neighborin' country folk 'round," she joins the conversation.

"Aye, ma'am. This kindly Knight offered to see this lass safely home, he has," BJ carries on in the best brogue she can muster.

"He has, has he?" She turns to Jake, "That be very thoughtful of ya, sir. Long as yar intentions be honorable." She gazes from him to Cheryl, and back.

"Only the best of, Madam," he assures her, then continues, "Seems Milady's carriage is in need of tending to, so I've offered to have a look-see with the hope I might cure what ails it."

"Good man, ya are, lad." Millie then turns her attention to BJ. "Well, Lass, you've a lovely home now. Things are lookin' up fer ya. I'll be here bright an' early come Monday morn to tend the wee lasses, and see what great adventures we can get on with this week coming."

"Thank you so much, Millie. We'll see you, then." The pair hug goodbye.

BJ hugs Cheryl goodbye, also whispering to her, "Just breathe. It will all be fine. He won't bite." She physically encounters Cheryl's giggle in her embrace and pulls back to see her face.

Cheryl whispers back, "He said that too, but then he added 'unless you ask really nice'." She again blushes.

Over Cheryl's shoulder, BJ catches Brady slap Jake on the back and say, "'Bout time you took a step, 'stead of pussyfootin' 'round another five years."

She wonders if they've honestly been playing cat and mouse for five years already? She hugs her friend once more, then lets her go to be on her way before she gets cold feet.

Once everyone leaves, the house seems profoundly quiet, but not in a lonely way, in a cozy, homey way. She goes about getting the girls settled down in their new room. She puts Chenoa in the beautiful crib with a few toys and asks, "Chumani, will you please stay in the room, and play, and keep an eye on your little sister while I go and get things unloaded from the car?"

"Sure. There's so much to look at. Mommy? I'm hungry."

"I know, Sweetie. We didn't have lunch, and it's about time for dinner already. I have to bring our stuff in from the car, and find our food so I can fix you something, OK?"

"OK."

Jason and Emily see BJ unloading the car. Emily takes Riyon into play with Chumani and helps with Chenoa. Jason goes to help carry things in.

"You don't have to help," BJ insists to them both.

"We don't have to. We want to," Jason informs.

"The children and I were discussing how delicious hot pizza and ice-cold beverages sound. I hope you don't mind, but we're about to order delivery."

The expressions on the faces of both Kemps, letting her know the offer, in fact, is not up for discussion, causes BJ to sigh, realizing it does sound good, and she won't have to find and fix anything, so she agrees.

After dinner, the Kemps retire to their house, and BJ puts the girls to bed. She collapses on her brand-new double reclining love seat and reclines. From there, she surveys everything. All the new furniture, fresh paint, nature based and inspired knick-knack décor... It is all so overwhelming. She cries. Tears of joy for all the wonderful people who have taken her little family under their wing and helped give them a fresh start on life. She is sure that other than the births of her girls, she's never felt such pure happiness. She is engulfed in something else by these people. Something so special she's only experienced with her daughters. Love. She supposes her parents loved her in some way, but she'd been a disappointment to them both. She never quite measured up to being an adequate substitute for the son her father desperately wanted, and because she tried so hard to be, she, then was never quite girlie enough to please her mother. As for her husband? She was sure he'd been incapable of loving anything other than his drugs and alcohol. Not even his daughter, whom he rarely paid any attention to, let alone shown her any love. BJ naively thought Matt cared for her, and with time, he'd love her, and she'd help him get clean. How utterly naive and wrong she'd been.

However, these people she met in the past couple months, who have no connection to them, have shown them more love than she thought was possible, especially considering they are still relative strangers.

Going to her room to get ready for bed, she becomes so excited to spend her first night in her new bed, in her new room, in her new home. As she drifts off to sleep, her thoughts return to her earlier musings. She wonders what it would be like to have a man love her as much as these people seem to?

Her dreams are a jumble of visions dominated by a 6'4" molded Adonis body, topped with a head of thick chestnut brown hair, masterfully sculpted features, ornamented with eyes of sparkling amber cut glass. Somewhere in her dream state, she is conscious of a thought that her descriptive dream narrative is sounding like a romance character description.

14

The sun rises brightly Sunday morning, signaling the start of a bright new chapter in the McCallister trio's lives. BJ quickly decided she wants to christen their new place with its first home-cooked Sunday dinner. After getting the girls up, fed and dressed, and deciding it isn't too ungodly an hour to be calling people, she dials Cheryl first. "Good morning, Cheryl. I hope I didn't wake you?"

"No. How was your first night of sleep in your own Home?"

"It was great. I'm wondering, do you have plans this afternoon?"

"No. Why, what's up?"

"I want to make my first Sunday dinner in my new place and would love to share it with you and the Kemps. Would you be interested in joining us for a home-cooked meal, about 2:30 or 3?"

"That sounds delightful. I would love to join you."

"Great! By the way, how did your evening go with Jake?" There is a long pause. BJ isn't sure if she should have asked.

Then, with a slightly wistful, shy tone, Cheryl responds. "It was very...nice?...interesting?...umm, I'm not good at that sort of thing. You know, making small talk, getting to know someone. I was pretty nervous, but Jake was a perfect gentleman. He checked out my car, figured out what was wrong, went and bought the parts and fixed it. Afterward, we sat and talked for a couple hours, then he went home."

"Why don't you give him a call and see if he wants to join us for dinner today. That would be nice."

"I don't think I would be comfortable doing that. I wouldn't want him to think I'm asking him on a date or something." Cheryl is too reserved to be that bold.

"Did he give you his number?"

"Yes, he said to give him a call if I have any more trouble with my car."

"Fine. If it will make it easier, call him and tell him I want to invite him, but that you aren't sure about giving out his personal number, so I asked you to call him to invite him for me."

Cheryl again is quiet for a moment. "Yeah, I guess that would be OK. Then it wouldn't be 'me' asking. Right? I can do that."

"Right. We're heading out to the store. I'll plan on seeing you both around 2:30'ish. Bye for now."

"Bye"

BJ and the girls stop by the front house on their way to the car.

"Good morning," Emily greets the trio. "How was your first night?"

"Wonderful!" BJ sighs. "We're going grocery shopping. We're wondering if the three of you have plans this afternoon, as we'd like to invite you to Sunday dinner around 2:30 or 3:00. I've also invited my friends Cheryl and Jake from work. I'm going to call and invite Millie and Brady, too.

"That sounds lovely, dear, and may I say, a welcome blessing to have someone else do the cooking for once." Emily chuckles. "Is there anything I can bring or do to help?"

"No, thank you. You've already done so much for us. This is in no way sufficient repayment, but it's a start."

"You don't have to repay anything. We do for you because we want to help. A home-cooked meal cooked from your heart will be more than adequate, thanks. We'll see you around 2:30. Have fun shopping."

BJ makes her plant-based version of her favorite Sunday dinner she remembers from childhood. Oven-baked seitan 'Roast' covered with homemade vegan Au Jus, sides of freshly made mashed potatoes with rich brown no beef-beef gravy, cooked carrots, Harvard beets, corn, pickles, black olives and crescent rolls with oat butter.

Emily pops over after BJ and the girls return from the store and asks, "May Jason and I take the girls out to play with Riyon by the pool for the afternoon? That way you can immerse yourself in your cooking without distraction."

"That would be immensely helpful and greatly appreciated," BJ responds.

Cheryl and Jake arrive at quarter to two...together... Millie and Brady also arrive five minutes later.

Dinner goes off without a hitch. BJ feels good about how well it all came together after not cooking much over the past year, truthfully, far longer than that, since there wasn't often much to cook in regard to nice meals during her marriage. She is proud that her first meal and entertaining venture are a success. Though she feels a bit self-conscious when everyone oo's & aah's over how delicious the meal is. She is inwardly pleasantly surprised, especially after she informs them that the entire meal is plant-based

Friday, two weeks later, rolls around, and midday, BJ is in the break room when Cheryl enters. "Hey, Cheryl. I made another huge meal last night with lots of leftovers, which I brought for lunch to share. Would you like to join me?"

"You've been cooking up a storm since you got your place," Cheryl notes, smiling.

"I never knew how much I enjoy cooking. Probably because I never had money to buy more than the bare essentials or a nice place to do the cooking."

"You're good at it, too. That dinner you made last Sunday was so delicious, I can close my eyes and still taste it. Yum." She licks her lips appreciatively as if she actually can still taste it.

"Eh, hmm," Jake clears his throat as he enters the break room just in time to witness the exaggerated lip licking. Cheryl blushes scarlet. He walks to her, gives her a wink and a hug, whispering, "Was that for my benefit? Because if you want a kiss, all you need to do is ask. Although that is a very nice manner of invitation." He kisses her sweetly.

BJ can't help smiling, ear-to-ear, at the scene playing out before her. She is so happy for her friends who are finally getting together. She learned from Cheryl that she had liked him since she began working at Fenton Warehouse five years ago, but that she'd been so shy that she'd done all she could to stay clear of him. He finally told her the night he drove her home from BJ's Welcome Home evening that he's been attracted to her since the moment she appeared at Fenton, but didn't want to push things, saying he figured the best things in life are worth the wait.

BJ, so touched by it all, is brought to tears. Crying is something she seldom allows herself to do. It helps nothing, but these were, yet again, happy tears. She seems to be having quite a few of those lately.

Cheryl and Jake take seats next to each other across the table from BJ, who motions for them to dig into the buffet of leftovers she brought.

"How are the housewarming party plans for this Sunday coming along?" Jake asks, conversationally.

"Great," Cheryl assures, mouth half full.

"I assume you will be there?" BJ queries, looking pointedly from one to the other of the pair before her.

"Ah, but of course. Armageddon couldn't keep me from a night with my two favorite women in the world." Jake winks at her and places a light kiss on Cheryl's cheek.

"You, smooth talker you. Cheryl, I think you have a keeper," BJ announces.

Cheryl looks into Jake's eyes, "Yep. I agree."

RJ spent the past few weeks bouncing from city to city all across the country. Eight cities in all, having various meetings and outings with one or more clients in each city. His days are packed with activities, but his nights continue to be filled with dreams and nightmares involving BJ. He is almost sure he prefers the nightmares revolving around her ordeal to the dreams of passionate moments and intimate rendezvous with her that play out in his few hours of sleep.

The client he is scheduled to meet with in the ninth city calls to tell him he needs to reschedule due to a family situation that came up. Under normal circumstances, RJ would have been a bit perturbed, but he actually welcomes the shortened trip. It will be nice to get home to be with his son, even though he talks to him regularly while he is away.

RJ changes his flight plan and boards the next available flight home early Sunday afternoon to surprise his son. Tomorrow they'll do something fun.

For BJ, Sunday morning thunders in with a jolt of excited electricity filling the air. Everyone seems all a buzz. Cheryl comes over early, and she and Jason get busy decorating for the housewarming party later that day. Emily and Millie are in the front house preparing food so as not to clutter up BJ's house; that way, it will be neat and tidy to show off to guests later.

Kristen comes early to wrangle and occupy all three children, as well as others as they arrive.

The band arrives, sets up, and strikes up some quiet background music while the clown with activities for the children gets underway.

A myriad of appetizers, potato and macaroni salads, meatless baked beans and other casseroles are laid out buffet style. The barbecue grills are lit. One for veggie bef burgers, chickun patties and grilled veggies. The second one is to be used for plant-based steaks and ribblets with Butch and Brady manning them. The array of aromas that fills the air is amazing. The band gradually picks up the tempo with every few songs, creating a lively party atmosphere.

Kemp family members, co-workers with their families, all begin arriving, and the buzz becomes a full-blown joy-filled cacophony. BJ is awash with introductions from every direction.

Emily stands surrounded by a throng of people. She motions for BJ to come over. "BJ, allow me to introduce you to my family. This is my eldest daughter, Amelia, and her husband Zachary."

As handshakes are exchanged, Amelia greets, "Please call us Mel, and Zach. It's a pleasure to meet you."

"Nice to meet you both."

"My second daughter, Delia, and her husband, Nathaniel."

"A pleasure." BJ again shakes hands.

"Likewise, and Del and Nate will do."

"Cornelia and her beau, Kavan."

"Neli, please. Nice to meet you."

"Thank you. You too."

"Last, but not least, my youngest, Ophelia, and...? Who do you have with you tonight?"

"Hi. I'm Ophie, and this is my friend Gil," Ophie introduces her escort to everyone.

"There are three little ones running around like hooligans somewhere, I'm sure you'll come across them at some point this evening. The older two are ours, Austin, nine, and Aurora, she's seven." Amelia points out her two.

"Six-year-old Jed is ours," Del supplies as he runs past.

"Wow, you have such a big family." BJ shakes her head. "I probably won't remember all the names, but I'll do my best," she tells the group.

"Don't worry. You'll have plenty of time and opportunity to learn them," Mel assures.

"Where are your girls, we've heard so much about?" Neli asks.

"They're around somewhere with one of their babysitters," BJ answers, looking around for them.

"How many babysitters do you have?" Gil asks.

"Two. I have one who cares for my girls five days a week when I'm at my day job, and another one takes care of them four nights a week when I work my second job," BJ explains.

"When do you have time to spend with your girls?" Kavan asks, bewildered by how much she must work and be away from them.

"Three evenings a week and during the day on Saturdays and Sundays." BJ realizes that to these young men, and maybe to all of the family members before her, it must seem she is away from her girls too much, and may seem like she's an absent parent, but...

"I commend you," Zach pipes up, seeing the wheels of her mind begin spinning, and the expression that crosses her face shows her worry about how that may sound to someone who doesn't understand her circumstances. "Wow. You truly are dedicated to and love your girls so much to work that hard to provide for them. That shows how strong a woman you are. I bet there's nothing you wouldn't do to give them the best life you can. I'm sure you and your girls understand it isn't necessarily the amount of time you spend together, it's how you spend the time you have. From what Mom says, you have wonderful children, which is a testament to how good a mother you are," Zach concludes, smiling at BJ.

Tears well in BJ's eyes. It is overwhelming to have someone speak up for and defend her like that, and he's only just met her.

"I'm hungry," Del breaks the tension. "Let's grab some of the delicious-smelling food."

The cluster begins separating with parting comments such as "We'll talk again in a bit." "Pleasure to meet you." "Welcome to Kemp House"

Zach and Mel stay behind. "Are you OK?" Mel asks, seeing the unshed tears.

"Yes, thank you," she responds, then turns to Zach. "Thank you very much for what you said."

"I meant every word. Mom told us enough about you that we understand you are a great Mom and proud woman. It's an honor to be here tonight to welcome you to your new home here at Kemp House." Zach takes her hand, then hugs her.

Mel puts her arms around BJ as well. "Welcome. They call this a housewarming party, but I know you make any where you are a warm place to be. Now let's go eat! I'm starved."

The party is in full swing. Music, dancing, and children running around. Adults are trying to hold conversations over the din. Dusk arrives, and the ambient lighting turns on. All the crew from the docks have come and brought their significant others and children. Buddy let Josie off for the night so she could attend, and he even left his manager in charge for a few hours so he could come. Kristen's parents did the same. BJ can't believe how many people are there. The most amazing thing to her is that they are there For Her! In her honor. To welcome her. It is surreal.

The energy level is at maximum, loud and uproarious, when inexplicably, BJ experiences a drastic, noticeable drop like a single balloon in a cluster that reached maximum capacity and bursts.

The band is still playing, the children are still squealing, the waterfall can still be heard, but the adult noise suddenly dissipates to a hum, a low murmur.

BJ glances around, curious as to what is taking place. She realizes a portion of the eyes seem to be looking at her, and the rest are looking at... what? She turns to follow the direction of their gaze.

There, standing just inside the gate to the backyard, stands the object of their attention.

The band quiets. The children, obviously noticing the drop in sound level, look up from their playing to see what the adults are all looking at.

"Uncle RJ!"

"Daddy!"

The duet of voices sings out as both children go running from where they've been playing toward the man standing there looking as perplexed and befuddled as BJ is in the moment.

As the pair reach their target, "Oops, I mean, Mr. Fenton," Chumani corrects her faux pas, then glances from Riyon to Mr. Fenton. "Do you know my mommy's boss too?" She asks.

"This is my Daddy," Riyon answers.

Chumani's face lights up like a mercury light as she turns to search out her mother, then spotting her, she calls out, "Mommy, Mr. Fenton is Riyon's Daddy! Isn't that cool?"

BJ stands stock-still as the weight of that tidbit of information sparks a string of thoughts exploding in her head.

RJ bends and scoops up his son in one arm and Chumani in the other. "What's going on here?" he asks the pair loudly enough for all to hear, then looks around at the crowd filling the backyard of his home, taking in all the familiar faces. His siblings with their families. Employees with theirs.

"We're having a 'House Heating Party' for Chumani, Chenoa, and Ms. BJ," Riyon announces, full of excitement.

Emily steps in front of her son as his expressions race through incomprehension, realization, fury, then settle on his mother's face as she corrects, "It's a house *Warming* party, Riyon."

"Same thing. Warming. Heating."

"If you're Riyon's daddy, that means you live here too!" Chumani proclaims. "Yay! Isn't that neat, Mommy?" The look on her mommy's face concerns her, and she squirms to get out of Mr. Fenton's arms. "Mommy?" RJ sets her down. She runs to her mommy. "What's wrong, Mommy?"

Cheryl comes to stand next to BJ, as do Millie, Zach, and Mel. Jason goes to stand next to his wife as Jake approaches RJ. "How's it going, bro? This is a surprise. We didn't expect you to be home for a few more days."

RJ glares at Jake, Mère, and Jason. "I feel like the parent returning home from vacation early to find the kids having a wild party. Would someone like to tell me what the hell is going on?"

"Daddy, you're not s'pose to say bad words, and I already told you, we're havin' a house heating party for Ms. BJ, and her girls."

Emily takes her son's arm, "Let's step in the house and talk. Riyon Dear, you go play while I explain things to your daddy."

"Sure, as hell would like someone to explain to *me* what the hell is going on," BJ announces.

Brady tells the band to start playing again. They start with some background type music, as they had earlier in the evening.

"Mommy? You never say bad words, and you said one twice."

"I'm sorry, Sweetie. Mommy will wash my mouth later. Right now, will you go play with Riyon for a while?"

"OK, but are you OK?"

"I'll be fine, baby girl."

Chumani walks away as BJ turns to look at the adults who have gathered around her.

Cheryl lowers her eyes, reverting to her shy guarded manner.

Mel casts a glance at Millie.

"Awk. Don'a be lookin' at me tha' way. It'll all come out in the warsh," she assures as she walks away.

BJ now peers at Mel and Zach, pleadingly.

"Short version?" Mel asks rhetorically, "RJ Fenton is my big brother, your slightly chauvinistic boss. Our parents, Mère and Jason, learned about you from Millie and decided they want to help you and your beautiful girls. They wanted to have you settled in and comfortable in your new home before you discovered they are your boss's parents. They didn't tell him their plan because they knew he'd have issues with it, and be all bent out of shape about having an employee, especially a female, living with him."

BJ's eyes nearly pop out of their sockets. "Excuse me? I am not living with him!" she spits out through gritted teeth.

"Correction. On the same property."

"That can change easily enough," BJ states.

Zach chimes in once again: "Earlier, I stated that I'm pretty sure you'll do anything to provide the best life you can for your girls. You don't strike me as the kind of woman who would back down from any fight if it meant taking care of them properly. If you had a better option than living here, you'd have been there. Don't blow up a bridge to a better life because there's an ogre living under it. You're on it. Walk right on over him."

BJ thinks about that. He has a point. She stood up to this ogre a few times already. Why would she back down now? Her girls deserve this nice place to live. However, the deceitfulness she's just discovered of the Kemps... *wait a minute!* The thought strikes her like a lightning bolt. She peers at her friend Cheryl, then around the crowd; the crew, Millie, Brady, the Kemp, or more correctly, the Fenton siblings, all the people who have made her feel so welcome and cared for. "You all knew?" her voice full and booming. All those near enough to hear her over the band glance from one to another, with mere facial expressions and head nods, began confirming they'd all known.

BJ's thoughts are conflicted. Betrayal by and deep caring compassion from these people, vying for prominence. These people are either so callous that they didn't care how upsetting their secretiveness would eventually be for her. Or they care so much that they've all been willing to play along to bring her this amazing, joy-filled night. It is evident that no one expected The Boss to show up tonight.

15

"What the hell are you thinking? I can't have an employee living in my house. Especially a female!" RJ burst out at his parents.

"Calm down, Dear," Emily soothes.

"Calm down? That woman already thinks I'm a chauvinistic buffoon. Now, when I have to kick her and her two darling daughters out, sending them back to living in a motel, she'll genuinely hate me and have every right to."

"Don't worry, Son. You won't be kicking them out, so she won't have *that* to hate you for."

"Mère, I cannot have her living in my house."

"That's exactly why you have nothing to worry about. She's not living in *your* house. She's living in *her* house."

At RJ's shocked expression, Jason fills in the blanks.

"Ms. McCallister and her darling daughters are *renting* the newly refurbished pool house, which, you would have known already had you not flown off the handle like the buffoon you so aptly called yourself. That is why we are throwing her a housewarming party, which, again, if you used the brains gifted to you, you might have figured out. There would be no reason to have a housewarming if they were staying in the main house with us."

"Son, I know you have some warped issues pertaining to a female on the docks, but BJ has already proven to be a good dock hand. So, get over it. That young woman has done a hundred times more proving of her strength and fortitude than you can even imagine."

The information RJ garnered from the internet search rushes to his forethought. Eyeing his mother, he asks, "Did you do a background check on her, too?"

"TOO?" the Kemps query in unison, brows raised.

"No, Dear. *We* didn't do a background check. Did you?" Emily asks incredulously. RJ squirms under the scrutiny of Mère's too-knowing eyes. "Why would you do a background check on her?"

"I... I was curious. I wanted to make sure we didn't hire a criminal, a kidnapper or a fugitive with a surly past. Someone who might have some crazy person come looking for them and cause trouble. As a business owner, I have a legal right and responsibility to do a background check on new employees."

"And?" Jason prods. "What did you discover?"

RJ shakes his head, remembering what he discovered about this perplexing female. "You can't even imagine what that woman went through, specifically in the last year."

All RJ's blustering dissipates like the air letting out of a balloon all at once.

Emily looks from Jason to her son. She told Jason what BJ imparted to her almost glibly the night they went shopping. Her glibness about it all was obviously a coping mechanism.

"The accident?" is all Emily says.

RJ inhales sharply. "How..." he begins to ask.

"She told me. I shouldn't have been prying, but I'm glad I know. We'd already begun the process of helping her from what little Millie told us about them, but finding that out? Well, that solidified our resolve to do what we can."

Jason tries to brighten the mood. "So are you ready to swallow your pigheadedness and go back out to the party before your wet blanket arrival completely puts out the flames of fun we've all been experiencing, until you showed up? This is a celebration of a new chapter for them. There's no place for the sad memories tonight. So let's get out there."

Emily, Jason, and RJ emerge from the house, and once again the crowd quiets, though not as drastically as at RJ's first appearance.

RJ's and BJ's eyes meet from across the crowd. RJ smiles, bringing a scowl of curiosity to BJ's face. RJ strides across the patio toward BJ, grabbing the beer Jake holds out to him as he passes.

RJ stops in front of BJ. His sister Mel stands by her side. BJ is not holding a beverage. Looking to his sister, he holds up his beer and asks, "Got one of these around for her?"

Zach saw that BJ is drinking only nonalcoholic beer, so he grabs one from a cooler nearby, handing it to him, RJ opens them both, he hands the nonalc one to BJ, who takes it while still looking puzzled. He turns to the crowd and motions for the band to hold up a minute. Once everyone is quiet, he begins, "It's my understanding that, until I arrived, this was a pretty happening party in honor of the McCallister family getting a nice home to live in. It was not my intention to douse the excitement. So..." He turns back to BJ, holds up his beer in toast pose, "Here's to Ms. McCallister, Chumani, and Chenoa. May they be comfortable and happy in their new home. Sante!"

A chorus of "Sante" rings out.

"Maestro," he calls out, "Crank it up!" The band obliges. Turning back to BJ, "My apologies for having almost ruined your celebration by arriving home early."

"No need to apologize. It's your home to come to. I had no idea. If I knew, I never would have so much as given living here a thought, let alone done it. I'm sorry. The girls and I will move back to the motel a day this coming week, if you can wait that long."

"You'll do no such thing," his voice, deep resonance and forceful.

BJ's eyes shoot up to the face of the man-tower before her. Her expression, quizzical. RJ gazes at this chameleon woman. Taking in this evening's poised, extremely beautiful persona, to be added to the numerous sides of her he's already seen. He smiles, looking around the crowd at Mère, Jason and his siblings, "I fear I would be disowned by my family if you were to leave on my account." Then, looking her in the eye, eyes the deep blue of a fathomless ocean, he thinks of her past year of turmoil, and continues, "Hell, I wouldn't even want to be around myself if you left because of me." Realizing that sounds more telling than he is comfortable with, he continues, trying to regain his gruffer facade, "Your girls don't deserve to live in a motel, or worse."

Taking offense at his statement, BJ squares her shoulders and retorts, "Well, they already have lived in worse, through no fault of mine. I do what I have to do to care for my children and provide them with the best conditions I possibly can with what resources I have available."

Realizing he sounded judgmental, RJ wipes a hand across his face, exhaling heavily. "Look," he begins, again looking into her eyes, a mistake which is nearly his undoing. "I didn't mean to sound... like a pompous ass. I know you're a good mother and do whatever it takes for your girls. What I should have said, meant to say, is that none of you deserve to live in a motel, or worse. Again, I apologize, which is not something I generally have to do often, but it seems I have to do quite a lot with you."

"Whatever." BJ isn't going to let him off the hook quite that easy. "I have no idea what I ever did to cause you to have such a low opinion of me and my abilities in every facet of my life. However, I have no intention of continuing to prove myself to you over and over. I've proven I'm a good dock hand, and that's the only area of my life you need to be concerned with. As for your need to repeatedly apologize to me? If you don't like needing to apologize for rude comments or actions, may I suggest you cease acting and speaking rudely? Like I tell Chumani, if you don't say or do things wrong or mean, you've nothing to apologize for. Think before you act or speak," BJ pauses, takes a deep breath, "Now, if you don't mind, and even if you do, I intend to go back to enjoying the evening, celebrating our having a nice place to live, however short-lived that situation may be. Excuse me, Mr. Fenton." BJ strides off in the direction of her daughters, who are with Millie and Emily.

As BJ approaches, Millie enthuses gaily, "Aye, glad I am that bit's over. Not quite how we 'spected thangs to play out, but maybe for the better this way, with all us 'round for moral support, an' him seein' ya already been welcomed ta the fold, as they say."

BJ eyes the two ladies, cautiously schooling her expression, desperately trying to veil the anger, hurt and betrayal filling her. The fact remains that the love emanating from these women, from everyone here, save one, still fills her beyond measure. She understands they all seem to have the best interests of her little family at heart; she just isn't sure she likes the manner in which they have all been so deceptive and secretive.

"BJ, Dear," Emily says, wrapping her arms around her, hugging her thoroughly, with more sincerity than BJ ever remembers experiencing from anyone other than her girls. "I know you must be feeling deceived, even betrayed," she begins.

"Darn. Here I thought I was doing a pretty darn good job of maintaining a bland expression," BJ attempts to lighten the mood, her own mood specifically.

Emily and Millie chuckle with her; "I hate to tell you, but your eyes belie what your face tries to hide. As it's been said, 'The eyes are the window to the soul', and your crystal blue eyes are spotlessly clear windows at that."

The love expressed by Emily's features is BJ's undoing. Tears well in her eyes.

"'Tis 'nough of this nonsense," Millie interrupts, "There be plenty water 'round here without yar addin' to it with yar salty bits."

Emily and BJ laugh at Millie's way with words. Taking a deep breath, BJ calls out, "Let's Party!"

BJ scoops up Chumani, who's been playing nearby, swings her round, saying, "You haven't gone for a swim yet tonight."

Chumani giggles as Mommy tickles her. "No, I don't have on my bathing suit."

"Awk, no mind that. Yar clothes be warsh and dryable," BJ does an adequate impersonation of Millie's accent. "Ready to go in, are ya?"

"Yes, I mean no, I mean…" Chumani is still giggling, "Help!" she calls out playfully, "The Mommy Tickle Monster is getting me."

"I'll save you, Chumani!" Riyon comes running to the rescue and begins tickling BJ, who laughs, and alternates tickling him as well.

"Me thinks these two hooligans need coolin' down, don'cha know." BJ directs her inquiring expression at Emily to gauge her reaction to the idea of Riyon going into the pool fully clothed, then remembers his father is there, and it should be his decision; she turns her inquisition toward RJ, whose smile at that moment could have powered the entire party and more.

Realizing she is seeking approval to put his son into the water, he holds out both hands palm up while shrugging. Accepting that as approval, BJ latches onto Riyon, still holding the squirming Chumani, shouts "Here we go!", and jumps in with both children in tow. The entire crowd erupts with gasps and laughter.

"Well, I'll be jiggered," is Millie's reaction.

"Land sakes alive," is Emily's response. She glimpses her son's reaction, which is one of utter surprise, as the threesome emerges through the surface of the water, gasping and laughing.

"That was fun!" Riyon announces. Both children begin trying to dunk BJ.

"Help! Help!" she calls out joyfully, making halfhearted attempts to escape.

Riyon doggy paddles next to her and whispers, "Let's get my dad."

Chumani overhears, "YEAH! Let's. I'll go this way, you go that way, Riyon and Mommy can go that way." Chumani secretively points to lay out their plan of attack.

For a split second, BJ panics at the idea, then, at the speed of a hummingbird's wings, throws caution aside. "OK, but we gotta make it look like we're just getting out to dry off and eat. Go over and stay close to him. Wait until you see me give the thumbs up to signal attack. Got it?"

"Got it," they agree in unison. They splash about a minute or two longer, then begin getting out of the pool.

Riyon goes straight to his dad. Chumani accepts the towel Kristen brings her, then heads toward RJ, too. "That was cool," Riyon is telling his father.

"It was so fun," Chumani enthuses as she joins them.

BJ circles around behind RJ undetected. Well, at least undetected by RJ. Others seem to be eyeing the threesome, anticipating what they surmise is about to take place.

"It sure looked like fun," RJ affirms.

"Hey, Bro, can I borrow your phone a minute? I left mine in the car," Jake draws RJ's attention away from BJ's blindsided approach while the kids keep up the excited chatter about trying to dunk BJ. RJ thoughtlessly hands his phone to his friend.

Ophie steps in front of her big brother, wraps her arms around him for a big hug, saying, "With all the commotion, I didn't get my hug yet." After her brother returns the gesture, wrapping his arms around her, Neli pick-pockets his wallet.

"Hey, what are you doing?" he asks.

"Whatever it takes to catch my big brother's attention," she responds teasingly as she frolics a few feet away, taking the wallet with her.

"If you want money from me, little sis, all you have to do is ask," he tells her playfully.

"Cool," Del chimes in. "I want your car." She unlatches the hook of his key ring from his belt loop and snatches his keys.

Stunned, RJ looks to Mère. "Are we in financial trouble, and resorting to becoming a band of pickpockets and thieves?" he asks jokingly above the sounds of music and chatter.

Seeing he's been efficiently stripped of valuable non-waterproof items, BJ gives the signal to the children, who each latch onto a lower limb of the oak tree of a man and begin pulling, effectively compromising his balance as BJ comes up from behind, wraps her arms around his waist, digs her feet in firmly as she begins pushing the man tower toward the pool. The crowd erupts, cheering them on. RJ sputters, "What the...?" he tries tugging loose the little vice clamp arms around his legs. "What...? Who...?" he tries to glimpse who the larger person is helping from behind when he realizes that one is also wet against him. As the thought that there is only one person, other than the kids, who is wet reaches his mind, the realization *that* is no longer true immediately becomes evident as he finds himself submerged in the silent depths of the pool.

The uproarious applause, cheers, and laughter that greet his ears as his head breaches the surface are almost deafening. He swirls around searching out the culprits of this assault. He first spots his son and Chumani, who are already making their way safely toward the edge in the shallow end.

BJ emerges near him. After wiping the water from her face, she experiences the heat of the amber-flaming glare of her opponent. It is time to high-tail it out of there, and fast, before the water begins to boil. In an instant, his expression switches from anger to be replaced with what BJ can only describe as mischievousness. *"All the more reason to flee, and fast,"* her inner voice warns. She turns, diving under the water, and away from the devilish grin she just witnessed. Unfortunately, his 6'4" frame means his arm span is 6'4" as well, which covers nearly half the width of the pool, making it virtually impossible to get past him, so she dives deeper. He follows. His grasp is that of a steel manacle, halting her escape. She struggles diligently against his grip, trying to break free.

"What the hell are you doing?" his thoughts rail against his actions. *"Now that you have hold of her, what do you intend to do?"* His eyes open. A moment of panic crosses BJ's face until she finds him looking at her, then it turns to determination to break free from his touch. He doesn't know how it is possible, but the temperature of the water is rapidly

increasing, or is it his temperature? All of a sudden, the need for air is overwhelming, and he is sure she is probably about to run out of oxygen as well, so he swims for the surface, bringing her along, kicking and flailing. They breach the surface simultaneously, both gasping for air, though he doesn't let loose his grip around her slender waist.

"Let me go!" BJ demands, coughing and sputtering.

"Not a chance," is RJ's aggravatingly calm response.

"I said, let me go," BJ grinds out defiantly.

"You honestly think you can get away with a stunt like that without payback?"

BJ minimizes her squirming, stares him squarely in the eye, "And exactly how do you propose to pay me back? I'm already wet," she states vehemently, then instantly regrets her choice of words as a gleam of excitement sparks in his eyes that is nothing to do with the party atmosphere surrounding them and is absolutely not G, PG, or even R-rated.

"Yes, I bet," his voice is rich, and thick as sweet molasses, and abhorrently conceited. Not an inkling of warning given, he kisses her. Long and hard.

For a brief moment, she welcomes the hot contact of his mouth on hers, then her common sense comes flooding back. She pushes at his chest, so strong and wonderfully taut it is beneath her palms. *"Snap out of it!"* her logical mind screams. She places her hands on his face, pushing his head back, breaking the contact of the kiss, then... SLAP! Her hand makes second contact with his face.

His grasp loosens ever so slightly. Their eyes meet. "Damn!" His voice now deeper, raspy, quiet, "I'm sorry," he finds himself saying, yet again, to this woman. "That was uncalled for..." He begins

"Uncalled for?" She spats at him. "Like hell it was. You deserved that, and more."

"Really?" The gleam returns to his eyes. "Shall we go another round?" RJ peers pointedly at her mouth, licking his lips.

BJ stares at him, thoroughly confused. Is this a sadistic man who enjoys being hit? In a flash, it strikes her. He meant that his action was uncalled for. Her hot-headed, hair-trigger response caused her to respond inappropriately, making her choice of words come across, yet again, a bit provocative.

"Oh... No... I thought you meant my slapping you..."

"Yes, I know what you thought. I just couldn't resist teasing you." His smirk and wink somehow make her relax a bit, still encircled in his arms, looped about her.

BJ notes that she is still treading water, her feet occasionally brushing against his legs, as she tries to keep her head above water. Next, she realizes, he doesn't seem to be exerting any effort to keep himself afloat when it dawns on her that at his height at this area of the pool, he is probably standing. She glances down to confirm his feet are on solid ground. The sight that catches her eye is not that of his legs or feet, but that of a different appendage straining against the loose material of his business slacks. Her eyes pop as her head jerks back up to view the amused expression on his face.

"Do you think you could stop squirming against me for a bit?" he speaks ever so quietly, for her ears only. "I'll support you so you won't go under," he assures her.

BJ becomes stock-still. The look of horror on her beautiful face causes RJ to chuckle and smile before saying, "I think I need to swim a few laps before attempting to disembark from the pool..."

"Fully clothed?" BJ inquires, surprised.

"Unless, of course, you prefer I disrobe right here, right now, and give you my clothing," he pauses at the next horrified look that crashes onto her face. "That's what I thought. As I was saying...I need to swim a bit. I'm letting you know, I'm about to let go of you... for now," he winks again.

A warm flush engulfs not only her face, but her entire body.

RJ smirks, gives her a little shove in the direction of the shallow end so she's able to touch the bottom, then swims off in the opposite direction.

It is at that moment that BJ remembers the throng of people standing around witnessing everything that just transpired. Her face blushes with embarrassment as she climbs out of the pool. Cheryl stands holding a huge beach towel, which BJ gratefully accepts, wraps around herself, and hides her face in.

"How about you go change into dry clothes?" Cheryl suggests.

"Good idea." BJ enters her new home dripping wet, closes the door, strips, then wraps the towel around her before heading to her room. A few minutes later, clad in dry clothing, she steps into the bathroom to take stock of the state of her hair and face. *"Oh well,"* she thinks. She wipes away a few smudges of mascara, applies fresh lip gloss, runs the brush through her sopping hair, and ties it up in a high ponytail. *"So much for all the time spent earlier curling it to look nice for once,"* she thinks.

The thought that she needs to go back out there and face all those people after the scene that just played out strikes fear in her as she walks toward the door. *"Here goes nothing."*

16

Surprisingly, BJ finds everyone still mingling around, some dancing, chatting as if the episode never happened. She finds herself searching the crowd for RJ to determine where not to go when a voice comes from behind.

"He's in the house composing himself and redressing as well." It is Jason Kemp. "Are you alright?" BJ's momentary questioning expression prompts him to clarify, "Are you alright about... Everything?"

BJ draws a deep cleansing breath before answering, "I have selfishly decided that this is not the time to be concerned about anything other than enjoying this evening, this magical experience, the likes I've never experienced or even witnessed before. As for tomorrow, and what happens next? To quote a song from my youth,"

The big, fatherly man envelopes her in a deep, loving embrace. Her arms wrap around his waist to hug him back. When he gently withdraws, "BJ," when she lifts her gaze in response, he continues, "It is an honor to have you be a part of our lives."

BJ isn't sure how to respond to that, so she simply smiles, "Thank you."

"Some of the guests are beginning to head out, but want to say goodbye to you first," he informs, guiding her toward the gate where people are gathering, waiting to bid her goodnight. Yet another new experience for BJ as a guest of honor.

RJ chooses not to return to the party right away. Instead, he stands lurking in the shadows, peering out the window from behind the curtain, watching the festivities winding down. The band finishes and begins packing up. RJ turns on the outdoor surround sound, opting for a bit more soothing music to bring the evening to a close as the non-Fenton-Kemp clan, employees and their families depart first. Watching how they all embrace BJ in parting hugs, he notes her expression change from one of pure awe that these people are bestowing affection upon her and her daughters to one of grateful acceptance that they are.

"I'm telling Mère you're spying," comes the playful sound of his third sister, Neli. She winds her arms around her big brother's waist.

"I was just..."

"I know what you were 'just' doing. You were spying on a beautiful woman who somehow succeeded in breaching a crack in that tough guy armor of yours."

RJ opens his mouth to argue, but is silenced by the look of knowing in his little sister's eyes.

"Don't worry, I'll keep your secret... for now, though after that scene earlier I'm pretty sure you're the only one that hasn't figured out how this story should... dare I say, will end." She ends the hug, walking away, "Are you coming back out, or do I need to tell Mère where you're hiding since she's who sent me to find you?"

RJ follows Neli out.

"There you are, bro. Where have you been hiding?"

RJ shoots Neli a warning look. She smiles in return, mouthing, "You owe me."

"I took a quick shower to wash off the chlorine."

"And cool down?" his lifelong buddy teases.

RJ's face flushes, a first-time occurrence, and his best friend doesn't miss it. "Wow," is Jake's response.

"Well, Bro, we need to be going, as we both have to be at work early in the morning, and our boss doesn't take kindly to employees arriving late. Considering it seems he likes to show up *way* early—like *days* early," Jake teases.

At that moment, Jake's arm around Cheryl's waist registers in RJ's brain, and he does a quick replay of what his buddy said. "Did you just say WE need to be going?"

"Ah, nice of you to finally get your wits about you long enough to remember there are actually other people at this event tonight. Yes, I said we, as in Cheryl and I. Together finally. Thanks, in part, to your fair maiden."

RJ's confusion, evident by his expression, Jake clarifies, "BJ, you dumb ass."

"She's not *my* anything. Except my employee," RJ retorts.

"And your tenant," Cheryl supplies, smiling.

"And your Damsel-in-Distress. Like Cheryl is mine." Jake winks, giving her a squeeze.

Seeing the expressions pass between the two lovebirds before him, RJ says in jest, "Get a room."

"Look who's talking," Zach, who's been standing observing the conversation, awaiting his chance to tell his brother-in-law goodnight, chimes in. "Hell, we were all taking bets on who thought the 'real' you was abducted by aliens, and finally replaced with a real human."

Numerous people in earshot join in on the laughter.

"Some of us," Nate imparts as he too joins the conversation, "were taking bets as to whether you would completely forget there were, oh, I don't know, like fifty-some people standing around observing, and have a make-out session right there in the middle of a well-lit, sparkling, clean pool. By the way... the babysitters took action, and corralled your kids along with the others, and took them to the play equipment around back just in case."

RJ has never in his life been so embarrassed and appalled by his actions. He looks around at the group of jovial faces, beaming smiles. "My apologies to all of you, and everyone who is here. I promise you, nothing like that will ever happen again."

"Damn! I knew when he said he was going in the house to *change,* we should have stopped him. The aliens returned this guy and took back the human RJ," Zach announces jokingly, to which everyone laughs.

RJ spots BJ engaged in parting conversation with others. Returning his attention to Jake and Cheryl, he says, "For the record, BJ is far from being anyone's Damsel-in-Distress. Least of all mine. She's too independent."

"Remember, strong independent women often are so because they *have* to be. It's not always a choice, and even if it is by choice, that doesn't mean they wouldn't appreciate a helping hand occasionally. Emily and Jason were smart enough to know that. That's why we are all here tonight, after all." Jake imparts a bit of wisdom.

"Kristen put Chenoa ta bed a while ago. I took Chumani in an' got her tucked inta bed as well, but no' without the promise I would 'ave her Mommy *an'* Mr. Fenton come tell her goodnight," Millie fills BJ in and informs her of the deal struck with the wee lass, before saying her final goodnight.

"Thank you. I'll check on her. She's probably already sleeping. We will not be starting any practices to intrude on the Kemps or Fentons."

Soon, all the goodbyes are over, and the only ones remaining are the residents.

BJ steps soundlessly into the girls' room.

"Hi, Mommy."

"Hey, baby girl. You should be asleep."

"I was waiting to tell you how much fun today was."

"Yes, it was a lot of fun, wasn't it? Now you need to go to sleep. We'll talk about it tomorrow.

"Where's Mr. Fenton? I want to tell him goodnight, too. Isn't it cool that it ended up that he's Riyon's daddy, and we live by him? Now he doesn't have to come to the motel to visit us 'cause we can see him every day, and..."

"Sweetie, stop."

"Why, Mommy?"

BJ puts her face in her hands, drawing a calming breath before she begins. "Mr. Fenton is Mommy's boss. He's also Riyon's daddy. He runs a business all day, and he travels a lot, so when he's home, he needs to be with his son and spend time with his own family. You wouldn't want Mommy to go spend time with someone else's kids at bedtime, and leave you, right?"

"No, I guess not."

"Riyon needs his Daddy with him every second he can get with him. You don't have a Daddy, and Riyon doesn't have a Mommy. So, like I have to be both Mommy and Daddy for you and Chenoa, Mr. Fenton needs to be both for Riyon. You understand?"

Chumani nods. "Least Mr. Fenton and Riyon have Mémère and Misho too. I just wish…"

"Honey, let Mommy explain something. We are renting this house from very nice people, but we won't be imposing ourselves on them."

"What does 'posing mean?"

"*Imposing*, and it means that we can't bother or annoy them. They have their family, relatives, and friends, and they all have their own lives to live. *Our* family is still only the three of us, and always will be." Chumani tears up. "Sweetie, don't cry. I understand that it's hard to be around people with lots of loving family members, and wish we had that too, but that's not the kind of family we have. I'm sorry that all you have is me. I try hard to be the best me I can be, to make up for you not having anyone else. I understand right now that may not seem like enough for you, but I hope one day you will understand and appreciate everything." She scoops Chumani into her arms, hugging her tightly, both with tears streaming down their faces. A hand lightly touches her back, and thinking it is probably Jason's, she only tenses slightly.

Sensing someone's presence, Chumani opens her eyes. "Mr. Fenton!" she exclaims, causing BJ to tense rigidly.

RJ kneels down next to the pair of crying females, placing a comforting hand on Chumani's back, too, as the little one leans back in her mommy's arms to look at him. Using the hand that was on BJ's back, he wipes the tears from Chumani's cheeks.

"Hey, there, Sweetie. Don't cry," he says, his voice deep and thick with emotion from witnessing and overhearing this private moment.

"Mommy's crying too," Chumani informs, sniffling.

RJ swallows hard, then looks to BJ's face, seeing the tears, he repeats the action of wiping them from her cheeks as well, and repeats, "Don't cry."

"Mommy said you couldn't come say goodnight, 'cause you have your own family and need to be with Riyon, 'specially at bedtime, 'cause he doesn't have a Mommy."

"That's right. I do need to be there with him as much as possible, including at bedtime. But Millie told me you wanted to say goodnight too, so I've come over to tell you goodnight before Riyon, and I hit the sack. However," RJ turns his attention to BJ before continuing, "Riyon requests Ms. BJ, please come over there so he may tell you goodnight as well."

BJ's look of surprise brings smiles to RJ and Chumani. "See, Mommy. Riyon likes you like I like Mr. Fenton."

"I'll sit with Chumani while you go tell my son goodnight."

"But…"

"But what?" RJ asks as Chumani crawls from her mother's arms into RJ's when he sits on the edge of her bed.

"Go, Mommy. Riyon's waiting for you. You don't want him to cry like I did when I thought Mr. Fenton wasn't coming, do you?"

"No, Sweetie, I don't want anyone to cry."

"We'll be right here when you come back. K?"

BJ rises and heads for the door, glancing back at her daughter sitting so comfortably on her boss's lap. The sight tugs at her heart. With tears welling, she leaves the room.

Emily shows BJ to Riyon's room.

"Hey there, big fella. I hear you want to see me."

"Yeah, I want to tell you how cool it is that you helped us push my daddy in the pool. That was so fun."

"Yes, it was fun, wasn't it?" BJ smiles, realizing she has never done anything so silly, and how much she enjoyed it.

"I want to tell you that I am *really* glad you guys came to live here. It is so nice having you, Chumani, and baby Chenoa here. It's kinda like our family got bigger. It's cool," he looks thoughtful for a moment. "Do you sing lullabies to your girls?"

"Yes, most nights I do. Why?"

"Could you sing one to me? Daddy reads, but he doesn't sing, and Mémère says she can't carry a tune in a bucket, whatever that means. I think that means she can't sing."

BJ smiles. "Yes, that's what that is supposed to mean. I'm not a great singer, but I'll sing to you if you'd like."

"Yes, please."

BJ sings the songs she sings to her girls each night. Riyon closes his eyes. Smiling, he whispers as she sings, "This is what it's like to have a Mommy." Tears again well up, a lump in her throat threatens to prevent her from continuing to sing. She swallows hard and continues. It doesn't take long for the steady, even breathing of sleep to envelop the miniature of her boss. The thought strikes her how very much this young man resembles his father, broaching the question in her mind, why didn't she recognize the similarities before? Why didn't she make the connection? There are so many signals and signs she missed.

When she finishes singing, she returns to her place to find Chumani sleeping soundly in RJ's arms. The sight overwhelms her, once again raising tears to breach their floodgates. RJ looks up as she enters the room, whispering, "She asked if I could hold her until she was asleep," he explains. "I'm afraid to put her down for fear of waking her," he fibs. He is really just sitting there holding her, looking at her, noticing how much she resembles her mother. Sorrow for her lack of a father envelops him with the same intensity as it does for his son's lack of a mother. Situations so different, yet so similar. BJ helps him carefully lay her daughter in her bed, covering her with her favorite blankie, then, as quiet as the whisper of an evening breeze, they leave the room after peeking at Chenoa, who still sleeps soundly, giving credence to the saying *slept like a baby.*

"Thanks…"

"I didn't…"

They both begin at once after entering the great room.

"Go ahead…" they speak again at once, causing them both to chuckle lightly. This time, BJ just points at him, smiling.

"What I was about to say was, I didn't mean to eavesdrop, nor did I intend to override what you told Chumani about my not being able to come say good night. I apologize for both. Damn!" he curses under his breath, smiling. "I have not apologized to anyone, or even this much at all, in my life, yet I find myself apologizing to you constantly." He shakes his head in disbelief. "What were you saying?"

I was saying thank you for coming to say good night to Chumani. You didn't have to. That was very nice of you."

"I have to admit it wasn't a difficult decision. When Millie told me I wanted to come, but as you told your daughter, I too thought that I needed to be there for my son, who promptly became excited at the idea of a 'parent exchange' as he put it. I was forcefully informed that I must come to Chumani so you could go to him," he smiles, a touch of hurt in his expression, she isn't quite sure is real or contrived.

"I see," BJ says thoughtfully. "So, what you're saying is your son is a mini you in all manners, including being a mini dictator?" She smiles to soften the sting of her words.

"Ouch," RJ replies playfully as he is sure she at least halfway meant the accusation to be taken. He looks thoughtful for a moment. "Is that how I come across? A dictator? Am I that bad?" he asks her seriously.

"I can only speak from my own experiences and observations. I do sense with much of the crew, while you must have their respect as their boss, sometimes it seems they more fear you than respect you." BJ goes on in response to the slightly stricken look that washes over his handsome features, "Don't get me wrong. I'm not saying you're a bad boss, but there's a fine line between ruling with an iron fist and *leading* your troops to greatness. You've almost found that balance, but seem to still be a bit more of a ruler than a leader."

"Wow. Thank you for your candor. That's refreshing. Other than my family, the only one who is candid with me is Jake, and he's basically my brother." At her questioning expression, he explains, "Our parents were best friends. His dad worked with my father for my grandfather before my father took over the business. Jake and I were born two weeks apart. We were raised together. Our families did everything together, from holidays to vacations, you name it. He was my only 'sibling' for ten years until my sisters began showing up."

RJ is sure BJ's wistful expression is due to her not having any siblings at all. He is going to have to be careful not to let on how much knowledge he has about her due to all the background checking he's done, even after his initial search with Drew. He found all sorts of public records, and some not so public, revolving around all that took place after the horrifying accident that took what little family she had. The financial raping that took place was unconscionable. The fact that this woman and two children have survived all they have is a grand testament to the fortitude of the woman standing mere steps from him. Seeing her standing there looking relaxed in his presence brings back a rush of memories of what transpired between them earlier in the evening.

"Um, about earlier..." BJ tenses, causing him to regret bringing it up, but he continues, "I can't remember if I apologized for that yet, since I seem to be apologizing to you so much the apologies are all kind of blurring together," his laugh, temperate to abate the tension on the face of the beautiful woman before him.

It works, evidenced by the expression she graces him with when she raises her eyes to meet his. "Sad thing is, you're right. There have been so many apologies, I don't even remember if you apologized for that horrifying escapade," her tone, a morsel of anger tempered with a smidgen of teasing.

His brows raise in mock surprise, instantly followed by a childlike pout of hurt. "Horrifying?" Then, more seriously, "Was it honestly that bad?"

The smoldering look that washes away the moments before playful expression causes BJ to inhale sharply. Her chest constricts; she swallows hard and blushes. She lowers her eyes in hopes he doesn't catch how the memory affects her. Too late.

Without conscious thought, in a gentle swiftness, RJ closes the gap of mere feet between them. His index finger gently lifts BJ's chin. A myriad of emotions flash in the depths of the fathomless pools that are her eyes. On his next breath, he is inhaling her essence as their mouths meet in a feather-light embrace. His inhalation deepens, filling his lungs with her. When finally, he exhales, the sensation is as if he just inhaled and experienced the purest breath of life. His eyes open to mere slits to take in the sight of her. She is a vision of serenity, as if floating in a still, calm pond on a lazy summer afternoon.

Somewhere in the recesses of RJ's mind, three words, which thread through a variety of popular songs' lyrics, begin floating there. The tingling sensation that envelopes him is undoubtedly what makes them such popular lyrics. His heart whispers, this is what it is to experience a last first kiss.

With the lightness of touch of the finest feather, RJ's index finger still holds BJ's chin. Her eyes flash fear, excitement, desire and her mouth goes bone dry with the sharp, heated breath she inhales, causing the tip of her tongue to peek out to moisten her lips. Deep desire is evident in the sparkling amber eyes caressing her face that halt when they meet the deep blue of her own. BJ's heart whispers to her, *"If this is to be my last first kiss, or even my last kiss, I can die content."*

RJ closes the breath of space between them, his hot, hungry lips ever so gently connecting with BJ's delicate, moist mouth. In a wink of a moment, she is floating where there is no time, no space, only sensation and what a glorious sensation it is. So glorious, in fact, she doesn't even realize the loss of contact from the feather-light embrace of the warm, moist mouth that moments before was caressing hers. Time pauses. When BJ's eyes ease open, she finds herself looking straight into RJ's.

"Was that a bit less horrifying?" he asks, his resonant voice a mere whisper.

BJ's mind screams, *"NO! More horrifying than ever! Because it felt so wonderfully amazing, and it shouldn't. I should be slapping, hitting, and pushing you away."* However, what she wants to do instead is melt into his arms. *"Run!"* Screams one part of her. *"Enjoy,"* soothes another part of her. What she answers aloud, "A bit."

He smiles, thinking *"That will do... for now."* His response aloud, "Glad to hear that."

<h1 style="text-align:center">17</h1>

"BJ?" RJ speaks her name softly, with reverence. Her eyes respond along with a soft, "Hmm?"

"I don't understand *this* yet," he gestures, indicating the two of them, "I'm pretty sure you don't either. Think we can agree to let it be, take baby steps, and see where it goes?" She doesn't answer right away, and he continues, "Trust me, I'm as scared as you are."

Her expression, one of incredulity; he nods in confirmation.

"What are you scared of?" she asks.

It is his turn to not respond right away. She waits.

"You. What I feel for...you, your girls. How I'm acting, reacting, to everything to do with you. It's...not like me. I...I don't 'do' emotional entanglements. Yet, I'm experiencing something...feelings I never have. Not for anyone. It's all new to me, and it's scaring the hell out of me," he ends with a soft self-disapproving shake of his head, and laugh at himself.

BJ isn't quite sure how to respond to his open candor. She is pretty sure that, too, is not something he does, at least not often. She thinks of what Emily told her about her son, whom, at the time, BJ had no idea that man and this one were one and the same, but now, recalling Emily's words about her son not loving any woman, not even his son's mother, makes what he says now ring true and make sense. She has to be careful not to let on that his mother imparted personal information about him, even though she didn't know it was about him.

"Not sure your idea is the best plan."

RJ smiles, trying to ease some of the tension, "You mean you'd rather not take baby steps and just plunge full steam ahead?"

"Nooo."

"What are you scared of?"

"For starters? You're my boss," BJ reminds him.

"True. What else?" he prods.

BJ thinks a moment, then decides, since he is being honest with her, the least she can do is reciprocate that honesty. "Being hurt again...emotionally, and physically. Having my girls become emotionally attached to someone they can lose. I don't want them hurt."

"So, you're already planning to break up with me, and we haven't even gotten together yet?" he teases. "Wow. I've heard of planning ahead, but..." he winks. "I understand you not wanting the girls to become attached, therefore hoping they never get hurt. Unfortunately, Chumani seems to already like me...*whole lots...*" he finishes in a child-like manner.

A bit exasperated by that thought, BJ turns to step out of the loop of his arms she realizes she is still in.

RJ lets her go, though he does so against his will. Hating the emptiness of his arms, the rapid distance as she steps away, he fights his desire to draw her back.

"Are you OK?" he asks after she stands there with her back to him for some time. She doesn't respond, he steps to her, touches her shoulder, she jolts at his touch, her eyes full with fear. "I'm sorry, I didn't mean to startle you." Again, he asks, "Are you OK?"

"Yes. No! I don't know. I... don't need *this*. I don't want complications. I need to make a stable life for my daughters and myself without the risk of any more drama, trauma and pain. I can't allow my foolish feelings to jeopardize my goals for a solid, secure, free from disappointment, happy life for my girls. I can't do....*this*... not slow, not fast, not at all."

The strained pain in her voice, the tears clogging her throat as she speaks, causes him to pause until she draws in a deep, calming breath before saying, "I hear you. I understand what you're saying. However, you and I both know from experience, it's not possible to predict the outcome of any plans or circumstances. We both have proof of that in our lives, including... this."

BJ turns to look at him as he speaks, compassion in his eyes, he continues, "It's obvious neither of us had any intentions of anything of this nature evolving between us... or at all.

She snorts softly. "Exactly."

"But like with all other circumstances we've experienced in our lives, the fact of the matter is we have to take them as they come, and deal with them in the best manner possible for all involved. Are you willing to walk away and risk missing out on *what could have been*? Miss something possibly amazing?"

BJ looks him straight in the eye, "Yes. You have no idea what I've survived or what I've lost due to decisions I've made. I understand better than most the risks involved with every choice made every second. That's why I know that I would rather pass up on... *this*, and lose *this* now before I become, before the girls become, so invested that the loss would cause yet another devastating which we already survived once, I doubt we could survive again."

Her pain, so palpable, it is as if it is his own. It takes more willpower than he believes he is capable of to not take her in his arms and tell her he knows all about it. Not now. Things are moving too rapidly. He isn't thinking clearly. RJ needs to back off. They both just stand there another minute, the air crackling with tension. Finally, RJ draws a deep, steadying breath before saying, "It's late. I should go. See you tomorrow at work?"

In that instant, BJ remembers who this man is. Her boss, the man she overheard her coworkers discussing his trip to seduce and conquer various prospects. Evidently, he didn't sate his voracious appetite while away. How could she have forgotten and allowed herself to become one more prospect, worse, she almost allowed herself to become yet another conquest?

"Of course, I'll be there and, I imagine, since you're back from your... *prospecting...* trip," BJ emphasizes the term with disdain, "that you will be too, at least until your next one."

RJ isn't sure what just transpired, why her tone sounds so angry, contemptuous. He decides they are both tired and reeling from all the activity of the past few hours. What he does know is that he likes the BJ of a few minutes ago a whole lot better than this rigid, angry beauty before him now.

"Even though this trip got cut short, somehow it still seemed too long. Funny how when I was younger, I used to love taking these extended trips. Date after date of packed activity was exhilarating. Now? All I could think of was getting home, seeing my son..." he lets the sentence hang. Not finishing the thought, rambling on in his mind, *"you, your girls."*

"Well, I'm sure when you were younger your...*stamina* was much better."

Again, her tone is disdainful and...? Hurt? No, that can't be, but something is going through that pretty head. He is too tired and confused to try to figure it out tonight. Though he still has an ounce of teasing left in him to try to bring an upward curve to the soft lips he kissed a short while ago, the ones he wishes he were kissing again right now.

"Are you implying that I'm getting too old to do long business trips?"

"Business trips? Is that what you call them?" BJ thinks to herself... or did she? Seeing the shocked, puzzled expression on the masculine face mere feet away, she realizes she must have spoken those questions aloud.

"Yeees," RJ draws out the word, his tone a bit puzzled, "When one travels to conduct business, that is generally the term used."

"Oh, I didn't... I mean, I knew that. It's just... never mind... I'm tired. We need to get to bed... I mean, I need to get to sleep," she stammers. "I have to be up early to go to work. I wouldn't want my boss to think I'm getting any preferential treatment by being allowed to arrive late, even if it is his fault that I won't be getting enough sleep tonight," her tone less angry, with a hint more sarcasm.

A devilish gleam sparks in his amber eyes, "Because you'll be having sweet dreams of me?" he inquires, brows fluttering.

"No," she states sternly, but a telltale blush creeps across her face at the thought that maybe she will dream of him, his kisses.

"Well, since I believe your boss may have a similar issue tonight, I think he'll be a bit more understanding than normal tomorrow." The devilish gleam that sparked moments ago is now in full flame, fueling BJ's slight blush to full blaze.

RJ steps toward the door, pauses, turns back to BJ, kisses her rosy cheek, saying, "Goodnight, BJ. Don't worry if you're late tomorrow; I'll clear it with the boss." RJ leaves before BJ can respond. Before he can find another reason to stay.

BJ locks the door, turns off the lights, goes straight to her room, puts on her sleep clothes, and climbs into her queen-sized bed. As she snuggles down into the comfy, earth-toned, nature-inspired bedding, closing her eyes, she is so ready for sleep to carry her off, when all of a sudden, thoughts of her discussion with Emily regarding the purchase of such a large bed come rushing back to her. *"One never knows, Dear, one day you may have adult company to share it with."*

BJ wonders if Emily would be horrified at the thought of the possibility of that 'adult company' being her son? With the full intensity of a stage spotlight sparking to life, the thought strikes BJ; *Or? Is that what Emily's intention has been all along?*

BJ drifts into fitful sleep just as RJ predicted. Her exhausted mind races with thoughts and dreams of her with RJ, RJ spending time with her girls, the five of them spending time together...

RJ drifts into fitful sleep just as he feared. His mind races with thoughts and dreams of BJ. His discovery of the accident ignited a desire to find out more about her, but the occasional skittishness and glimmers of fear from this otherwise steadfast, unwavering woman, his desire to learn even more. Just before his sleep deepens beyond thought, he decides to delve deeper into her past.

The alarm rings, and it is as though she didn't sleep a wink. However, she will not be late. She won't allow the happenings of yesterday to afford her any special privileges. She's not giving her boss that to hold against her in some later circumstance.

The alarm rings, and RJ wakes with two things BJ said last night that kept replaying in his mind even as he slept... and still are...*"Being hurt again...emotionally and physically...* and *"You have no idea what I've survived or what I've lost due to decisions I've made."* RJ's resolve is set. He is going to discuss his decision to delve deeper into BJ's past with Jason, maybe get his help researching.

While BJ is preparing her cup of coffee, she recalls something Millic said last night as she was leaving, *"The wee lasses will probably be a tad tired in the morn'. You should jus' let 'em sleep, an' I can get 'em up and fed whene'er they wake."*

BJ doesn't really want to do that because she wants to be with her girls every moment she can. However, as things have played out, she is so tired she decides to take Millie up on the idea this one time.

On her drive to work, with a little self-talk, she also decides that she isn't going to allow the events of yesterday to adversely affect her mood today or any day. She chooses to maintain her joy of having a nice place, at least temporarily, to raise her girls.

"Morning, BJ," Jake greets her on the dock.

"Morning, Jake," BJ responds in her usual bright, cheery mood.

Jake expected a different mood from her this morning due to the incidents of last night. However, it seems BJ decided to pick which portions of last evening she wants to remember and pretend the embarrassing moments never happened. It seems the crew came to the same decision. As for RJ's mood? It is mostly back to normal. Cantankerous as usual, if not a bit more so, but with an unusual something about him that not even Jake witnessed in their lifetime. A peculiar look seems to appear on RJ's face when he comes out to the dock and spots BJ working, appearing to not take note of his presence. Jake can only describe it as 'hurt'. Though it is fleeting and the day rolls on.

The rest of the week finds BJ doing her best to remain aloof and unaffected, with RJ daily more puzzled by her ability to easily do so.

18

"Good morning, my little man," RJ greets his son early on this overcast Monday, a week after the party. "So today is the big day. Your very first day of school. How are you feeling about that?"

"I'm OK. I'm not scared or nothin', but..." Riyon pauses, looking thoughtful.

"But what, buddy?"

"I've been thinking. Chumani is the same age as me. Isn't she supposed to be starting school, too? It would be so cool if we were going together. That way, I could watch out for her. Make it so she wouldn't be scared."

RJ looks at Mère questioningly.

"Oh my. With all that's been going on, it seems none of us gave it a thought that she should be registered for school as well. Though she wouldn't be attending school with you, Riyon," she concludes, looking at her grandson.

"Why not?"

"Well, Dear," she begins glancing at RJ as she explains, "you'll be attending a private school, which costs a lot of money, and Ms. BJ wouldn't be able to afford to send Chumani there, so Chumani will have to be enrolled in a public school."

"That's not fair! That sucks. Then I want to go to Public school so I can go with Chumani."

"Watch your language, young man." Mémère admonishes her grandson, then looks at her son. "Well?"

"Well, what? My son will not be attending public school."

"Then I won't go to school at all. I'll stay home with Chumani," Riyon states belligerently.

"We can offer to pay for Chumani's tuition," Emily states encouragingly.

"She's too damn proud, she'd never accept that."

"Watch your language, young man," Emily now admonishes her son. "What if there were a scholarship of sorts that she qualified for? She'd never have to know."

RJ looks at his mother, knowing that if he doesn't handle this, she will.

"Fine Mère. I'll handle the 'scholarship'. You handle getting her to go for it, and enroll Chumani." He turns to his son, "I know we teach you not to lie or keep secrets, but this one time, at least for now, I'm requesting you say nothing about this conversation. Are we clear?"

"If it means Chumani gets to go to school with me, I'll take this to the grave." He smiles hugely at Daddy's and Mémère's quizzical expressions. "I heard that on TV."

They laugh.

"OK, good. You better hurry and finish your breakfast, or you're going to be late for your very first day of school, and that will not look good on your school transcripts for sure. Get a move on," RJ encourages.

RJ and Riyon arrive at school right on time. RJ escorts his son to his classroom. Not realizing how emotional that small act would turn out to be, RJ is caught off guard when tears sting his eyes as a myriad of thoughts rush through his mind. *"Holy cow, my son is growing up... This is the first day of thirteen-plus years of school, homework, projects, activities, sports, dances, girls... How will BJ handle Chumani's first day of school? However, the thoughts that grab him hardest are: How can Riyon's mother be OK with not experiencing any of this?... How could any woman simply walk away from a being she created, and never look back?"*

"See you tonight, Daddy," Riyon says, giving his father a huge hug then walks away confidently.

After Riyon is out of earshot, a mother standing nearby warns, "Enjoy those goodbye hugs while they last. This is my 3rd time through this. Trust me it doesn't take long for them to feel the peer pressure that hugging your parents goodbye is for sissies. Too bad his mother couldn't be here for his first day. No job is worth missing special moments like these. They're grown in the blink of an eye. She'll regret it one day, mark my word."

RJ feels conflicted about this strange woman's bold, blunt statements, especially about his son's mother. He knows she has no way of knowing there is no mother in the picture, still it seems pretty bold to assume his mother had chosen work over this landmark event. Yet, her comment makes him wonder if Riyon's mother is somewhere thinking about missing this event and regretting her absence.

Knowing it is probably rude not to respond at all, RJ chooses the simple response of, "Thanks," then walks away.

RJ meets with the headmaster. Though he doesn't want to go into too many details, he needs to provide some explanation: "My parents have rented our pool house to an employee of mine, who is a struggling single mother. Her daughter is the same age as my son, Riyon, and should be enrolled in school. Due to all the recent upheaval in their lives, that fact is not yet attended to. My son, Riyon, and her daughter, Chumani, have become very close. Riyon is adamant that it will be best for Chumani to attend school with him. However, this mother's pride would not allow her to accept what she would consider to be charity from my family if we offer to pay. My mother suggested we circumvent that refusal by creating a 'Scholarship' of sorts that could be offered when my mother brings Ms. McCallister here to check into enrolling Chumani. This pretense of a scholarship would be strictly for Ms. McCallister's daughter and must remain anonymous."

Mr. Teasdale listens closely, "Understood, but as you well know, we have application requirements such as family background checks, financial stability, and such for all our students that would have to be performed before consideration for enrollment."

"I have already done all the background checks you could ever need, and then some. I will send you copies of what I have by private messenger this afternoon. As for her financial stability, I will be silently responsible for any and all fees incurred for Chumani. Since Ms. McCallister is my employee, there is no need for you to contact her employer, as I'm standing before you now." RJ makes his position clear. "I will release Ms. McCallister early from work today to come here with my mother, whom you know very well from many years of dealings since my sisters and I all attended here. You will bypass the rigorous questioning and make this as smooth as possible for Ms. Mc-Callister. As you will discover from the reports I will forward to you, this young woman needs, and more importantly, deserves something in her life to go smoothly. Speaking of the information in the reports, you, Sir, are the ONLY person authorized to view them. You are not allowed to share the information they contain with anyone." Head Master Teasdale nods his understanding. "I trust once you've read the files, you will understand the sensitive nature. Ms. McCallister doesn't even know I have knowledge of any of the information. That's how it will stay. Do I make myself clear?"

The headmaster is a formidable man in his own right, not some weasel of a man to be pushed around, but the Fenton/Kemp family is a long-standing major contributor to this establishment, and he has no intention of rocking that particular boat. Besides, Mr. RJ Fenton is vouching for this woman. That is not a commonplace occurrence. "Yes, Sir. Perfectly clear."

RJ writes out a check for the first full year of Chumani's tuition and hands it to Mr. Teasdale. "Chumani McCallister will be in class tomorrow. The *same* class as my son."

"Yes, I understand."

"Good day to you."

"And to you, Mr. Fenton."

Once back at the warehouse, RJ emerges from his office and steps out onto the dock.

"BJ!" the boss calls out above the noise. She looks up to figure out who is calling her. RJ motions for her to come over.

She finishes what she is doing, then confidently struts over, trying to maintain the air and aloofness of nothing more than an employee. "What's up, Boss? What can I do for you?"

There is but a millisecond of heated emotion that sparks in his eyes, brought on by the question, but she hasn't missed it. She glances away.

RJ clears his throat. He sat for more than an hour planning out how to approach this. "It was brought to my attention this morning by Riyon that Chumani should also have been enrolled in Kindergarten and starting school today, as they are the same age."

Mixed flashes of emotions race across BJ's features, which RJ can already tell, some are of self-reprimand for not having thought of that, and taken care of it already. Some are defiance stemming from her fear that he or anyone would find her inadequate in her motherly duties. He chooses to rush headlong into his prepared speech before allowing her a chance to spout off.

"Riyon is of the adamant opinion that Chumani *must* attend school with him, so that he can take care of her so she won't be picked on."

BJ's expression softens. She finds it very touching and endearing that Riyon and Chumani have become so close.

"I was sure with all the chaos and upheaval of your being new to the area, new jobs, moving, etc., with so much going on, that thought probably hasn't even crossed your mind. Due to the ultimatum given to me by Riyon, I was forced to possibly overstep my boundaries as your boss, and..." he let that hang before going on. "Well, I took it upon myself to speak with the headmaster, and set an appointment for this afternoon for you to go enroll Chumani. Mère offered to pick you up here, and drive you over, and help you in any way she can, as she's been through the process five, no, six times now; she can help streamline the ordeal. She'll be arriving around 3 this afternoon."

BJ's brain is racing, trying to keep up with everything he is saying. Her mind catches on a few specific words he uttered.

"Headmaster? That sounds like a private school, and what kind of ultimatum did a 5-year-old give to cause you to, as you put it, overstep your boundaries so drastically?"

"Yes, it is a private school."

"There is no way in Hell I can afford private school!"

"Then I guess it's a good thing we're not in Hell," he smiles devilishly. "Mr. Teasdale informed me that there happens to be one full scholarship still available for this term. As for the Ultimatum? Riyon said if Chumani doesn't attend school with him, he is dropping out tomorrow." BJ looks surprised. "I'm sure you can understand the thought of having my son be a dropout on the second day of kindergarten is more than enough incentive to push me to not only step over the boundaries, but to jump, run, even dance over them, if necessary," he concludes, smiling, seeing her stern look crack a bit too.

"Fine. I'll go talk to the *headmaster*," she emphasizes the words with a touch of disdain. "Though I'm not promising that I'll agree to put my daughter in private school. Even though there may be financial help for the tuition, I'm sure the uniforms, the myriad other supplies, and activities will be costly, and more than I can afford."

"Mr. Teasdale assured me this particular scholarship covers everything."

"As I said, I'll go talk to this Mr. Teasdale, but no promises. As for your potential kindergarten dropout? If you need me to, I'll help explain it to him."

RJ is pretty darn sure that won't be necessary. "Fine. I'll let you face his wrath," he chuckles.

"Is there anything else you need me for, or may I return to work?" Damn, she knew before he spoke, she did it again.

"There are many things that come to mind that I might need you for, but..."

How can his amber eyes smolder and twinkle at the same time? BJ rolls her eyes, sighing with exasperation at his soft laughter as she walks away with the heat from his eyes singeing her back as they follow.

"Hello, dear," Emily's welcome genial as BJ gets in the front seat of her air-conditioned car that afternoon.

"Hello, Emily. I apologize for putting you out like this. I could have driven myself."

"Nonsense, dear. You're not putting me out, and yes, I know you could have driven yourself and handled the dealings with Mr. Teasdale. It's just that I've been through this so many times already, I thought it might be easier to have me along in case you have questions or concerns."

"Thank you." Then after a few moments, "It's likely after one look at me, this Headmaster will find any reason he can, not to allow my daughter in his school. I can't imagine there are any other students attending there whose mothers work at all, let alone are dockhands. We're not your typical private school kind of folk. Pretty sure I could never fit into their social circle."

"BJ, dear, you listen to me right now. I will have no more of that kind of talk from you." BJ has never heard Mrs. Kemp's tone of voice so stern or angry. "You have absolutely nothing to be ashamed of. You are a beautiful, strong, working mother. As for the other mothers? They have so many lessons to learn, and it's high time they do. Who better for them to learn them from than you? You have so much to offer to so many people. You are a shining example of the strength of a real mother, a real *Woman*. I'm sorry, dear, I didn't mean to get so worked up. However, I detest the thought of you thinking you're not good enough, that these mothers with rich husbands or family money are in any way better than you. You are a hundred times better than every one of them, and I don't want you to ever think, or believe otherwise."

BJ mulls over Emily's words before responding, "Thank you."

Arriving at the school a short time later, BJ's first impression is 'old money'. Before her stands an Ivy League-style two-story, well-maintained historic red brick building with areas covered in dark green wall-climbing ivy, surrounded by manicured lawns. Surely, it doesn't look child-friendly.

First to exit the car, BJ walks toward one side of the parking lot and peers beyond the front administrative structure to view a secondary building. It is a much larger building with a bold wood beam construction. While still rather ominous in stature, it blends in much better with the forested area surrounding the manicured lawns and the stuffy looking brick building. Though the structures still appear a bit rigid, the outdoor areas are stark contrasts with their vibrant multi-colored playground equipment of slides, swing sets, tunnels, teeter-totters and historic merry-go-round intermixed with natural elements such as a woodland styled suspension bridge, rock climbing wall and tree-house fort, making the outdoor experience quite appealing.

"I hope the building interiors are as appealing as the play areas." BJ mumbles.

"I think you'll be pleasantly surprised with the interior's similar mix of aesthetics. Shall we?" Emily smiles encouragingly.

"I guess I'm as ready as I'll ever be, but first let me tell you what I told your son. I agreed to come talk to this, Mr. Teasdale. However, I'm not making any promises that I will enroll Chumani here. Your son explained that there might be some kind of tuition scholarship, and he assured me it is 'all inclusive', but I don't want to subject Chumani to a situation where, if extracurricular activities arise that cost more money than I can afford, she would then be left out. That wouldn't be fair to her."

"I understand, dear. We'll find out what this scholarship is all about and go from there. OK?"

Drawing a deep steadying breath, BJ agrees, "OK."

Mr. Teasdale receives the files from RJ just after lunch and reads them. He finds himself repeatedly saying things such as 'Oh my goodness', 'Oh my God', 'Oh, no', 'You've got to be kidding me'. He even finds himself wiping tears from his face. RJ is correct when he says, *"This young woman needs, and more importantly, deserves something in her life to go smoothly."* He can understand why Mr. Fenton desires to help this woman. Determined to play his part in the situation, Mr. Teasdale prepares for the arrival of Ms. McCallister.

19

"Mrs. Kemp. Always a pleasure to see you," the black suit and tie attired, Mr. Teasdale, greets, extending his hand cordially to both women. "This must be the young woman your son spoke to me about this morning," he comments, shaking hands with BJ. "Wow, you have a very firm handshake, Ms.?"

"McCallister, BJ McCallister. My apologies, I'm so sorry. I hope I didn't cause you discomfort."

"Oh, no. What I meant is, it's nice to exchange a true handshake with a confident woman. Please come with me to my office."

As the ladies follow Headmaster Teasdale toward his office, BJ takes in as much of her surroundings as possible, including Mr. Teasdale. Approximately 5'8", buzz-cut thinning white hair with a white full goatee and mustache. He is moderately built, and his attire and demeanor fit well with the buttermilk biscuit walls with colonial mahogany wood trim and matching floors.

Once everyone is seated in the office, Mr. Teasdale inquires, "Can I get either of you something to drink?"

"Coffee would be nice, thank you," Emily responds

"No, thank you. I'm fine," BJ answers.

"Are you sure? Not even a glass of water?"

"OK, sure, that will be fine. I don't want to put anyone out."

"No worries," he buzzes the outer office, "Mary Jane, can you please bring in two coffees and a water? Thank you."

"Let's get things rolling. In speaking to Mr. Fenton this morning, I understand you're new to the area, and having been so busy moving and beginning a new job, the thought of your first child starting school was not at the top of your priority list."

"Actually, truth be told, I don't think that was even on my priority list. We have had numerous life-changing issues occur over the past year, and I guess the fact that my baby is actually of school age somehow escaped my thoughts."

Emily looks pointedly at Mr. Teasdale, reminding him to tread cautiously so as not to let on that he is privy to any knowledge of BJ's past. Emily called earlier to ensure Mr. Teasdale received the package that RJ had delivered by messenger. They talked at length about how this appointment needs to be handled.

"It's always difficult to realize our little ones are growing up. Particularly understandable if you've been experiencing disruption in the day-to-day flow of life. Now you're here, and as they say, 'All's well that ends well'. Here are some information pamphlets about our school." He hands a stack of papers to BJ. He catches her overwhelmed expression. "Not to worry, Ms. McCallister, there's no need to read them right now; there's no test on the information." He smiles.

"The most important issues I'm concerned with are the tuition, uniform costs, supply fees, and other incidental costs."

Mr. Teasdale looks at each woman pointedly, convincingly, before saying, "Oh, didn't Mr. Fenton explain? He mentioned when we spoke this morning that might be an issue, and inquired if there are any discounts or a low-rate payment plan that might help. I told him how very fortunate you are that we have available, one fully funded scholarship, which we haven't utilized, as it has very specific stipulations set forth by the scholarship benefactor. Not only must it be used to assist someone deserving who is currently without adequate means to afford to attend our school, but it is only allowed to be used for a female child entering kindergarten." At BJ's skeptical expression, he continues, "This philanthropist wants a young girl just starting out to have all the amazing benefits an education from our establishment can afford her. I'm not privy to all the details of this contributor, as it is an anonymously supported fund. So, facts are that you are currently unable to afford enrollment here for your daughter, and she happens to be starting kindergarten. In my opinion, that's fate."

Emily smiles broadly, "You see, Dear. The stars seem to all be in perfect alignment. What more could you ask for?"

"That all sounds wonderful, but as I asked once already, what kinds of fees other than the tuition covered by the scholarship might be incurred throughout the term?"

"I'm sorry, Ms. McCallister. I guess I'm not making myself clear on that. This benefactor will pay for Everything! Uniforms, books, supplies, field trips and school lunch. You name it, they intend to cover it all."

"Everything?" BJ asks.

"Yes, ma'am. Everything."

"What do I need to do to determine if we qualify?"

"Nothing. We already know you live within the district since Mr. Fenton mentioned you are renting from Mrs. Kemp. He also mentioned you are employed by him, so if needed, we can have him fax over wage history, with your permission, of course. We will need a copy of your daughter's birth certificate, which I understand may need some searching for after a move, so when you can dig that up, and social security numbers for you both, that kind of thing for registration purposes, but as far as the scholarship is concerned, it's a done deal. In fact, I can assure you this benefactor will be extremely glad to hear that your daughter will be enrolling and benefiting from these funds. Please, take the registration forms home with you, fill them out this evening, if possible, and find the necessary documents when you can. Take this voucher to the store listed on it sometime today, and pick up your daughter's first couple of uniforms, then we will see your daughter here tomorrow morning for her first day of school."

BJ's mind is once again well on its way to overload as they leave the headmaster's office.

"We'll pick up Riyon while we're here."

"He's still here?" BJ asks, surprised. "I thought kindergarten was only half-days."

Oh dear, Emily senses a touch of panic in BJ's tone. "Yes, public schools do start kindergartners with only half days, but some private schools go ahead and begin them with full days like all the other grade levels. That's not a problem for you, is it, Dear? I mean, since you're at work the whole day already."

"Oh, crud, I forgot about getting her to and from school," BJ's voice takes on an air of slight panic.

"No need for concern. That's one more of the beautiful things about her attending the same school as Riyon. Millie can continue caring for Chenoa, and Chumani can ride with us, as either Jason or I will drive the two 'big kids' to and from school."

Riyon spots them and comes running.

"Mémère, I didn't know you were picking me up. Why are you here, Ms. BJ?"

"Well," she begins explaining, taking his hand, as they all walk toward Mémère's car so Emily can drive BJ back to Fenton Warehouse to her car.

"Nice to see that your mommy could at least make it to pick you up from school on your first day," the lady who'd spoken to RJ that morning comments as she passes.

Riyon wraps both his arms around BJ's hand and forearm possessively and smiles hugely up at BJ. Unsure what to say and seeing his beaming smile, BJ just doesn't respond.

Upon telling Riyon that they came to enroll Chumani in school so she'd be coming with him starting tomorrow, Riyon shouts, "Yes!" doing a fist pump and pull.

Emily interjects, "However, young man, when we arrive home, you are to say nothing about it to Chumani. You will let Ms. BJ tell her when she gets home. Is that understood?"

"Yes, Mémère. I understand," then to BJ, "Can I be there when you tell her, though?"

"Of course. So how was your first day?"

"It was good, but tomorrow will be better if Chumani gets to be there too."

BJ arrives home only a few minutes after Emily and Riyon. She finds everyone out by the pool, including RJ.

"Hi, Mommy." Chumani comes running.

"Hey, baby girl. How are you?"

"Good. Riyon was telling us all about his very first day of school. Sounds like he had fun. Tell my mommy about your day," Chumani urges Riyon.

"Hey, Chumani, Sweetie," BJ gets her daughter's attention.

"What, Mommy?"

"I have something I want to talk to you about. Can you come here and sit with me for a minute?" BJ sits down on one of the chaise lounge chairs. Chumani comes over and sits with her.

"What's wrong, Mommy?" she asks, concerned compassion far beyond her years in her tone.

"Nothing is wrong, Sweetie. You know Mommy has been very busy with work, moving, and so many things. I kind of lost track of the fact that you're getting so big, and, well, you are supposed to be starting kindergarten too, like Riyon did today. I'm wondering how you would feel about attending school with Riyon tomorrow," BJ witnesses her daughter's angelic little face begin to glow, "and every day after that?"

Chumani's eyes widen to the size of saucers. "You mean it? Really? I get to go to school, and I get to go with Riyon?" BJ nods. "Yippee! Yippee! Yippee!" Chumani hugs her mom, then she and Riyon begin jumping around like jumping beans. Chumani's spirited reaction to this surprise makes everyone happy that she is so happy. Emily and Jason are chatting with the children about the exciting news. BJ knows she should probably mention the comment made by the woman today to RJ, and decides to take this moment to do just that. So, she asks him, "May I speak to you a moment?" She indicates stepping aside from the others.

"An incident occurred today after school, which in and of itself is of no consequence, though I found what she said very strange. I have no clue why she said what she did, but it was Riyon's reaction I feel you should know about." BJ describes Riyon's reaction.

RJ explains the woman's comments of that morning, "She must have assumed you were his mother, which, as you said, is of little or no concern. As for Riyon's reaction. You're probably right, it should probably be discouraged right away before it becomes an issue, though on the other hand, it was only a one-time honest mistake, and it probably will never happen again. I don't see a point of making much of an issue out of it for a one-time occurrence. If something like this happens again, we'll have a talk with him."

"It's your call. He's your son. I agree, I just thought you should know."

Chumani's vivaciousness shows no signs of diminishing anytime soon. It is, in fact, still in at full throttle later that evening after dinner, when BJ takes her daughters to the store with the voucher to pick up Chumani's first school uniforms.

At work the next day, BJ continues to ignore him. What does he expect? It isn't like she has any idea that he worked everything out so their children can attend school together.

Scowling, RJ stands watching the dock activity, his grumpy expression intensifies daily. Why do these moments when BJ is ignoring his presence bother him? She goes on with her work as if nothing ever took place between them. Is she honestly unfazed by the incidents of Sunday night? *"Crymonie sakes!"* RJ utters vehemently to himself. followed by an internal chat, *"You're acting like a heartsick teenager. What do you care if she's impervious to your lapses of control? Damn, you should be glad. At least it seems she's taken better control of herself and isn't dwelling on your momentary foible. She's not letting it permeate her every thought like you are.”* RJ silently scolds.

“Boss...? Boss?” Butch's questioning tone finally penetrates RJ's brain, and he realizes he's been obliviously standing there staring, lost in his thoughts.

“What?” he snaps, he is so ticked at himself. He draws a lung-filling calming breath and continues, “Sorry, I didn't mean to snap. I was thinking about something, and didn't hear you. What can I do for you?”

Butch follows the direction of the boss's stare and is sure he has a pretty good idea of 'Who', not 'What', RJ is thinking about. The smirk on his face lets his boss know it even before he speaks. “It damn well better not take the two of you as long to come to your senses as it took Jake and Cheryl,” the gruff dock hand's blunt statement earns him a stern look from the boss.

“State your business or go back to work.”

Chuckling, Butch decides to let it drop and gets on with the business at hand.

20

"Ma-ma, ma-ma," Chenoa's baby voice creeps through the morning after fog of yet another fitful, short Friday night sleep. *"Do not be grumpy with your girls."* BJ counsels herself even before she opens her eyes. *"It's not their fault your wayward brain keeps having dreams of Mr. Fenton, or rather nightmares, causing you to feel sleep deprived.* "Why, she wonders, is her mind so obsessed with thoughts of the man when she sleeps? She is finding it fairly easy to push thoughts of him out of her mind when she is awake. She keeps busy with working both jobs, caring for their new home, and spending every second she can with her girls. She worried at first that living in such close quarters would be an issue, but truth be told, her concern that she'd have to deal with him at work all day, and then be around him every evening at home, didn't manifest. In fact, she's caught herself disappointed more than once this week that she hasn't seen even a glimpse of him, other than occasionally at work, since Monday night.

"Mommy?" comes the soft sound of Chumani's voice near her ear.

"Good morning, Sweetie. Mommy's getting up." She sits up, scooping her daughter into her arms and nuzzling her neck as she does. Chumani squirms and giggles playfully calling out "stop", but not really meaning it, as she enjoys the tickling and cuddling from her mommy. The duo goes to Chenoa, who was still calling out, "Mamma," and so, their morning routine begins.

BJ stands making breakfast while the girls sit watching Saturday morning cartoons. Sounds float in from outside, and her heart skips a beat, whether in dread or excitement, she isn't sure. She opens the kitchen window as it is a beautiful, warm, sunny morning.

"Yummm! Ms. BJ must be making breakfast. I can smell it. Doesn't it smell good, Daddy?"

"Surely does, buddy."

Riyon and Mr. Fenton's voices reach Chumani's ears, and she goes running to the sliding glass door leading to the patio. Swiftly, she opens it, calling out, "Mr. Fenton, Mr. Fenton," and out the door she goes.

"Chumani," BJ calls after her. But Chumani ignores her mother; instead, she runs and throws her arms around RJ's leg.

"Good morning, Miss Chumani," RJ returns the girl's enthusiastic greeting by scooping her up into his arms for a real hug.

"I've missed you," she exclaims fervently.

"I've missed you, too," he states honestly.

"Chenoa misses you, too. She's in the house watching cartoons. You should go see her since she can't come out here."

"I'm not sure that's such a good idea. It smells like Mommy is making you breakfast, and I don't want to intrude."

"You wouldn't be 'truding. I know," she says as she squirms out of his arms, finishing as she bolts back towards the door, "you can eat breakfast with us like you did that other time. Mommy, can Mr. Fenton and Riyon eat breakfast with us?" She hollers upon entering the house.

RJ and Riyon follow to the door, "Chumani, sweetie?" When she turns back to the door, RJ states, "We don't want to intrude on your morning with your mommy. We'll be here hanging out for the day. How about you eat breakfast with your family, and in a while, if Mommy says it's OK, you can come spend some time with us out here?"

"I want you to eat with us like before, but with Riyon this time, too," she states pleadingly, turning doleful eyes to her mother, "Please, Mommy?" she begs.

BJ breathes a heavy sigh, her internal emotions waging war with her. She wants to scream *NO!* She also wants to sing out *Yes!*

"Sure smells good," Riyon chimes in. That did BJ in. She can fight herself and turn RJ away without a concern for hurting his feelings, but the adorable little mini RJ was a different story.

RJ wants to show BJ that he, too, can pretend he is unaffected by last week's episodes. She doesn't seem to want him to join them for breakfast, but he doesn't want to hurt Chumani's feelings and make her think he doesn't want to be around *her*. He can tell that these little girls could use a decent father figure in their lives, just as his son could use a mother figure in his. What to do? Make Chumani happy by coercing BJ to let them join in, or make BJ happy by adamantly declining the child's invite. He handles major business decisions easier than this.

"We're having scrambled eggs, veggie smokie links, toast, and OJ. Riyon, please help Chumani set 2 more places at the table for you and your daddy."

OK, then, evidently, she isn't having as difficult a time making a decision as he is.

"Yes!" Chumani cheers, then heads to do as told.

RJ looks at BJ, who comes to the door.

"Do you know how to make toast?" is all she says to him as she heads back to the kitchen.

Wordlessly, RJ follows and begins his appointed chore. Chenoa crawls toward him, calling out, "Uppie, uppie." So, while the toast is toasting, he picks her up, bringing her to the kitchen to assist him. The whole morning plays out quite surreal. Everything they do fits together. Their interactions in the kitchen seem to flow seamlessly, as do their interactions with all three children. The activities of getting everyone to the table, eating and doing dishes all occur so naturally, as if they'd been working together as a family all along.

"Do you have plans for your day?" RJ inquires, standing very near as BJ surveys the scene before her of all three children playing companionably on the living room floor.

"Nothing special, just running to the store for a few necessities, and going to work this evening as usual." They both stand there for a couple of minutes watching the children.

"Riyon and I plan to spend the day hanging out by the pool. We were wondering if you'd like to join us. We can make it a pool party. Mère and Jason said they will be gone for the early part of the day. Riyon and I thought we'd be master barbecue chefs and cook lundin for everyone."

BJ's head tips up at that. "Did you say 'lundin'? She asks, surprised.

"Yes, you know a meal between breakfast and lunch is called 'brunch'. 'Lundin' is what we call...

"A meal between lunch and dinner. I came up with that years ago."

"So did I. Guess great minds do think alike," he smiles. "If my son and I do all the cooking, will you ladies join us?"

BJ hesitates, thinking, *"First breakfast together, then lundin all in the same day? What next? Don't even go there,"* she warns her wandering mind.

"I don't know. Like I said, I need to go to the store, and...."

"So, do I. We can all go together, do our shopping, then come back. You can relax the rest of the day until you have to go to work. What's there to think about?"

He's fairly sure of what she is thinking about, and is definitely sure of what he is thinking about.

Their internal dialogues run rampant;

"We both need to stop our respective nonsense. She needs to chill and not get so worked up over us spending time together. It's no big deal. I'm trying to make the best of the situation for the sake of the kids and to keep tensions at a minimum for everyone else. However, I really need to keep my wandering thoughts from sounding like scenes from risqué romance novels or worse."

"What's there to think about, he asks. I'll tell you what there is to think about. The fact that it seems so comfortable spending time with them. The fact that I must put an end to doing so, because the longer I let it continue, the harder it will be on the girls, and on me when it ultimately ends. On the other hand, for the time being, since we are still living here, and I don't want

to lock the girls away inside, and I surely don't expect them to do that either, and since this is 'community space,' what can it hurt to enjoy it with them? It's no different than if we lived in an apartment building with a pool, and the neighbors got together for a barbecue."

"Fine."

"Fine?"

"Yes, that's what I said. Fine."

"OK, then." RJ wants to involve the kids before she has a chance to change her mind.

"Hey, do you two think you can clean up your toys lightning fast so we can all go to the store to get food for our pool party?"

Riyon and Chumani look at each other, eyes bulging, "Pool party?" They exclaim in unison, then immediately proceed to hurriedly pick up all their toys.

"Guess that answers that. I need to go to the big house. How long do you need to get ready to go?"

BJ thinks a moment. "Is ten minutes too long?" her inquiry apprehensive, recalling Matthew's volatile hatred that she couldn't simply walk out the door at the drop of a hat. He didn't understand there are things that need doing before taking off somewhere.

"Ten minutes? That's it? Never mind..."

"I'm sorry, I can be ready in five. Is that better?" BJ's voice almost sounds panicked. He looks at her sympathetically, realizing this must have been an issue with her husband.

"No, BJ, that's not better. That's worse. As I was about to say, never mind your prep time, there's no way I can be ready in ten minutes. If you can, you're a heck of a lot faster than any woman I've ever met, and faster than I am." He smiles cheerily. "Do you think you can be patient, and give me say twenty minutes?"

"Really? I mean, twenty would be much better for us too, but..."

"I get it, you're probably used to being rushed by someone in your past." She nods. RJ turns face-to-face with BJ. She looks down submissively. In a partial replay of the other night, RJ uses his index finger under her chin to gently tilt her head up to look at him. "I don't ever want you to feel pressured by me in any situation. Whoever caused the emotional pain that made you feel so unworthy and fearful is a moron. You do not need to be afraid anymore. More importantly, you deserve to be treated well. You deserve to have a good life, to be cared about, and taken care of. You deserve to be loved," he speaks in a whisper.

BJ's eyes are bright silver-blue with the hint of fear still there until his last words, when a momentary flash of calm blue overcomes them. Promptly, sheer panic strikes. BJ jolts back.

RJ reaches out to tenderly halt her retreat. "Don't bolt. Don't fear me, BJ. I won't hurt you...or your girls. Let me help you learn to blend the strong, confident dock hand BJ with the compassionate mother, and friend BJ, and send the terrified BJ packing for good."

BJ lets the arm he takes hold of relax. He smiles. "I'll hurry so you won't become upset with *me* for making you wait," he teases with a wink.

BJ responds in an uncharacteristic fashion by sticking her tongue out, taking RJ so completely by surprise that he laughs outright.

"Chumani, let Riyon go with his daddy to get ready to go to the store. Mr. Fenton says they won't be ready for *twenty minutes*. That's way more time than it will take us three *ladies* to be ready. We'll be waiting by the car when you finish primping," BJ finishes with a feigned pompous air, then struts over to pick up Chenoa.

RJ turns to Riyon, "Guess we'd better hurry, buddy. Never a good thing to leave a lady waiting."

"Probably a whole lot worse to leave three of them waiting, then, huh?" Riyon surmises, causing both adults to laugh out loud.

"You're a very smart young man, Riyon." BJ compliments.

Twenty minutes later, three females stand in the driveway feigning impatience.

Jason finds Emily covertly peeking out from behind their curtains. "Who are you spying on?"

"I'm not spying. I'm watching."

"Semantics. 'Watching' who?"

"Our girls. I happened to witness our boys join them for breakfast, and it appears the girls are waiting by Rainier's truck. Apparently, they're going somewhere together." Emily informs her husband.

"Really?" Jason's interest is piqued, and he joins his wife near the window. From there, they watch the five of them load into RJ's crew cab pickup and leave. The couple smiles, sighing contentedly.

BJ steps, a couple of feet away from the cart to retrieve an item from a shelf across the aisle, eliciting a screech of disapproval from Chenoa. RJ steps in, conversing with Baby Chenoa. Hearing baby talk in his rich, deep tone brings a smile to BJ.

"Well, if I hadn't seen and heard it myself, I would never have believed RJ Fenton would be caught dead talking baby talk," comes the affluent-sounding female voice from the woman approaching from the other end of the aisle as BJ places the item in the cart.

At that moment, Chumani calls out, "Mommy, can we get some of these? Please?"

Riyon tugs at RJ's leg, "Daddy, please, can we get these? They're really good. We had some at school."

The female voice continues, "Or married with...three children?"

RJ looks up. "Priscilla," with minimum acknowledgment, then says to Riyon, "Let me see what it is." After looking at the packages Riyon and Chumani are holding, he looks to BJ to find out what her thoughts are about the item.

"Only one package, *if* you can agree on a flavor."

"Raspberry," Chumani calls out.

"Orange," Riyon speaks simultaneously, then realizing Chumani chose a different flavor, unhesitatingly concedes, "OK, raspberry this time, but can we get orange next time?"

"OK," Chumani agrees.

That crisis handled, RJ turns his attention to the well-dressed, voluptuous, leggy woman standing there observing the exchange.

"If they're that well-behaved all the time, you two need to write a book on parenting. I would ask what you've been up to, but it's obvious you've been busy since the last time I saw you."

"Yes, well, it has been a very long time."

"This little...family scenario is the last thing anyone would ever have imagined you to be part of. I don't know how I didn't feel the chill of hell freezing," the woman says with amusement.

"I imagine ice wouldn't notice that particular change in climate," RJ retorts bluntly. "I trust all is as usual with you. I don't want to be rude, but we have shopping to finish. Many children become bored and impatient with the act of shopping, something I'm sure you've never experienced. However, we do need to be going. Thanks for saying hello."

RJ proceeds forward, pushing the cart containing Chenoa, with the other three taking their cue and moving on down the aisle with him.

Once in the truck for the return ride home, the kids all securely in the rear seat, chatting excitedly, BJ asks, "May I ask you something?"

"Sure."

"The incident with that woman in the store..." she pauses, unsure of how to ask.

"She was someone I dated a few times *many* years ago."

"What I was wondering was... why didn't you correct her when she made reference to all of us as being a 'little family'?"

RJ questioned himself about that, also. "I guess...I just figured since it's none of her business, let her think what she wants. Besides, I'm sure that will guarantee I'll never hear from her again," he ends with a light chuckle, adding, "I think she may actually be allergic to children," they laugh.

BJ figures since it pertains to his life, and has nothing to do with her, if he wants to allow that woman to make assumptions, so be it.

21

Mondays arrive in the same manner each week, leaving RJ in awe at how well BJ seems to be able to repeatedly turn off the activities of each weekend and ignore his presence. He realizes he should be glad that she seems to have enough restraint for them both.

He experiences occasional questioning glances from employees and catches intermittent whispers, which BJ effectively pays no heed to.

With Halloween still three weeks from today, this week promises to grant everyone a respite from major activities and general chaos. Kind of a calm before the storm of activities and events of the impending holiday season about to begin.

Midday Saturday, BJ pulls her rather old laptop computer from the bottom of the box she packed it in. BJ plugs it in and logs in. She hasn't bothered with it for months. Once it boots up, she accesses her email account, not expecting other than junk and spam mail, which she intends to click select-all-delete. However, there in her inbox, she finds an email from Yul Conner, Attorney at Law. Loathing for this man instantly sets fire to her gut before she even opens the message. Doing her best to regain calm, she reads...

Dear Ms. McCallister,

The law offices of Conner & Cheetum have been attempting to reach you to initiate a payment arrangement for the outstanding balances owed by you for the following:

Property taxes due on the house of your deceased parents.

Closing costs due for the short sale of your parents' house.

Your parents past due legal fees owed.

All of which you became responsible for upon their deaths.

You also became responsible for the following upon the death of your husband:

Four months unpaid rent plus ongoing late fees.

Past due utility bills: gas, water, and electricity at the rental.

You are also responsible for your own outstanding, past due medical bills for:

OBGYN Doctor fees.

Labor and Delivery charges

NICU service charges.

Hospital stay fees.

As well as your legal fees owed to this law firm for our assistance in the above-mentioned matters.

We have all been sufficiently patient in awaiting your response to set up proper payment arrangements.

Should you not respond in a timely manner to this notification with an adequate in good faith initial payment for each item listed, we will have no recourse but to press charges against you.

Should you choose not to show up for the hearing and trial, a bench warrant will be issued for your arrest. Once arrested, you will most likely lose custody of your children.

We look forward to your expedient response and payment.

Sincerely, Yul Conner, Esq.

Closing her eyes, counting to ten, inhaling slowly and holding the breath for the count of five; exhaling to the count of five and repeating the breathing technique twice more before opening her eyes is the calming procedure BJ performs at this time to avoid losing her temper over the desperate attempts to get money from her, and the heavy handed threatening use of the loss of her children in the form of unethical scare tactics.

BJ proceeds to select all, being sure to uncheck that solo message to exclude it when she then clicks delete all selected items. She also copies and pastes the message she received and then dictates a response message, which she might send if she can figure out a way to do so without there being any way for it to be tracked to this location.

To: Mr. Conner of Conner and Cheetum Law Firm.

"As I told you before, Mr. Conner, if I had the money to pay for my legal fees, I would... and I will... Someday.

Regarding the medical bills? Take those up with Matthew's insurance company. I was still covered on his policy at the time of his death, and upon his death, should have remained covered for the grace period of six months due to pregnancy being a fully covered existing condition.

With respect to the rent and utilities, those were all in Matthew's name because he didn't want me to have any access to or any say where those were concerned, so good luck getting their money from a dead man.

As for the rest of it, which are all debts of my deceased parents? Not my bills. Not—My—Problem.

Now, to address your cold-hearted attempt to use the threat of loss of my children to scare me. Should you choose to continue to harass me, be assured that will be added to the list of perpetrated infractions and offenses committed by Conner and Cheetum, Attorneys at Law.

To be clear: the woman you were dealing with in the past was in a diminished capacity and state of mind due to spousal mental abuse and domestic violence, combined with the sudden, tragic loss of three family members, while being under the influence of pregnancy-altered hormones. I have since recovered from those issues. Now, and furthermore, you will be dealing with the real me. A strong of mind and body, take-no-prisoners mentality, intelligent, independent woman. I suggest you back off.

Sincerely, BJ McCallister

Due to a late night last night and a busy early morning, both girls have gone down for naps, so the house is quiet. BJ now steps away from her computer to go refill her water glass in the kitchen.

She inhales deeply, drawing herself back to the peaceful alone time she intended to enjoy this afternoon. She stands gazing at the towering Western White Pines, Giant Sequoia saplings, multiple California Incense Cedars and Juniper bushes alongside the Japanese Maple, Desert peach, apple and crabapple trees above the mixture of ground covers, which create a glorious natural sanctuary for a variety of furry wildlife critters and a birdwatcher's paradise.

Hearing the stirrings of Chumani and Chenoa waking, she takes in one last cleansing and calming breath and a final quick scan of the glory of Mother Nature, then heads to tend to her girls.

"Hello, ladies. Did you sleep well?"

"Hi, Mommy. Yes, can I get up now?"

"Of course. Go potty while I change your sister, and we'll meet you in the living room."

"OK."

"Hello, Chenoa. How are you doing? Did you have a good nap?" BJ converses with her youngest as she begins the diaper-changing process. "Sometimes I wish you were as advanced as your big sister was. She walked and was potty trained by the time she was your age. Other times I'm glad you're maturing at a bit slower pace so I can enjoy this baby time a little longer."

"Ms. BJ?"

Riyon and RJ cautiously step into the pool-house.

"Uh! I hear Riyon," BJ says in a childlike voice.

RJ instructs, "Wait here, son."

Chenoa begins to wiggle to go see their friends. "Hold still a second."

"We'll be right out. Come on in, guys."

"On my way, Riyon," Chumani calls out from the bathroom.

RJ walks to the dining table to sit while they wait. The still visible screen of the open laptop catches his attention, glances at the screen and seeing the addressee is the lawyer BJ had dealings with after the accident, he covertly snaps a few photos of the screens of the received message as well as one of her response to read later, being sure to return to the spot it was on, then sends the computer into sleep mode.

BJ sets Chenoa on the floor, and she immediately begins to crawl, lickety-split, toward the other room. The sounds of Chenoa squealing with delight at finding two of her favorite people, reaches BJ as she completes cleanup of her task and is now making her way toward the great room just as Chumani pops into the hall, making her way to the same destination.

"Hey, guys," BJ greets.

To avoid her knowing he's been at the table and inadvertently seen the screen, he puts the computer in sleep mode, then scoops up the nap re-energized darling and is enjoying her favorite greeting and show of affection of two-handed face patting. RJ giggles, makes silly faces and noises and generally entertains the cherub in his arms.

"Hi, Ms. BJ. Hi, Chumani. What are you ladies up to?" Riyon inquires.

Chumani responds as BJ joyfully watches her baby girl and this extraordinary man sharing these silly yet touching moments. She slips her phone out of her pocket and snaps a few pictures of the sweet sight.

Noticing her laptop is still open, she surreptitiously goes over to it and thankfully finds it has gone into black-screen sleep mode. She closes, unplugs, and stows it back in the box in her room. When she returns, she finds RJ has set Chenoa down, and she is playing with Riyon and Chumani.

"Ms. BJ, are Chumani and Chenoa busy today, or can they play outside with me and Daddy, too, for a while? We thought you might have things to do, and we can keep them busy for you. But if you're not busy, you can play with us too, cause that would be cool!"

"Or maybe if Ms. BJ isn't busy, she might enjoy some quiet alone time to rest before work tonight," RJ offers.

BJ ponders the idea.

"We'd love for you to play with us, but Mr. Fenton's idea is cool too. Me and Chenoa took naps while you cleaned, so maybe you can take a nap so you're not so tired."

"We'll take real good care of them for you, Ms. BJ, so you don't have to worry, and we'll stay here in case you get rested and want to come play with us too," Riyon assures.

"OK, that sounds like a good plan. I'll sit under the trees outside the kitchen and read. While you girls go have some fun with Riyon."

The afternoon plays out in a comfortable manner as BJ sits reading a romance novel she picked up during their travels, thinking she might one day have free time to get lost in a happily-ever-after adult Fairy Tale. At first, she occasionally becomes distracted by the gleeful sounds of her girls enjoying their time with the Kemp family, as she also hears Emily and Jason have joined the activities.

Eventually, BJ allows the story to sweep her away to an unknown world of a strong woman and her two sons dealing with the tragic loss of their wonderful husband and father. An investigation gets underway into whether it was truly an accident or if the sleezy banker had something to do with the incident. When a handsome foreign stranger shows up at her doorstep looking for a few days of odd jobs in exchange for a place to set up his tent for a few nights and a meal or two as he is passing through the small town on his travels across the country.

So lost in the story does BJ become that time passes unnoticed, until Chumani creeps around the corner, trying not to startle her mommy, and quietly informs her, "Hi, Mommy. Mémère cooked dinner for everybody, and she is serving it by the pool. She said to ask you to please come eat."

Startled by how late it has gotten, BJ quickly dog-ears the page in her book. "Thank you, sweetie. I didn't realize how late it is. Did you and your sister have a good time with Riyon?" She asks as they walk hand in hand toward the patio.

"We had so much fun. We played on the playground and then went to the side yard and played Frisbee, and football, and tag and a game called kick-the-can that they taught us. Mémère, Misho and Mr. Fenton took turns helping Chenoa play 'cause she's so little. Did you enjoy the book you read?"

"I'm so glad you had such a great time, and yes, I really enjoyed the book I was reading. I got so interested in it that I lost track of time. I'm so sorry," she informs everyone as they arrive at the table.

Emily responds, "That's wonderful, and do not apologize. That is exactly what we hoped for. The children got to play, and you got to do something just for yourself without worry. Now we'll eat, and Kristen will be here to take over with the girls later, so you can go to work well rested. I call that a successful day."

"Agreed," Misho and RJ reply in unison.

22

S itting out by the pool enjoying a little quiet time after finishing their Friday evening dinner, Riyon and RJ, hear occasional sounds from the pool house where Kristen is caring for Chumani and Chenoa.

"Daddy?"

"Yes, son."

"Halloween is only a couple of weeks away and Chumani and I decided what we want to be."

"What did you decide on?"

"She wants to be an Indian Princess, and I want to be an Indian Warrior. But we need costumes. Can we go tomorrow to buy them?"

"An Indian Princess, and a Warrior, huh?"

"Yup."

"Sure, I'll take you tomorrow to find an Indian costume."

"Can we all go together? Chumani said Ms. BJ doesn't buy store-bought costumes. She gets stuff and makes them a'riginal."

RJ experiences a moment of hurt at the thought that Riyon doesn't want to go costume shopping with him alone. However, in the same instant, he is glad his son wants the girls to join them, because truth be told, he is looking forward to weekends more and more as each one finds them all spending time together doing one thing or another.

"Well, we'll have to find out if they're available and want to go with us. If they aren't, you and I can still go, and I can try to do it the way you say Ms. BJ does it."

"OK."

"Morning, Daddy. Can we go ask if they can go shopping with us today?" Riyon asks eagerly, early the next morning.

"Morning, buddy. We need to wait a while. Remember, Ms. BJ works until late at night on the weekends, so she needs to sleep in to be well rested."

"I know, but they're already up. Ms. BJ's making breakfast. I heard them talking when I was out practicing being an Indian warrior. I was sneaking around real quiet so they didn't know I was there spying on them."

RJ isn't sure if, as a father, he should scold his son for spying or praise him for utilizing his imagination.

"Still, we should let them have their morning together without intruding. OK?"

"OK." Riyon's enthusiasm deflates.

"Mommy. Can we go shopping for Halloween costume stuff today? Riyon and I decided what we want to be." With an air of majesty, she intones her title. "I'm an Indian Princess, and Riyon is an Indian Warrior, so he can protect me. I told Riyon you don't buy pre-made stuff, and that you'd help with his costume too. He's asking Mr. Fenton if they can go with us today."

BJ sighs, resigning herself to the fact that as long as they live here, and the kids have anything to say about it, there are always going to be issues with keeping their lives separate. She isn't quite sure if that is a good thing or...?

"They're up," Chumani enthuses as soon as RJ and Riyon appear, walking out to the patio with their breakfast plates to sit at the umbrella table. "Can we eat out there with them?" She asks as she grabs her bowl of cereal, heading for and opening the door, calling out, "Morning."

"Chumani," BJ calls as she goes after her, forgetting she is still clad in only her short, satin V-necked nightie and panties. She takes but only two steps out the door when she remembers, and stops dead in her tracks.

Too late. RJ, already alert to their presence, glances up and sees the scantily clad, sleep-disheveled BJ standing mere yards away.

BJ hurriedly retreats into the house, bringing a smirk to RJ's face. Chumani continues on her mission of joining the boys for breakfast. "I asked my mommy. Did you ask your daddy?" She speaks to Riyon.

"Yeah, he said it's OK with him if it's OK with Ms. BJ."

"Mommy didn't answer yet, but I know she'll say yes, since Daddy said yes."

RJ's heart skips a beat. He is sure it is just a slip of the tongue, but...

BJ catches it too, as she is returning from donning a robe, carrying Chenoa, who, spying RJ, squeals with excitement, and reaches for him. Their eyes meet. Both draw in deep breaths, deciding to let it slide as the unintentional slip they both are sure it is.

"Good morning," BJ greets amiably.

"Morning," RJ responds politely, hoping to disguise the husky, heated tone of voice he fears will give away the wanderings of his thoughts. The robe does nothing to abate the image of what lurks beneath the satin that mirrors the vibrant blue of the morning sky and BJ's eyes.

"Mommy, Mr. Fenton said they can go with us if you say yes. Pleeease?" Chumani draws out the word pleadingly.

BJ looks at RJ for confirmation of his agreement. "What can I say? I've only ever bought pre-made costumes, which I now hear aren't the most desirable. I guess I'm in for a training session today to learn 'how to create your own *a'riginal* costume.'"

"Ah. I see. Well, then, I suppose I have no choice in the matter. We can't have Master Riyon face a life doomed to store-bought, cookie-cutter costumes now, can we?"

"Nope!" Chumani confirms.

"I need to do a bit of house cleaning this morning before we can go, so,"

"We can help you clean house!" Riyon announces, looking to his dad for agreement. "We don't have to clean the big house 'cause Mémère has a cleaning lady. Right Daddy? If we help, you'll be done faster, so we can go sooner. Right, Daddy?"

The adults look at each other. "Can't argue with that logic," RJ acquiesces.

BJ sighs heavily, brows raised, "You have a point, Riyon. Give us a few minutes to change our clothes, then we'll get started." She reaches for Chenoa, who is still complacently sitting on RJ's lap, sucking her thumb. The lapels of BJ's robe fall open as she leans forward to retrieve her daughter, revealing a glimpse of the open neckline of BJ's nightie beneath, a movement which catches RJ's attention. His eyes shoot to hers. They both swallow hard in unison. Clearing his throat to enable speaking around the lump that instantly forms, RJ says to his son. "Let's leave the ladies to their personal time while we clean up the breakfast dishes."

On the drive to the thrift store in town, RJ tells BJ about the family-friendly Halloween party at his sister's on Saturday, the day after Halloween. "We're hoping you and the girls will join us." Sensing her immediate hesitancy, he continues, "It would be another way for you to meet people. Maybe other parents."

Overhearing the adults' conversation, Riyon shouts, "Yeah! That would be cool, and so much more fun if you guys go too."

"Can we go, Mommy? Pleeese?" Chumani once again draws out her please in pleading fashion.

"Chumani," BJ speaks, her tone admonishing. "You need to not beg and plead. Simply ask Mommy a question, and be prepared for whatever answer I give. Understand?"

"Yes, Mommy." Chumani's tone switches from excited to dejected in a millisecond.

"Don't get all mopey. I only want to be sure you don't become accustomed to me *always* agreeing to everything you ask.

"I know, Mommy. I didn't forget the rules. Just sometimes the rules get a little blurry when I get too excited."

RJ laughs, and BJ shoots him a disapproving glance, though she can barely contain her own smile.

"Can we go?" Chumani prompts.

BJ clears her throat, expelling breath heavily, "Oh, alright, I..." The squeals of excitement drown out the remainder of her sentence, "...suppose we can go."

"What are you and Daddy dressing as?" Riyon asks jubilantly.

BJ looks at RJ questioningly. "Yes, it is a costume party."

"Oh."

Chumani and Riyon pipe up, shouting out various ideas they have of what their parents should go as.

"You could go as King and Queen," is Chumani's first suggestion.

"Or cowboy and cowgirl," Riyon suggests

"Or knight and princess. Or the same as us." Chumani throws out two more ideas

"Ooor..." Riyon draws everyone's attention, "a bride and groom," which is followed by silence.

BJ is the first to recover, "Our costumes don't have to be paired. We can go as things unrelated. I have always wanted to be an Indian Maiden. Chumani, Chenoa, and I could go as squaw, princess, and papoose. Riyon, you can be the warrior protector of all three of us."

"Yeah, and Daddy can be the handsome cowboy that tries to steal you away from our tribe."

"Yeah!" Chumani agrees, and Chenoa, caught up in the excitement of their voices, joyously babbles her two cents' worth of agreement.

After arriving at the thrift store, they are standing looking at various items to create the outfits for the children, when BJ senses a sudden tension exuding from RJ. She shivers, then turns to discover his rigid stance effectively filling the aisle, almost as if shielding her and the children. His head turns slightly in her direction as he whispers over his shoulder, "BJ. Take the kids and walk away. Now."

"Is something…"

"Don't ask. Just do it!" he states almost harshly, then in a gentler tone, "Please?"

BJ turns without further question. "Hey guys, let's go look over here at some other things." She maneuvers the cart containing Chenoa with one hand, using the other hand to direct the other two, moving them further down the aisle.

A woman approaches from the opposite end of the aisle, saying, "Is that him?"

Every nerve ending in BJ's body goes on alert. There is no longer a reason to question RJ's actions.

"Walk away, Staci. You're so good at it." The calm, menacing tone is not one BJ ever heard coming from RJ, though she heard it more than enough times from her deceased husband for years.

"Please? Let me see him," the woman's voice is woeful.

"No."

"But I'm his…"

"No, you are not! You are nothing! Do not make a scene. Walk away now." RJ's voice strains with anger he struggles to contain.

"Daddy?" Riyon, hearing the stern tone of his father's voice, is concerned as he tries to move past BJ to go to his daddy.

"Sweetie, stay here," BJ requests firmly.

"Stay with Mommy, Riyon," Chumani encourages, also sensing the tension, having experienced and lived through tense situations like this oh so many times. "She'll protect you like she always does."

Staci, overhearing, shoots RJ a curious, questioning look.

"None of your business."

"You don't have to tell him anything. Just let me see him. Please?"

BJ, physically blocking Staci's view of the son she abandoned, detects the pleading in the woman's voice; turns and touches RJ's arm, interrupting. She stares intently into the other woman's eyes, stating softly yet menacingly, "You may *see*, but if you utter one word out of line, and you know exactly what I mean, you will be sorry. Do I make myself clear?"

Staci looks at the two adults. RJ looks at BJ.

"Perfectly clear," Staci assures.

BJ takes charge of the situation at this point. Stepping aside, she moves the children a bit closer, saying in her usual jovial tone, "Hey, guys, this is Staci." Looking and speaking specifically to Riyon, "Miss Staci was a friend of your daddy's many years ago." Then, turning to Staci, she continues, "This is Riyon, Chumani, and Chenoa," indicating each in turn as she speaks.

Staci's quizzical look is left questioning as she bends and extends her hand first to Riyon, "Pleasure to meet you." Riyon and Chumani each shake her hand in turn. Chumani, still sensing the tension, steps protectively closer to Riyon, eyeing this woman who made Mr. Fenton's voice angry.

Staci straightens and steps back. "You're a very handsome young man...and you are a very lovely young lady." She then looks at Chenoa, "Such a cute baby."

"Thank you," BJ responds. "It was good to meet you. I don't mean to be rude, but we're a bit pressed for time and need to finish our shopping. If you'll excuse us?" She turns to the children, "Say Goodbye to Miss Staci."

"G'bye"

"Bye."

BJ turns her attention to RJ, and, without thought, touches his arm, "Shall we, Rainier?"

His shocked expression is fleeting and nearly imperceptible. Staci's, however, is blatantly obvious.

RJ looks pointedly at Staci and bids emphatically, "Adieu, Staci."

Understanding that particular form of goodbye in French is most often utilized as a final farewell, as in last goodbyes to deceased or those you choose never to have contact with again, BJ wonders momentarily if Staci ever learned that. No matter. BJ is sure the tone of RJ's voice and the fiery look in his eyes make that abundantly clear.

The five of them walk away without looking back.

They finish their shopping, with BJ doing a variety of silly things, such as holding up various outrageous articles of clothing she comes across and asking if she'd look good in them. The moods of the children rebound far quicker than RJ's, so she takes extreme measures, holding up a slightly risqué item of lingerie, saying, "Maybe I should wear this to the party, then when I return home after it's over, I won't even have to change to go to bed. What do you think?" She speaks to Riyon and Chumani, but sneaks a glance at RJ's expression. *Score!* The deep, angry tension of moments before eases first to a mischievous grin, followed in a nanosecond by a more or less seductive smirk.

Riyon pipes up. "I think you *should* get that, then one of these days we can all have a slumber party, and you can wear that." A devilish expression, a youthful twin of his father's, comes over his young innocent features, transforming them to wise beyond his years. "I know Daddy would like that!" he waggles his eyebrows at his father.

The shocked expressions that burst onto the faces of the two adults send the children, quickly followed by the adults, into near-hysterical fits of laughter. When the bouts of laughter die down a bit, "He's your son!" BJ reminds.

That statement brings forth an instant reminder of the incident earlier. He smiles broadly, "Yes, he is *my* son," he states, filled with extreme pride.

On the ride home, RJ ventures to ask, "Would you mind telling me how you found out my name?"

"When I was getting to know Mrs. Emily Kemp, she told me various stories of her wonderful, amazing son, Rainier. I knew you as RJ Fenton, chauvinistic boss, and owner of Fenton Warehouse, with no clue you and he were one and the same. However, she didn't say what the J stands for."

"Julian. You sure chose one hell of a moment to let that cat out of the bag. I do believe it made a very pointed statement in the moment, since she never knew my true name."

"Seriously? But you were going to marry her," BJ says in hushed confusion.

RJ checks to be sure the children are still engrossed in their own conversation and matches BJ's volume.

"I shall assume your obvious understanding of who that was, and the back story to it is also something my mother told you about."

"Yes."

"So, yes, I planned to marry her, but not because I loved her. I've never loved a woman before. Never thought I was capable. She was someone I spent time with occasionally. We weren't even considered a couple. Even with what seem to be the best precautions, accidents still happen. Though I no longer view the outcome as an accident but rather...destiny, but in no way an accident. I wouldn't change the outcome for the world. He's taught me how to authentically love."

Back at the house, the children are excited to show their amazing costume finds to Mémère and Misho. They are carrying on with such exuberance and excitement, RJ takes the opportunity to nudge BJ off to the side. "About earlier," he begins, first looking away with a far-off expression, then into BJ's eyes. "Thank You. From the bottom of my heart."

BJ senses how affected he is by the whole ordeal, she lays a hand on his arm, spurring him to go on.

"If you hadn't stepped in, I don't know what I would have done. I was so close to losing control. I wanted to shout at her, ask her what kind of a woman would disappear without a trace for five years, then calmly walk up to me as if nothing ever happened. Hell, in that moment, I felt like I wanted to smack her! I have never in my life, ever even come close to desiring to cause physical or any other kind of pain or harm to any woman, until that moment. I'm glad you stepped in. Just having your presence beside me doused my anger."

RJ covers the hand BJ placed on his arm with his own, brings it to his lips, kisses it, then places it against his chest over his heart.

The thumping of his heart vibrates her hand where it rests. First sure it is pounding from the residual angst of earlier, then, seeing the look that crosses his features in the next moment, she is pretty sure there is something else also contributing to the rapid beat of his big heart.

Emotional blinders obscure their view as their eyes lock. In that moment, there is nothing but the emotional bewitchment he is experiencing cast by this bewitching woman. RJ's head lowers ever so slowly toward hers, half expecting her to withdraw. He moistens his lips. Her lips part. They touch. Both inhale the essence of the other as they had previously. The kiss deepens. Seconds later...The cocoon of imaginary solitude is torn wide open.

"Oooo, you're kiiisssing," comes the sound of two small voices, followed by the sounds of lips smacking.

Their mouths separate, both smiling, resting forehead to forehead.

"OK, you two yahoos, leave your parents alone," Jason corrals the looky-loos.

The brows of both kissers furrow at the pluralization of the word parent. They each were singular in their parenting, yet lately they'd been, in essence, co-parenting.

RJ senses BJ tense. He doesn't think he can stand it if she withdraws from him again. He needs to hold on to this moment without scaring her. He must find a way to keep moving this forward. He kisses her again. Not quite as softly, yet not intensely. This kiss speaks of his need not to backtrack from where they are in this moment. This kiss pleads with her to give them a chance. He lifts his head, looking into the windows of her soul, opening the windows to his own soul, hoping she can see the sincerity behind his next words, "Please, don't walk away from me."

BJ understands that simple request holds a vast array of emotions and hides volumes of pain. She stares into the glowing embers, which serve as RJ's eyes, praying years past have taught her better judgment. "OK."

That simple yet totally complex answer places fathomless trust in him to never hurt her or her daughters.

RJ takes both of her hands in his and answers that unasked question. "OK."

Chenoa begins to whimper. "Duty calls," BJ states calmly, turning to go to her daughter. RJ maintains his gentle grasp of her hand and walks with her to Chenoa.

"Ma-ma," Chenoa beams at the sight of her mother reaching for and accepting her from Emily.

Emily beams at the sight of RJ and BJ holding hands. Chumani and Riyon laugh and giggle once again, making smooching sounds.

Jason smiles broadly as he looks about, absorbing the scene taking place around him. "Place your orders, everyone. I'm buying burgers for dinner," he announces, determining there is enough going on that adding preparing a meal to the agenda before BJ needs to leave for work just doesn't make sense.

23

"You sure look happy tonight, Sugar," Josie tells BJ, a couple of hours into their shift.

"I am, Josie. I am," is all she has time to reply in the moment.

A short time later, BJ is doling out the drinks to one of her tables and a male customer she's not seen there before begins, "Hey, baby cakes. How about you take your well-deserved break, meet me out back, and I'll show you a good time. I'll even 'tip' you real nice."

"No, thank you," BJ's response firm, yet polite.

"Aww, come on, darling. You know you want some of this." He looks pointedly toward the evident bulge in his jeans.

"Not a chance, pal, but I'm sure you can find some lonely drunk in here to take you up on that offer."

As she steps away, the man, who is apparently mentally challenged at the moment due to all the blood being drained from his pea-sized brain, makes the grave mistake of reaching under BJ's skirt and grabbing her inner thigh, causing her to nearly dump her tray of drinks.

The regulars nearby step back, sensing a storm about to erupt. Josie appears, grabs BJ's tray, freeing her hands. The newcomer is still smiling, but not for long. Catching him by surprise, BJ reaches behind her, grabs the man's wrist and removes his hand from between her legs. She then yanks him to his feet, hurling him a good ten feet. The crowd momentarily falls silent. The band halts. The man regains his balance, looks around, embarrassed, and makes his second grave mistake of the evening by lunging toward BJ, shouting vehemently, "You little bitch!"

To which she replies sassily, "Not Yours."

He grabs for her.

With precision, she kicks the swollen appendage between his legs. He doubles over and collapses to his knees. BJ grabs a handful of hair on his head, tilting it back so he can see the seriousness on her face, "If thine hand or thine dick offends thee or me, I'll gladly remove them both, *for free.*"

The crowd bursts out laughing.

A shiver of chills rushes through her, triggered by the awareness of the gentle giant now standing at her side.

RJ came to Buddy's for a nightcap. OK, to see BJ. He witnesses the entire incident and rises to defend the woman he loves... *wait, he'll analyze that thought later...* but it is no surprise to him that she is entirely capable of handling the situation on her own.

The bouncer also appears along with the local cop he notified, who usually stays near the joint on busy nights to avoid drunks getting behind the wheel of their cars and to deal with the occasional barroom brawl. This was a first. *'Cocktail waitress takes down drunk man.'*

The bouncer pulls the man to his feet, and the officer begins to cuff him.

"You bitch. I'll show you," he tries to lurch at BJ again.

She doesn't so much as flinch. Instead, she takes one step forward, staring the man straight in the eyes. The Officer pulls him back, saying, "You know, dude, I'm cuffing you for your own safety. I believe if I were to let you go right now, she would finish you off."

"And if she doesn't, I *will!*" RJ speaks, towering over many in the bar, specifically BJ's assailant.

The officer takes note of RJ's protective arm now around BJ comfortingly. It doesn't take a detective to deduce she's his, and he means what he says. "There's that too. Actually, from the looks on the majority of the folks in this place, you don't stand a chance if I walk away from you. I'll leave it up to you. Would you like to go with me into 'protective' custody or would you prefer I release you here, and now?"

The man looks around the room at all the glaring faces. "Fine. Arrest me. See if I care."

"That's the first smart choice you've made this evening," the officer tells the man as he steers him toward the door.

An uproarious cheer goes up throughout the bar as everyone applauds. BJ blushes at the attention, then, seeing her boss, Buddy, approaching, she stiffens, fearing he's upset with her for misconduct, since the rules clearly state 'NO Fighting for any reason'. Buddy stops directly in front of her. Again, the crowd silences. He nods to RJ, still at her side, arm draped lazily at her waist.

"I'm afraid I must relieve you of your position here as cocktail server..."

Pretty much everyone in the place gasps and begins to mutter. A few of Buddy's long-standing good ole boys pipe up.

"Now just you wait a gall-darn minute. You can't do that."

"Absolutely not."

Buddy holds up his hand to silence the crowd. "I can, and I will. This is My bar. I'll do what I think is best for it." He turns to BJ. "Sorry, my dear, you're no longer a cocktail server at this establishment...I think I need to promote you to bouncer," he announces loudly, smiling broadly. "One round on the house for everyone."

The crowd roars their approval and begins placing orders for their free round. "Go clock out, have a drink, and go home with your man. You're done for the night."

"Thank you for the offer of the bouncer position, but I need the tips I get from my serving position."

"I understand. I think we can work something out. Maybe give you more time with your family," he looks at RJ and winks. "We'll talk tomorrow."

As BJ turns to go to the back room to clock out, Buddy says, "I'm sorry that guy was such a jerk. But I sure am glad you taught him a thing or two."

Josie follows BJ to the back room. "Well, well, I see your handsome Knight was here ready to defend your honor. Although you proved you can damn well hold your own. You OK, Sugar?" she asks, concerned.

"Yes, I'm fine. Thank you. Yes, he is here, though I didn't know until he stepped next to me."

"He arrived shortly before the fireworks began," Josie informs her. "So how are things? Between the two of you?"

BJ's smile speaks volumes. She blushes, shyly responding, "Improving."

Josie hugs BJ, saying, "Well, I for one am damn happy for that. You deserve a good man. Now git out of here. I'll take care of your station and side work tonight. I'll bag up your tips and have Buddy put them in the safe for you."

"Oh, no. Don't do that. If you're taking over my tables and doing my side work, keep the tips." BJ instructs her friend.

"Not a chance. Them good ole boys will take care of me, too. Don't you worry. Now git." She hugs her goodbye.

RJ follows BJ home. He gets caught at a couple of red lights, causing him to arrive a few minutes after her. He sits out by the pool in the cool evening air. He can see shadows of BJ and Kristen and hear BJ explaining briefly why she is home early. After Kristen leaves, RJ goes to check on BJ and tell her goodnight.

"Oh! Hi. I didn't think I'd be seeing you again tonight. I thought..."

"You thought for one second that I could go to bed without checking on you after all that's transpired today?"

They both pause to think over all that took place in this one day. Remembering back to BJ appearing in her barely-there nightie this morning, the Staci incident, their kisses, then tonight. Did all that literally happen today?

"Wow. A lot happened in this one day."

"Indeed," RJ agrees. "I would like to recapture a few of the better moments of the day," he speaks smoothly as he steps closer to BJ, crossing the threshold of the doorway without invitation, then closes the door behind him, his devilish grin glowing in the dim lighting of the room. He places his hands on BJ's hips, drawing her near.

BJ is staring at his broad chest, finding it difficult to breathe.

RJ sucks in a deep breath.

BJ raises her eyes to his face, his expression filled with...? What? What is it there on his face?

"I'm not sure if this is the right time or place for this, but..." He pauses and makes intense eye contact with BJ. With so much going on in this one day, they are milky blue with emotions. His reflection there ignites his smile. "I... think...No. I know...I love you, Breezy Jo McCallister."

Numerous shocked thoughts and emotions collide. *Did he really say what I think he said? Didn't he say earlier today that he never loved a woman? He stated it in past tense. I'm tired, I must be hallucinating. My brain is on overload, I must already be in bed sleeping, and this is a dream. A damn good one, but a dream all the same.*

RJ stands frozen, watching the expressions race across her features. He can't remember a time in his life being this insecure, scared and uncertain of his decision to put voice to anything. However, this unfamiliar feeling for this woman is making him, as the old adage says, more nervous than a cat in a room full of rocking chairs.

RJ is struck by a thought which springs to the forefront of his mind, *"What if she rejects me?"* Hot on the heels of that distressing question, *"What if my admission scares her off?*

Jumbled emotions cross RJ's handsome features. He looks at one moment scared, nervous, worried, and insecure.

She is experiencing all that intensified. The realization that they are in the same frame of mind, this uncharted territory for RJ, and, truth be told, for her as well, somehow calms her. She finally speaks softly with a hint of humor, "I think maybe my hearing was affected by the noise of the band and crowds at work tonight. I'm not quite sure I heard you correctly. Would you mind repeating that last statement?" Her teasing smile coaxes his in return.

He clears his throat, smirks and repeats, "I said...I love you, Breezy Jo McCallister."

Suddenly, it dawns on her that he is using her full name. Brows furrowed; "Excuse me, Rainier Julian, what did you call me?" BJ asks, feigning anger.

"I called you the most beautiful name I've ever heard: A name so perfectly fitting for you. Breezy Jo."

"And how did you find out that particular piece of information?"

"Promise you won't be mad."

BJ looks skeptically at him.

"Promise?"

"I'll promise to at least control any anger, but I can't promise I won't feel any."

"OK, then agree that if you're angry, you'll only be angry at me."

She can tell he's trying to protect someone. "OK. Fine, I'll only be mad at you. Now tell me how you found out?"

Sheepishly, eyes downcast, "I took advantage of a sick little girl." Her brow furrows. "The night I spent at the motel, taking care of the girls. Chumani wanted to know what RJ stands for. I convinced her to tell me what BJ stands for in exchange for me telling her what RJ stands for."

"You sneaky, deceptive man, you." She gently pummels his chest, laughingly saying, "How dare you take advantage of a sick child, any child, for that matter. You've known all this time?"

"Yes, and I must say, though most of the time you are a very Breezy sort of girl, tonight, and a few other times I've noted, you're more of a gale force wind kinda gal," bringing chuckles from them both.

Their laughter subsides. They seem to realize at the same moment they're still standing in the same spot, although RJ's hands have gone from resting on BJ's hips to them linked behind her back, encircling her waist. Silence falls.

BJ looks up at this gorgeous hunk of man, taking in every detail of his features: from his rich olive complexion, his sparkling amber eyes atop dimpled cheeks supported by a strong masculine jaw, and such kissable lips. She wonders what it would feel like to run her fingers through that thick thatch of chestnut brown hair.

Hesitant, she begins, "About what you said…"

"Hey," he interrupts. "I didn't say it to pressure you in any way. Don't feel like you're required to say it back. I probably should have waited, found a better time, but… I'm new at this," he smiles. "I've never said that to any woman, never felt this for any woman. I guess I got a little anxious to tell someone, and figured without a doubt you should be the first to know."

"I appreciate that." She looks away, but not before the deep blue pools appear about to overflow.

"Hey, come sit with me." He maneuvers her to the love-seat, and they sit down together.

"RJ, I…"

"Shh. Don't speak. Just be. This has been one heck of a day with so many different emotions running rampant for both of us. Do you mind if I hold you a while? I just want to be with you."

"Sounds more amazing than you can imagine."

They recline both sections of the loveseat. RJ lies back, taking BJ with him, his arm around her shoulder, tucking her along his side. In a matter of moments, the steady, even breathing of sleep emanates from both.

The joyful singsong tone of Chumani's voice, like a feather duster carefully wiping away the cobwebs from the depths of their sleep, rouses the pair.

"Good morning, Mommy. Good morning, Mr. Fenton."

BJ is so very comfortable. She is dreaming that she is sleeping in RJ's embrace.

"Ummm."

The resonant sound from the comfortable, sleep-content man slithers into BJ's slowly waking mind, which is cocooned in this bliss.

She felt this way once before, that night at the motel when... BJ's eyes fly open to find Chumani standing next to her, smiling.

"Good morning, Mommy," her tone a chipper whisper. "Did you and Mr. Fenton sleep good?"

BJ's body attempts to jolt to an upright sitting position, but finds she is caught like an animal in a trap. Though she is pretty sure no animal trap is this comfortable.

RJ mumbles, "Where are you going?"

"Good morning, Mr. Fenton."

It is RJ who bolts upright, wiping his hands over his face repeatedly, trying to emerge from the fog that is his brain. He yawns boldly. Freed from her comfy trap, BJ sits up also.

"Good morning, Sweetie." BJ glances at the clock on the wall, "Eight o'clock? Oh, wow. I'm so sorry, Sweetie. It's so late." Chenoa! Her mind screams. "Your sister," BJ says, beginning to panic. Scrambling, she starts to get up to go to her baby.

"She's OK, Mommy. I changed her diaper and gave her a bottle."

BJ pauses, looking at her eldest daughter, beaming, ear to ear. "You did?" The surprise in her voice mingled with pride.

"Yup. I climbed into the crib with a clean diaper and wet wipes. Took off the smelly, soggy one, wiped her butt, and put on the clean one. I even put her jamma bottoms back on so she wouldn't be cold."

The three of them walk into the girls' room as she continues. "I put the dirty diaper in the pail, washed my hands, then went and got a bottle from the fridge, and gave it to her. I even turned on her favorite Care Bear DVD."

"Chumani, Mommy is *so* very proud of you. You did such a wonderful job taking care of your baby sister. I am so happy you know how to do all that, but you should have woken Mommy up so you didn't have to."

"I didn't *have* to do it. I wanted to. I love Chenoa, and I'm the big sister, so I need to help take care of her. Besides, I figured if you and Mr. Fenton fell asleep on the couch and didn't even make it to your bed, you both must'a been *Reeeally* tired. I wanted to let you sleep. Oh, and I already ate a bowl of cereal for breakfast too, so I'm good, and I gave Chenoa some dry Fruit Loops and Cheerios. She's good too."

The tears of joy and pride that begin rolling down BJ's cheeks are tinged with a smidgen of sadness that her little girl is growing up.

RJ gives BJ's shoulder a squeeze, then scoops up the smiling baby while BJ hugs Chumani tightly.

"Hello? Ms. BJ? Is my dad here?" They hear Riyon calling.

"We're in my room, Riyon," Chumani answers first.

Riyon enters smiling. "I figured since it didn't look like you even slept in your bed, and you weren't in the big house, and your truck is in the driveway, you must have stayed here last night," Riyon explains.

"Yup. They didn't even put their jammas on or make it to Mommy's bed. I found them asleep on the couch, still dressed just like this. Mommy is still wearing her uniform. They were *really* tired," Chumani explains the facts to Riyon.

The adults look at each other in amazement at how mature their two children sound about the whole situation, how they are carrying on almost as if the adults aren't there.

"Did you have breakfast? If not, I can fix you a bowl of cereal."

"Thanks, but I ate with Mémère and Misho."

"Wanna watch cartoons with me?" Chumani inquires.

"Sure." With that, the duo heads to the living room, leaving the adults somewhat stunned.

RJ takes note of the fact that Chumani pointed out that BJ is still wearing her server's uniform and offers, "How about I go enjoy cartoons with the gang while you shower and change?"

"Are you sure you wouldn't mind?"

"Absolutely," he says, kissing her forehead before walking out with Chenoa on his hip to go join the Saturday morning cartoon event.

A short while later, BJ emerges from showering and dressing for the day. Chenoa is standing at the loveseat playing with a toy, but when she catches sight of her mommy enter the room, she turns and steps away.

In a whispered gasp, the others hear BJ say, "Chenoa" as the little one takes her first step, which effectively turns the attention of the other three to look at the baby, affording everyone to witness Chenoa's next four of her first five steps before she plops down on her bottom then crawls the remainder of the way to her mother who scoops her up, hugging her effusively.

That evening, when BJ arrives for work at Buddy's, he asks her to come into the office. "I was serious last night. I thought about it today, and I have a new schedule to offer you. I know you make pretty good tips on Wednesdays and Fridays, so stick with those. Do you by any chance like sports?"

"Yes, I do."

"Good. I was thinking, and I know it will make your Mondays a bit long, but it will free up your Saturdays. You can be my new 'Bouncette' for Sunday and Monday night football, 5-10, no staying late, no side work. In the door by 5, out at 10. Hang around, making sure the rowdies don't get out of control. That should have you home early enough to get some sleep for your day job, and the pay is twenty an hour. What do you say? Start tomorrow?"

"Wow, OK. Sounds good. What should I wear?"

"Nice dark blue or black jeans, and these." He hands her two brand-new, bright yellow women's polo shirts. The silk screen on the left chest reads: Bouncette BJ, and the back reads in large black lettering: SECURITY Buddy's Lounge.

"You already made these today with my name? What if I said no?"

"Then you'd have some unique shirts to wear. But I knew you'd say yes," he smiles. "Now git out there and make some money."

24

Nigh on two weeks fly by in a flash. Morning of Halloween rises gloomy and gray, shrouded in early morning fog befitting the eeriness of the holiday.

BJ needs to make last-minute touches on all costumes to complete them. She made Native American-style dresses for Chumani and herself out of suede cloth items she found at the thrift store. She altered and embellished a leather vest for Riyon's outfit and made feathered, beaded headbands for the four of them. She's also made a bunting and papoose cradle board. She asked RJ if he needed any assistance with his outfit for the party, but she's been informed he has it handled.

BJ knocks at the back door of the big house. "Dear, there's no need for you to knock. You're welcome to come in anytime."

"Thank you, but I wouldn't feel right just walking into your home."

"Very well, then… for now," she winks. "What can I do for you?"

"I'm wondering if there is much trick-or-treating done around here or if there is somewhere better that you might suggest I could take the girls? I want to visit as many houses as we can in as short a time as possible, since I have to be at work at 9."

"Oh. Didn't Rainier speak to you about the plans?" Emily uses her son's given name.

"Plans? No. I haven't seen much of him this week."

"Well, we have only a few homes around here that get into the spirit of this particular holiday, so we take Riyon to Amelia's and Zachary's house, and he trick-or-treats with Aurora and Austin in their family-friendly neighborhood. Delia and Nathaniel also bring Jedidiah. I was sure you'd want to bring Chumani, and Chenoa too."

"Oh, I don't want to impose on your family activities."

"Nonsense, dear. You are family. Besides, everyone is looking forward to seeing you all again. I hope you don't mind, since I didn't hear otherwise, I assumed it was all settled. I told everyone you'd be there."

Emily's comment, *"You are family,"* strikes a minor chord in BJ's mind. A discordant melody. It sounds a bit off, yet is beautifully so right. The idea of seeing the others again and having the girls be able to trick-or-treat with the other children does sound fun. "If you're sure we won't be intruding."

"Not at all. In fact, even if I wasn't so determined to have you join us, I would never hear the end of it from any of my grandchildren or children if I didn't insist you attend." She pauses, "I do hope Rainier didn't forget to tell you about the Party Saturday."

"Yes, he told me about that."

"Did he tell you it's a costume party for young and old alike?"

BJ smiles, "Yes, I just completed the costumes for all three of us. You and Jason are going too, right? What are you going as?"

"Yes, we're going as Comte and Comtesse de la Succion de Sang." At BJ's quizzical look, Emily translates with a giggle, "Count and Countess of Blood Sucking, in other words, a couple of royal bloodsucking vampires." They laugh together.

"So, you'll go with us tomorrow evening, won't you? We figured since you have to go to work, you can just leave from there, and we'll bring the girls home with us and get them to bed."

BJ thought that through. "What time should I tell Kristen to come to babysit then?"

"We thought since she's a teenager, she'd probably enjoy the night off to celebrate. One of us will stay with the girls after we get them to bed."

"Oh. I don't want to impose..."

"Dear, let us get something clear from here on out. Whatever we offer to do or have you do with us is, and never will be, an imposition or intrusion. We absolutely adore all three of you. We thoroughly enjoy every moment we share with you." Emily sees a glimmer in BJ's eyes and fears she's spoken too sternly. Wrapping her arms around the younger woman, "I understand it may still be a bit difficult for you to grasp after past life experiences, but we truly care about you and your daughters."

Sniffling, tears trickling down her cheeks, "More than a bit difficult. Nearly incomprehensible," BJ responds with a lilt of laughter.

They finalize plans for the evening, including Emily offering to take care of the girls that evening while BJ works. That way, Kristen can have the night off.

"It's settled then," Emily confirms, releasing BJ.

BJ finishes dressing the girls in their costumes, gets mostly ready for work, except for donning her uniform, gathers the diaper bag, trick or treating bags, purse, keys and children, then heads to the car to load up and follow the Fenton-Kemps to their family's house.

"Such a beautiful Indian Princess," Jason compliments, appearing near the car.

"Thank you, Misho," Chumani accepts the compliment as the remainder of the Fenton-Kemp family appears.

"Everyone ready for a fun-filled night of trick-or-treating?" Emily asks.

Riyon and Chumani cheer. "Rainier, I was thinking it might be a good idea if you boys ride to the party with BJ since she doesn't know where we're going. Then she can go straight to work afterward, and we can bring both of you and the girls home."

"Good idea," he agrees. They all pile into the vehicles and are off.

BJ arrives home very late...or very early, depending on how you look at it. She glances at the clock when she walks in the door. It is quarter after 3:00. She finds RJ sleeping in a recliner. She tiptoes into the other room to check on her girls. She discovers Riyon in the top bunk, bringing a smile to her tired features, before heading to her room to change out of her uniform after this long, exhausting, insanely wild Halloween bar night. Deciding not to wake RJ, she returns to the living room with a blanket to cover him, but finds him awake and waiting.

"You look wiped out," he whispers in the dim glow of the night light.

She stumbles slightly as she approaches. He bolts to his feet to assist her. "Literally dizzy with exhaustion," she admits.

"Let me guide you to your room," he says as he is already maneuvering her that direction.

Turning back the covers and climbing in, she says, her voice barely audible, "You're welcome to crash here if you'd like."

After covering her, he walks to the other side of the bed, then, removing only his shirt, belt, shoes, and socks, he climbs in beside her.

Wrapping his arms around her, reveling in the glorious sensation, they drift off to sleep.

Morning breaks only a few short hours later. Hearing Chenoa beginning to fuss, RJ glances at the bedside clock, 7:30. He slips silently from the bed to go to her.

Riyon and Chumani are also awake. Chumani has already started the task of changing her sister's diaper, and Riyon already grabbed Chenoa's bottle.

"Hi, guys," he whispers.

"Hi, Daddy."

"Good morning, Mr. Fenton," they whisper their responses.

"You two are such big helpers." Continuing in whispers, he speaks to Chumani. "Your mommy had a very long, tiring night at work, and only got home a couple of hours ago. I'm thinking the four of us should go to the big house, and have breakfast with Mémère, and Misho, and let your mommy sleep."

"Good idea. We should take Chenoa's diaper bag in case we need to change her again."

"Good thinking. How about I finish dressing Chenoa, and you quietly get yourself dressed, OK?"

"Deal."

"I'll go tell Mémère and Misho we're on our way."

"Thank you, buddy. Be sure to be very quiet going out the door."

"I will," Riyon assures.

After breakfast, Chumani and Riyon play in the playroom of the big house, RJ takes a shower, Jason and Emily tend to household chores, and Chenoa.

It is approaching noon when Emily begins preparing lunch. She spies Chenoa napping on Misho's chest, where he sits dozing in his overstuffed chair in the living room. Surreptitiously, she sneaks taking a few pictures of the adorable scene to share with BJ later.

Entering the kitchen, the children overhear RJ and Emily talking quietly about something they didn't know about.

Seeing the looks of excited surprise on the two young faces, Emily begins, "You can say nothing about what you just heard. You cannot let on that you even know. Do you understand?"

"Yes, ma'am. We understand. It's a big surprise. We won't say a word," Riyon assures.

Chumani makes the motion of zipping her lips, locking them and throwing away the key.

"Good," the adults say in unison.

The sleepy silence of the house is incongruent with the sun peeking through the window blinds. BJ sits up, trying to clear her sleep-fogged brain. Seemingly right on cue, the front door opens tentatively, and Chumani peeks in as BJ steps from her cozy bedroom.

"Hi, Mommy. Did you sleep good?"

"Hi, Sweetie. Yes, I did. What's going on?"

"We all went to the big house to let you sleep. I'm here to find out if you woke up yet 'cause Mémère is making lunch, and wants to know if you're ready to eat something."

"I am pretty hungry. I'm going to clean up a bit first."

"OK, I'll go tell Mémère you're coming. See you in a little bit," she hugs her mommy.

Later that afternoon, Chumani asks enthusiastically. "Can we start getting ready for the party tonight? You didn't forget about the costume party Mr. Fenton told you about, did you?"

"No, Hunny, I didn't forget. We probably should get you in your costume while Chenoa is still napping."

"You too, Mommy. I can't wait to see all of us dressed up. We're going to have so much fun tonight. I just know it."

"I'm sure we will."

A while later, Riyon, in full Indian garb, knocks at the pool house door.

"Come in," Chumani calls out.

"Daddy asked me to come see if you ladies are ready."

"Finishing up," BJ informs from the bedroom.

"OK. Daddy said he'll be waiting at the car in 10 minutes if that works for you."

"That will be fine."

"I'll let him know. Wow, you look pretty, Ms. BJ," he finishes enthusiastically as she enters the living area carrying Chenoa. Chumani appears from behind her. "You look pretty, too, Chumani, and Chenoa is so cute."

"Thank you," BJ and Chumani reply in unison.

"You are a very handsome Warrior, Riyon," BJ compliments.

"Thank you, but wait 'til you see my Daddy."

Minutes later, Riyon escorts the ladies to the car. They stand awaiting RJ's appearance. They don't have to wait long. As he strides out the front door, BJ's heart jumps into overdrive at the sight of him.

Her expression must have given a hint to her inner feelings as she notes the smug smirk cross RJ's handsome features.

A sense of voyeurism settles over her, taking in dark brown cowboy boots striding in connection with long, strong, jean-clad legs and tight buttocks. A wide leather belt latched with a large turquoise and coral-adorned silver buckle around his narrow waist, securing the darkwash denims. Broad shoulders stretch taut the plaid material of the western-style shirt with its buckle-matching bolo tie. The outfit made complete with the dark brown cowboy hat atop his wavy chestnut brown hair.

BJ tries to gather her wits.

RJ smiles knowingly. "Everything OK?"

"Of course," she responds, turning her attention to the children.

"Let's load 'em up and move 'em out," she directs in wagon trail jargon. "Where are Emily and Jason?" She asks as they all pile into RJ's crew-cab truck.

"They headed over a little while ago to check if there are any last-minute details to help with," he explains before driving off.

Cars line both sides of the street in front of the spookily decorated house. He pulls the truck into the driveway, which seems to have barely enough room for one more vehicle. As they disembark, Riyon and Chumani begin to giggle quietly.

"What's so funny?" BJ asks

"Nothing," Riyon responds.

RJ is unbuckling Chenoa while BJ collects all their costume items and the diaper bag.

"Daddy, can we head in?" Riyon winks at his father out of sight from BJ.

"Sure. We'll be right behind you."

Off they go.

RJ comes around the side of the vehicle, approaching BJ. "I didn't have a chance to tell you tonight that you are the most beautiful Indian Maiden ever. I love your costume," he informs her after a brief survey of her beaded and fringed suede cloth dress, moccasins, and braided hair with a feathered headband. He brushes a light kiss on BJ's forehead before handing over Chenoa in her faux-fur bunting, then guides them up the walkway past the cobweb-laden trees of the fake graveyard with its ghouls, goblins, and skeletons. They reach the porch where a motion-sensor gatekeeper announces in an eerie voice, *"Welcome. All who pass through these gates beware. Surprises lurk everywhere,"* and concludes with a sinister laugh, *"Muah-ha-ha-ha."*

As RJ reaches for the doorknob, BJ states, "Wow, these people really go all out, don't they?"

To which he replies, "You have no idea," turns the knob, and ushers her into the darkened living space of the house.

"SURPRISE!!!" comes the chorus of voices ringing out as bright lights flick on to illuminate the room, and flashes begin sparking all around. BJ gasps and steps back into the solid safety of the man inches behind her.

"Happy Birthday, Mommy!" Chumani announces first, then is joined by an onslaught of voices repeating that greeting, and a spattering of "Woot, Woot," and the like.

Riyon and Chumani hug her legs, calling out cheerfully, "Were you surprised?"

"We got you!"

BJ, overwhelmed by the commotion swirling around, touches each of the little ones at her feet, then turns to look at RJ questioningly.

"Happy Birthday, BJ," is his simple smiled response.

"But...?"

Seeing the confusion and bewilderment on BJ's face, Cheryl appears at their side. She supplies the answer, "You filled out a job application, remember?" She smiles brightly, then begins ushering her into the room where co-workers from Fenton Warehouse, Buddy's lounge, Brady and Millie, Kristen and her Parents, all of RJ's sisters, and their families, Emily, and Jason all await.

"I'm so confused." She looks around, still puzzled.

Emily approaches and clarifies. "When Cheryl mentioned that your birthday is Nov. 1st, we decided to throw you a surprise party. We planned the whole thing under the guise of it being a Halloween Costume party, but actually, it's all for you. Happy Birthday," Emily concludes, hugging her. "Let me take this cherub so you can mingle and enjoy yourself."

With that, people in costumes of every sort begin coming up to BJ, hugging her and imparting their birthday wishes. Everyone seems so proud that they all were able to keep the plan a total secret and surprise her.

The events of the evening are a great success. There is a graveyard-themed cake with a tombstone that reads: RIP Youth, Hello, Big 3-o! There is plenty of food and drinks, games for young and old, music, and laughter.

About an hour into the evening, Millie comes up to BJ. "Dear, would ya be so kind as to come with me to the patio fer a wee bit?"

"Sure, Millie. What's up?" she asks as they go out the sliding door. "Ahk, jus' the wee matter of ya opening yar gifts is all."

BJ's jaw drops open at the sight of the gift-laden table before her. "But... I... Uh..."

"Close yar mouth, Dear or ya'll be catchin flies."

"But..." she looks at the ever-jovial woman beside her as tears begin to fill her eyes. "There are so many!" she exclaims in a whisper, words so filled with emotion she can barely speak.

Millie, seeing the overwhelmed disbelief evident on the lass's face, puts her arm 'round her, pulling her close. "Aye, lass, there are. This is wha' folks do fer the ones they love. There's always a first time fer experiencin' everythin' Luv." She winks at BJ. "Just breathe deep an' be gracious." She gives her a bit of a squeeze.

"Mommy! Look at all the presents for you!" Chumani enthuses.

"We'll help you," Riyon offers. "I'll give you presents to open. Chumani can take away the wrapping paper."

All the party attendees come out for the gift opening.

Jason brings over a chair. "Have a seat." BJ, still a bit flustered, sits, and Riyon brings the first gift for opening.

Gratitude exudes from the birthday girl the whole evening toward everyone, not only for their presents, but for their presence. The evening draws to a close. After thanking Del and Nate for hosting the party, the Fenton- Kemp- McCallister clan loads up and heads home.

2 5

"Hello?" BJ answers her cell as she pulls into the parking lot Monday morning. The past two weeks have zipped by. Thanksgiving is fast approaching, with the tragic anniversary hot on its heels.

"BJ?" The familiar-sounding voice inquires.

"Who's calling, please?" She avoids confirming who she is.

"BJ? This is Yul Conner of Conner and Cheetum Law Firm. I've been handling things for you regarding your parents' estate."

"Yes, Mr. Conner, I know who you are. What is the reason for your call?"

"Well, there is still the matter of the property tax arrears that need to be paid, as well as attorney's fees incurred due to your parents' legal issues. Along with all the other monies owed."

"Yes, well, as you stated, the fees are due to my parents' legal issues, and the property taxes were for property they owned, where I never resided. I don't know what to tell you other than, as my mother used to say, 'You can't get blood from a turnip.'"

"I'm not sure what a turnip has to do with this matter. However, we need to make arrangements for you to pay off your debts, or we'll be forced to take you to court and press charges for default."

BJ is ready to scream! "The turnip is an analogy, Sir. Turnips *have* no blood to give, and I have No Money to give. These are NOT my debts! They *were* my parents' and my husband's debts. Default Hell. I haven't defaulted on anything. It's Not My fault, my parents didn't know how to handle their finances, nor that my husband was an alcoholic drug addict who didn't pay the bills. So, go right ahead and take me to court. I still won't have any money for you," she screams at the man on the phone. She wishes she had figured a way to send the email response a while back without the IP address being able to be tracked here. She does not want this man to know where she is and risk him involving anyone here.

RJ spots BJ sitting in her car and walks over to check on her and to walk in with her. He overhears her talking on the phone, so he waits and listens. When her voice rises to a level he never expected to hear from her, he is alarmed. Her window is down a bit, allowing him to understand her every word clearly. He doesn't want to startle her, but he does want to intervene. He opens her car door and motions for her to hand him the phone. BJ is so distraught that she simply hands it over as tears begin to trickle. That is RJ's undoing.

"Hello. This is RJ Fenton with whom am I speaking?"

Mr. Conner is taken aback by the booming voice that assails his ears. "This is Yul Conner of Conner and Cheetum Law firm."

"Are you serious?" RJ thinks for a moment that this is a joke. His lawyers provided the individual name of the lawyer BJ has been dealing with, a Mr. Conner, and that alone is bad enough but... "Conner and Cheetum? Like 'Con her, and cheat him?'"

"Very serious, Sir, and no, not like that at all."

"Fine, Yul. You'll be hearing from my lawyers on this matter. Do not contact Ms. McCallister further. Do I make myself clear, Mr. Conner?"

"Yes, Sir. Mr. Fenton, was it?"

"Yes, RJ Fenton. Good day to you, Sir." With that, he ends the call.

BJ is still sitting in the seat, lightly crying, but doesn't comprehend why he is saying his lawyers will be in touch with Mr. Conner.

RJ takes her by the hand and draws her out of the car and into his arms comfortingly. "Let's go inside. It's a bit nippy out here. He gets her keys, locks her car, then guides her to his office. BJ stops crying and is gathering her wits.

"What just happened? What did he say to you to cause you to need your lawyers involved? I'm confused."

"Take a seat, Breezy."

BJ's head snaps up at the sound of her given name being used.

"Sit. Please?"

She sits. He sits across the desk from her.

"I didn't mean to eavesdrop. I saw you sitting in your car and came over to walk in with you. I arrived right as your voice escalated. I heard what you said."

"Sorry," BJ apologizes for raising her voice.

"You have nothing to apologize for." RJ hesitates, draws a deep steadying breath before forging ahead, knowing this may not go over well since he is sure that fiercely independent BJ will not be happy to find out how much knowledge RJ is privy to regarding the tumultuous struggles of her arcane past, nor how and when he acquired it.

"Are you OK?" he asks, concerned.

"Yes. Please explain why your lawyers will be contacting him."

RJ wipes his hands across his face. "It seems like forever ago when it was only a few months ago," he begins. "Right after I found out you'd been employed by Brady, before I knew anything about you. I was on a business trip. I was voicing my concerns over the situation with a longtime friend who suggested I do a background check on you to be sure you weren't running from the law."

BJ's eyes widen, and her jaw drops in disbelief. "You thought I was a criminal?"

"No! I was actually more concerned at that time that you might have some psychotic guy coming after you, who might bring harm to you or cause problems for my company. As I said, that was before I got to know you, and that was before you got under my skin," he tries to bring levity to the conversation. He pauses.

BJ looks at him, not sure she wants to hear any more, but she must know exactly how much he found out.

"Aaand?" she draws out the word. "What did you find?"

RJ shakes his head, remembering how perturbed his parents were when they found out that he'd done a background check.

"Everything," he states with calm certainty.

"Everything? Such as...?" she prods.

"Such as, the newspaper articles about the crash, the obituaries for your family..." Again, he pauses. "But I didn't stop there. I became more intrigued and delved deeper into other records and documents."

BJ stares blankly, not sure how to react to the information that he researched her past, thinking she is some kind of lowlife. How dare this man she allowed herself to fall in love with... *Wait! What did she just admit to herself? She'll deal with that some other time...* How dare he? How dare she? Geez, she must be stupid.

RJ continues. "What I discovered appalled me. I couldn't believe what I was reading. I was furious at the financial problems that you endured. So furious that I had my legal department look into the legalities of what transpired, and the manner in which they treated you. That's why I told Mr. Conner my lawyers will be contacting him, and that he is not to contact you directly ever again."

The expressive features before him experience the torment of trying to comprehend everything he's imparting regarding his unauthorized intervention due to his sincere desire to make things right for this enigmatic woman who has captured his heart and soul.

BJ struggles to grasp exactly what RJ is telling her. Her brain is on overload. The room is spinning. Or only her mind? So many emotions and thoughts vying for space in her brain. She wishes she could feel thrilled that this wonderful man decided to help her without her knowing. However, instead, she is enraged that this self-appointed, pompous ass went behind her back and took it upon himself to take control of a situation that has nothing to do with him. A situation that is her battle to fight. She is also furious that he, in actuality, has been lying to her all along, pitying her, taking her on like some charity case to improve his good Samaritan rating. How much of what is happening is based on lies and pity? Who all is in on it? How many of her newly acquired so-called friends are in on this pity party? Suddenly, it is all too much for BJ to wrap her mind around. She springs to her feet, runs out of the office, and straight to her car. "Keys? Where the heck did I put my keys?" she barks at herself. RJ is hot on her heels.

"BJ, wait! Listen to me..."

"Listen to you? Why? So, you can lie to me some more?"

Suddenly, she remembers he took her keys out of the ignition and locked the car. "Where are my keys?" she spits at him.

"You are not driving like this," he states calmly.

"What? Now you're going to tell me what I can and can't do?" BJ stands toe to toe with the man tower before her, "Look here, *Mr. Fenton*, I lived my life being controlled, first by my parents, then by my emotionally and physically abusive husband. I will never be told what to do by you or anyone ever again. Do I make myself clear?"

RJ smiles so as not to upset her further. He doesn't like that she is angry with him for trying to help. However, he does like that she is standing up to him in a manner he is sure she never did with her husband. That is a step in the right direction. RJ is unsure whether to play the *'I'm your Boss. If you leave, you risk losing your job' card* to prevent her from driving away angry or refuse to give her the keys and risk making her even more upset, if that is possible. Or should he offer to drive her home? He is saved from having to make that particular decision when she storms away and heads into work.

RJ follows, not too closely behind, watching as she steps onto the dock where the crew takes note of her mood and unanimously decide to give the raging female a wide berth; all except Jake, that is.

"Good morning, BJ," he greets in his ever-happy tone.

"Nothing good about it," she retorts.

RJ slinks his way close enough to hear his lifelong friend impart these words of wisdom.

"Ah, but you are so wrong. What's good about it is that you are alive, healthy, and loved by many. Don't you ever forget that." He steps nearer. When she stands from setting down a box, he wraps his arms around her in a brotherly bear hug.

"I have no idea what's eating you this morning, but let me just say this. Everyone makes mistakes. That doesn't mean they don't have good intentions behind their actions. Now I sense this state of upset you are experiencing might have something to do with our boss, and my lifelong best friend. Please listen closely to what I'm about to impart to you. RJ is *The* Absolute best man you will ever know. He doesn't often...OK, well, *never*... let's anyone affect him emotionally, so the fact that he has fallen in love with you makes you one very darn special person, and he's the kind of guy who will do whatever it takes to care for those he loves. Even though he may not always get it right the first time, he never does anything out of malice, and if he screws up, he will die trying to make it right. That said, let me make something clear to you..." He leans her back from where he's been still holding her in his brotherly embrace, and makes sure she is looking at him so he is sure she understands how serious he is when he continues... "That man means the World to me. I would give my life for him. So...don't you go breaking his heart. If you don't love him with all your heart, then walk out that door right now, and don't look back. Otherwise, cut him some slack. This is all new to him. He may not handle things perfectly right off the bat, but he will if you give him time." Jake kisses the top of BJ's head, ends his affectionate embrace, then walks away, leaving BJ to ponder all he said.

RJ now slinks away undetected and humbled by everything he overhears his best friend say.

A short while later, Jake approaches Butch, "Cover for me, will ya?" With eyebrows raised, he nods pointedly in BJ's direction. "I'm headed to talk to the boss."

"I got your back, my friend. Let me know when you figure out what happened. I do not like seeing our little Missy that upset. I'll give the boss my two cents' worth if need be."

Jake smiles. "Will do. No worries, I'll handle RJ if there's a need."

Butch is sure he will, too, since he is the older 'brother' of the two.

26

"Come in," the gruff answer comes from inside the office in response to Jake's knock. Upon entering, Jake finds his 'little brother' sitting behind his desk, head in hands. He's sure he's never seen his buddy so dejected.

"Spill," he commands.

RJ looks up at the firm tone of Jake's voice. "I thought it was Cheryl or Brady. What can I do for you?"

"You heard me. Spill," he reiterates.

He sighs, "It's a long story."

Pulling up the chair BJ vacated a while ago, he sits down. "No worries, I have all day, little brother. I'm pretty tight with the boss man. He won't mind paying me to listen to your screw up," Jake states flippantly.

RJ heaves a self-reproaching sigh. "This is the kind of thing that is the reason I don't do relationships." He begins to unload to the only person he ever felt utterly comfortable purging his woes to. "Where to start?"

"The beginning is usually the best place," Jake supplies.

"Once upon a time, an egg and a sperm got together and created a dumb ass that became me..."

They both chuckle. Jake is glad to find his 'brother from another mother' is still gifted with some humor.

"Actually, it all began when I laid eyes on one Breezy Jo McCallister....Damn! I promised not to tell anyone her real name."

"No worries, bro. Her secret's safe with me...even if it's not with you..." he snickers.

"Thanks. Anyway… That first day? I walked onto the dock, and the sight of her did something to me…twisted my innards."

Jake smirks. "I knew from the moment she agreed to Butch's challenge, she'd get to you."

"Yeah, well, getting to the crux of the matter, while I was on that business trip after meeting her, I couldn't get her off my mind. Drew Conrad suggested I do a background check on her."

"And you did?" Jake asks half-disbelievingly, even though he understands it makes good business sense, but still.

RJ lowers his gaze and his head. "Yes, Mère and Jason weren't too happy with me when they found out either. Anyway, we went online and searched her name, even though I supposedly didn't know her real name."

"How did you find out her real name?" Jake inquires.

RJ, yet again, lowers his head shamefully, looking up through lowered lashes, "I bribed her sick daughter."

"Damn man, have you no shame? Have you lost all your honor?" He is only half-teasing, yet still serious.

"Anyway, the search came up with a life story one can hardly believe is true, let alone believe that beautiful woman and two girls lived through. RJ recounts the sad tale of the accident.

Jake rears back in his chair, then forcefully forward. Heaving as if the wind had just been knocked out of him. "Are you kidding me?"

"No, and that's just the beginning. It gets worse."

"How the hell can it?" Jake is incredulous.

"There she was, 8 months pregnant. Both parents and husband dead in one fell swoop. This lawyer, get this: his name is Yul Conner of Conner and Cheetum law firm."

Jake's brows all but fly off the top of his head. "Seriously?"

RJ nods and continues. "Seems BJ's parents were trying to stave off foreclosure of their home, and hired this lawyer. They hadn't been successful. When they died, BJ was informed that she had to accept a short sale for the house at a price at or below what her parents owed on it. Plus they were something like 3 or 4 years in arrears on property taxes, owed outstanding lawyer and legal fees, plus she then had lawyers' fees to handle the proceedings after their deaths, compiled with three cremations, one burial plot, and 2 burials of the ash urns for her parents, To top it off BJ went into premature labor due to all the stress, which, then the insurance company refused to pay for the delivery, her hospital stay or the NICU for preemie Chenoa, because the insurance was through her husband's work and he died, so they *claimed* she was no longer covered. While she was dealing with all that turmoil, they returned to her apartment after Chenoa's release from the hospital 3 days after her birth, to find her husband hadn't been paying the rent and had been ignoring previous notifications to vacate. When they arrived home, she found an eviction notification on the front door. Mind you, Chenoa was born on December 21st. The notification stated she only had until Dec 31st to be out. She didn't know all the legalities and rights she had, so their scare tactics worked. From what my investigators found out, she sold pretty much everything she had, moved into her parents' place, hired an estate seller, sold off everything except what she and the girls needed and could fit in her station wagon. She was unemployed with nowhere to go and no one to turn to. So, on January 31st, the three of them became homeless. The investigators followed a trail of odd jobs she was able to do while having a preemie newborn and toddler in tow, and the three of them were living in her car. Sometime this summer, the lawyer contacted her after discovering a Bond her mother had in her maiden name, which listed BJ as the beneficiary. Seems the one decent thing the lawyer did was wire her the measly $3000 to survive on, shortly after which, they moved into the motel, and not long after that Brady somehow had the insight and guts to hire her, not even knowing any of this, and knowing I would be angry."

Jake sits there a bit, mulling over all he's just learned about the woman he already had great respect for, but now?... holds in the highest regard that of a Saint. "I take it this incident today is due at least in part to her finding out you knew all this, and didn't tell her you knew."

"Got it in one," RJ confirms. "Now, I think she thinks I view her as some charity case. That I've taken her on like a pet project. She thinks I'm deceptive, dishonest, nosy, and meddlesome."

"Agreed." Jake winks.

"I know. Anyway, I happened to overhear her arguing on the phone with Mr. Conner this morning, who is threatening to take her to court for everything they claim *she owes*. I took the phone and told him he'd be hearing from my lawyers, and not to contact BJ ever again."

"Ah, so not only have you developed feelings for her—I dare say fallen in love with her—but when you combine that with your newly acquired savior complex and her having an independent streak ten miles long, that explains the sparks flying this morning."

RJ shoots Jake a look when he says the part about falling in love with BJ, which Jake responds to now. "Yeah, Buddy. This, that you're feeling? Yeah, That's Love!"

RJ sighs very heavily. "I know. That's what I was afraid of, Doc. Is there a cure?"

"Afraid not, my friend. It's terminal. Pretty sure that's why wedding vows state 'til death do us part." They chuckle.

"Is there at least some sort of treatment to ease the pain?"

"Well, some of the best preventatives for the pain you're experiencing are huge doses of Truth, Honesty, Understanding and Patience. Taking into consideration everything you just told me, you need to be ready with mega doses of understanding, the next few weeks, since the anniversary of that whole mess is fast approaching."

"Yes, I know. Coupled with the mess that's about to begin in order to handle all the legal issues, I'm sensing that this is about to be a very tough month."

"I recommend that you not charge headlong on your white horse to save BJ. Rather, go to her and offer your moral support, then let her know that you will make all the resources at your disposal available to her free of charge with no strings attached. Purely out of care and concern for the well-being of her and the girls."

"Good idea. Thanks for reining me in, Jake. I don't know what I would do without you, brother." They both rise and exchange a sincere brotherly embrace.

"By the way, I didn't have a clue what was going on with BJ when I saw her come on the dock, but I knew there was something up, and I gave her some advice. Hope you don't mind, I told her you're in love with her, and that you're new to this 'love thing', so to cut you some slack. I can tell you this. She loves you too, and after what we've learned about her, I think this love thing is new to her too, so you need to cut her some slack as well."

"I overheard you. Thank you."

"Eavesdropper... Keep me posted."

"Will do. Again, thank you."

"Anytime." Jake turns back as he is about to walk out the door, "How much do Mère and Jason know?"

"I've told them everything. Pops has been helping keep up with the investigation and staying in touch with our lawyers."

Jake smiles hugely.

"What?"

"That is the first time I've heard you call him anything other than Jason."

"Yeah, well, guess I've been going through a lot of changes lately."

"All good ones, my friend, all good. Talk to you later."

"Later."

"Don't you look in a foul mood," Josie comments, seeing the scowling expression on BJ's face. "I pity anyone who gets out of line tonight. Pretty sure you'll make 'em regret it," she says lightheartedly.

BJ sighs. "Don't worry, I'm not likely to make anyone pay for someone else's screw-up."

"Uh oh. I'll have a few minutes after I drop off this round, we'll talk." Josie walks off, but returns in two minutes.

"OK. I'm free for a bit. Get to unloadin', Sugar."

"I don't want to..."

"Spill," she demands lovingly. "A good neighborhood bar, cocktail server ain't worth her salt if she ain't a good listener, and advice giver, and I am a damn good cocktail server if I do say so myself, and I do. Let 'er rip."

"All right. Fine. There's a whole lot about my past that you don't know about...that I thought no one around here knew. However, I found out this morning that Mr. Fenton has been digging into my past with private investigators and lawyers, and found out *everything*, and intends to have his lawyers handle 'fixing' it all."

"O...K... What part of him wanting to help you is bad?"

"I get as an employer, him doing a general background check. I'm more upset that he did deep research into all the legal matters of my past. He's known almost all of this since the beginning, and never told me he knew. All this so-called help he's been giving, they've all been giving, is just pity."

"First off, you're right, as your employer, we can give him doing the background check. That's common practice and plain old good business. Second, as a man in love, I'll give him delving deeper, and if he found something he thought he could assist you with, true, it would have been far better if he let you know he wanted to help rather than jumping in headlong, but since I'm pretty damn sure you've never killed anyone in your past, how bad can it be?"

Tears instantly flood BJ's eyes, and Josie realizes she must have said something that touched a nerve. She immediately puts an arm around BJ's waist, saying as she guides her in the direction of the ladies' room, "Let's step into my office." Once inside, Josie locks the door behind them. "Let it out, Sugar. Just let it all out," the older woman soothes.

"But I did kill someone," BJ begins sobbing, then purges all the nightmarish events of a year ago.

One of the other servers spies the exchange taking place before the other two servers head to the restroom. She nears and overhears the crying and realizes they need some time, so she lets Buddy know there is an issue being handled, so he won't be upset if he can't find the two of them. The other server assures him she'll keep watch of Josie's tables, and the bartender says he'll handle crowd control, which shouldn't be an issue since most of the crowd is regulars tonight.

Josie listens intently, schooling her features so as not to show the horror she feels for this gentle woman and what she endured.

"So..." BJ sniffles. "You see, I know the law says I owe all that money, and I'm not trying to run or hide from anything. I need to get settled and stable with my girls before making a payment arrangement to pay it all off. But they're being impatient. The call RJ overheard this morning was the lawyer threatening to take me to court for default," BJ concludes, sounding deflated.

Josie draws a long, deep, steadying breath before she begins, "Let me start by addressing your statement about Mr. 'Hunk' and his family doing for you out of pity. That's not true at all. No one is pitying you. Everyone, whether they know your past or not, does for you, loves you, because of the wonderful person you are, and for no other reason. That's a fact.

"Now tell me something, Sugar, is there anything you or anyone ever said or did that can be undone or unsaid?"

BJ thinks about it for a second and shakes her head no.

"Exactly. One second ago is history, and history cannot be rewritten. Let me set you straight once and for all, Sugar. You Did Not Kill your parents. That drunken bastard of a husband did that. You calling them for help was the right thing to do. There was no way on God's green earth that you or anyone could have predicted the events that followed that call. Everything happens for a reason, whether we perceive the events as good or bad in the human realm of things. We may not always, well, actually seldom, do we see the good in 'bad' situations and circumstances. That doesn't mean the good isn't there.

"You'd have never met Mr. Fenton, and his son, and been the cause of changing their lives for the better as you have, and the list of people whose lives you have touched goes on. You experienced all that you have to be the you that you are. To teach and show others it can be done, and to allow others the opportunity to give of themselves, thus helping to build a better them."

BJ stares at her friend. Processing everything she's just said. The wheels of her mind begin to spin uncontrollably, and she gives voice to some of the realizations that spring forth. "I never thought of any of the things that happened as having any good in them. But now... looking at things as you put it... If all that didn't happen, I would still be living 'that' life. Miserable. Always trying to please them. Never measuring up. Still being abused, and knocked around..."

"He beat you, too?" Josie asks incredulously.

"My parents when I was a kid, then my husband." BJ responds flatly, then goes on, "I would have stayed. Putting my girls at risk and allowing them to grow up not knowing there's a better way of life. That they deserve a better life."

"So, do You!" Josie supplies adamantly.

"It's been a struggle but..."

"Let me explain something to you. The mighty oak began its journey with the major struggle of cracking a tough nutshell, and trust me, it had many more struggles throughout its life. However, perseverance and faith during those times are why that mighty oak is an amazingly beautiful, magnificent success. Hang in there. The best things in life aren't necessarily the easiest, and the storms we withstand strengthen us. However, we must remember, as humans, we must also stay flexible like the willow tree, so when the storm winds blow, we can bend and move with the flow."

BJ smiles and snorts a contained chuckle. "Are you sure you're not a psychologist or philosopher?"

Josie laughs outright, "No, Sugar, I'm so much better than that. I'm a neighborhood bar cocktail server. Psychologists have the highfalutin' patients. Me? I deal mostly with down-in-the-dumps, drunks. A much better class of folks." They laugh together and return to the bar smiling, to the perplexed expressions of the rest of the crew and patrons.

27

BJ arrives home after her shift. Kristen is there with the girls, both of whom are snugly tucked in bed, soundly sleeping. After telling Kristen good night and seeing her off, she closes the door, leans against it and closes her eyes. She is startled by the light rapping on the door she is leaning against. She doesn't want to face RJ tonight. There is still too much running through her mind that she hasn't sorted out.

Rap, rap, rap. The sound comes again, followed by Emily's sweet, gentle voice. "BJ, dear? I need to speak with you if you can spare a moment."

She is fairly sure RJ would have told his parents of the morning's events and discussions. Though she doesn't want to get into it with Emily, she can't bring herself to be rude to the woman who has done so much for her little family. She pushes away from the door and opens it, trying to bring a smile to her face, "Hello, Mrs. Kemp."

Emily looks at this exhausted young woman before her. "Excuse me, dear," she begins with mock sternness, "What pray-tell have I done to be relegated to Mrs. Kemp again? I was sure we were way beyond those formalities."

BJ sighs, "I'm sorry, Emily."

"May I come in for a few minutes? I have some things I need to talk to you about. I know you're tired, but I will not be able to sleep if I don't clear up a few things."

BJ is not tired; she is beyond exhausted, but she doesn't want to be the cause of this woman's sleepless night. "Come in," she states as she moves away from the door, leaving her visitor to enter, then close the door behind her.

BJ walks over to the comfy love seat the Kemps bought for her use, and succumbs to its calling to sit. Emily sits perched on the edge of the love seat, taking in the depleted young woman next to her.

"Where to start?" Emily begins, "I guess the first thing I need to clear up is this. Jason and I chose to help you and your darling daughters purely from hearing Millie talk about the determined young woman Brady risked his job for by hiring because he knew she deserved a chance to provide for her daughters. Originally, there was no ulterior motive."

BJ looks up quizzically.

"Yes, dear. 'originally.' However, after hearing more about you, and hearing how my son reacted to you... Well, let's say an ulterior motive took root. I love my son in a way I'm sure you can understand as a mother and would do most anything to ensure his happiness. First, I thought it would be nice for him to date someone who isn't an airheaded bimbo."

BJ swallows a chuckle at the older woman's use of such a young person's terminology, a reaction Emily doesn't miss.

"I'm not so archaic that I don't know hip terms," she supplies jovially. "As I was saying, I originally wanted my son to be exposed to a better class of woman than he is usually in contact with. Someone with drive and determination, to show him the possibility of finding and falling in love with someone worthy of him, rather than spending the rest of his life alone.

"Meeting you was like fuel being tossed on our ulterior motive. We were already determined to have you rent from us, to help you provide the living arrangement you and your girls more than deserve. When you told me a few things about your past, I became even more determined to help you. When Rainier returned early, crashing our celebration, and I, *we all* witnessed the sparks and the fireworks that followed; the motive exploded right along with the two of you.

"When Rainier told us he'd done a background check on you, Jason and I were at once upset and intrigued that he felt compelled to know more about you. When he filled us in on the details he found out, we all became even more determined to do everything in our power to help you.

"It was shortly after that that Rainer got our lawyers involved. At that point, Jason took over most of the research and communications with them to find out all we could to sort out the sordid hell those vicious vultures put you through.

"I know on the one hand we probably should have told you, but in our defense, if we had, you more than likely wouldn't have accepted our help, and we'd have risked losing you to your pride; I couldn't fathom that. If you want to blame anyone, blame me. I begged them not to let on that we took it upon ourselves to become involved to get to the bottom of all the unethical, bad practices of all those involved and compile enough evidence against them to have leverage to achieve a positive outcome for you.

"Anything I would do to assist any of my children; I would do for you also. You see, it's not only Rainer who has fallen in love with you; every last one of us has. That includes both personal and work families."

BJ sits listening to and watching this elegant woman pour forth this information. The tears pooling in Emily's eyes on her last statement are genuine, causing the floodgates of BJ's own eyes to fail, letting loose the overflow and then some from her river of tears.

Conflicted, BJ isn't quite sure how to respond. The recently acquired information that these people hid their research and knowledge of her past from her threatens to overtake her with red-hot anger. Their deceit, however, is tempered by the fact that she has grown to love each of them. Combined with Emily's explanation for their reasons for not telling her because they evidently know her so well, they figured out how she would react, and since she is reacting just how they feared she would, can she blame them?

"I am sure there have been things in your life that you have done purely out of the goodness of your heart and had the recipient misunderstand your intent. Can you ever forgive us for our deceit, and come to understand we had only the best of intentions?"

BJ succumbs to the love she has for this woman and this family. Tears begin to trickle down the cheeks of both women. "I understand your reluctance to let me know you'd been checking up on me and everything you found out. Had I known, I would have disappeared. I thought about doing exactly that all day today. But now?" BJ shakes her head, snorting softly with a glimmer of a smile. "First Jake took me aside this morning and imparted his two cents worth without even knowing what I was upset about. Then tonight, Josie prodded me to let go the flood gates of the hell that was raging within me, then proceeded to utilize her years of bar room psychology training to impart her two cents worth. And now you've imparted your years of wisdom twenty cents worth.

"Since your family is basically giving me a second chance at a better life, I guess I can give you all a second chance. I suppose everyone deserves a second chance to set things straight, right?"

"Everyone?" Emily asks hopefully.

BJ looks into the glimmer of hope in Emily's eyes, knowing she is referring to her affording Rainier Julian Fenton III, a second chance.

Sighing heavily, "Yes, *Everyone*. But," she holds up a hand to the woman who is about to burst with joy, "there are conditions." She waits for Emily to school her enthusiasm before listing the conditions. "From this day forward, there will be no going behind my back. There will be total honesty from all parties at all times. You may help if you so choose, but *no one* may take control of my affairs."

Emily smiles at the strong young woman before her. "You've got it, dear." They hug. The kind of deep hug BJ had always hoped and dreamed of getting from her own mother. After long moments of embracing, Emily whispers, "I really should let you get some sleep. Thank you for allowing me to talk this out tonight. I wouldn't have been able to sleep a wink knowing you were upset." She rises to leave. "Good night, dear."

BJ lies in her bed alone in the dark. Her mind begins to mull over all that's been happening over the past few months. Exhaustion overcomes her as images of past and present mingle and jumble until finally the sweet bliss of thoughtless sleep overrides all else and she falls into a deep, dream-filled sleep.

Tuesday morning, RJ, seated at his desk, requests via com-link to the secretary's desk, "Cheryl, please tell BJ I need her to come to my office."

"Yes, Sir Mr. Fenton."

Cheryl witnessed some of yesterday's activity and has been filled in on the rest by Jake last evening. This formal request to speak to BJ seems...well, formal. Very much unlike his manner of late; since RJ and BJ have become much closer personally. She prefers the less formal atmosphere. However, this is her job, and he is her boss...

"BJ," Cheryl speaks as she approaches her hard at work friend.

"Hey, Cheryl. What's up?"

"Mr. Fenton," she speaks with the same formality she felt from the request, "would like to see you in his office."

"Now?"

"As he didn't specify otherwise, I would be inclined to make that assumption."

BJ looks at her friend, "Why so formal today?"

"It is the formality I sensed from the request." Cheryl feels a bit of an outsider in light of the information Jake imparted to her about BJ's past. She believes, had BJ viewed her as a true friend, she would have confided in her.

BJ, not knowing that RJ filled Jake in, who filled Cheryl in, eyes her friend quizzically and decides to let it slide for now. "Fine, I'll go as soon as I finish unloading this pallet jack."

Cheryl walks away, with BJ wondering if she did something to upset her friend. She'll deal with that later, but first she needs to face RJ.

Entering the boss's office, "You requested my presence?"

RJ looks up from his desk, taking in the stoic appearance of the woman before him. "Have a seat," he indicates the empty chair. She sits without relaxing her manner.

Earlier that morning, Emily filled her son in on the conversation she'd had with BJ late last night. He realizes he hasn't gone about things in the best manner.

"First, I want to express my deepest and most sincere apologies for going about so many things in such an inappropriate manner. Never did I mean to insult you, nor did I, at any time, intend to be controlling. I merely desired to take control, so to speak, to eliminate any and all of the stresses of your life that I can out of sympathy for all that you have endured."

BJ sits, staring at him.

"BJ, you are a very strong woman, both mentally and physically. However, during the time when all that chaos took place, you were justifiably hormonal due to pregnancy. That, coupled with the extreme losses of lives and material belongings, makes it completely understandable that at that time, and the months following, you were not capable of asserting the strength of personality we all know you possess. Considering those facts, my parents and I, as well as our lawyers, concur that you've been severely taken advantage of by the legal system.

"Although I was misguided in some of my strategies, I did have the forethought that you might feel obliged to repay me if we were to pay our lawyers for their services. Which is why the newest member of the law firm offered his services pro bono as a means of getting his feet wet, so to speak, with this as his first case. He has already found some interesting precedents and loopholes to work with that may pan out to be very helpful in resolving the legal issues at hand." RJ's tone is very businesslike. Like it was when she first met him. Gone is the playfulness of their more recent escapades. BJ doesn't like it and realizes it is her fault.

"Apology accepted. May I say something?"

"Of course."

"I need to express *my* deepest apologies for... for my overreaction," BJ lowers her eyes, "I... I don't want people pitying me. I don't want to become a burden on anyone, or have anyone feel responsible for us."

RJ rises and comes around the desk. He kneels next to BJ and lays a hand on hers, where it rests in her lap.

"Breezy?" Her head twitches slightly at the sound of her given name, but she doesn't look at him. In a soft, gentle voice, he asks, "Breezy, please answer this question. Are your girls a burden on you?"

Now her head snaps up to look at him. Anger flashes in her eyes. "NO! My girls are Not a burden to me!" she retorts vehemently.

Still in a gentle tone, "Do you feel responsible to care for and provide for them?"

"Of course!"

"Why?"

Some of BJ's vehemence quells. "They're my children. They *are* my responsibility."

"Would you ever want to see them suffer or go without?"

"I already have seen them suffer and go without," she states, hurt entering her voice.

"I'm sure that made you feel pretty horrible, didn't it?"

"Of course! Horrible, miserable, inadequate."

"You will do whatever it takes to care of them. Right?"

"Absolutely! As long as it's legal."

"Why?" he asks again, tenderly.

"Because I love them! I love them more than anyone can imagine."

"You're wrong," he says as she shoots another glare at him. "I don't have to imagine. Because I love my son just as much as you love your daughters, and...I love your daughters, and you that much too."

BJ's breath catches in her throat. She looks into RJ's eyes. Her own eyes stinging with unshed tears.

"I will do whatever it takes to care for the three of you. You will never be a burden to me. I'm choosing to be responsible for the three of you. I want to do for you because I love Chumani and Chenoa, but most importantly, I love you, Breezy Jo."

The unshed tears begin to flow. RJ wraps her in his arms, pulling her to her feet. Kissing the top of her head, her forehead, her tear-streaked cheeks, then with whispered softness, her lips.

BJ lies her head against his strong shoulder, tears still trickling down her cheeks. A soft giggle begins to emerge as the thought strikes her that this is the embodiment of the saying, *"A shoulder to cry on."*

RJ senses the change. Hearing the giggle as it begins to emanate from her, he asks, "What?"

"Thanks for being the proverbial shoulder to cry on."

RJ looks into her eyes. "Glad to be of service." He smiles with her.

"I need to get back to work. Yet again, I don't want my boss thinking I'm getting any preferential treatment," she reminds him of his long-ago statement, slips from his embrace, then heads to the door to leave the office.

"BJ?" She turns to look at him. "May I have your permission to continue to help sort out all these legal issues? Please?"

BJ stands looking into the eyes of the man who proclaimed his love for her and her girls, and finds his desire to do everything he can to 'make it all better' for them. Swallowing hard the lump of pride threatening to choke her, she replies, "As long as a meeting is set up to update me and I am kept informed on everything from here on, yes, you have my permission to continue *helping*," she emphasizes. "Thanks for asking," she smiles, and returns to work.

RJ stands there for long moments, staring blankly at the empty space she's just vacated, realizing the empty sensation he is experiencing in this moment is nothing compared to the bleak void he'd experience if she were seriously to be gone from his life.

He is on the phone with the lawyer within minutes, scheduling a meeting for Wednesday, 9 AM the following week to bring BJ up to speed on the findings.

"Josh, the young lawyer taking the lead on BJ's case, found several disturbing issues," Jason informs RJ and Emily as they sit down for dinner together that evening.

"Such as?" RJ inquires.

"There is a very tangled web he's unraveling. It seems that a wealthy individual wanted BJ's parents' house for a restoration for profit project, and they wouldn't sell, even though they were behind in taxes and payments. When her parents unexpectedly died, he and the bank seized the opportunity to hornswoggle BJ out of everything they could, which they did. Josh is preparing a letter of discovery to submit to them, and offering them a means to settle up without going through a lengthy, messy public trial."

"Here's hoping they agree to the settlement so she can not only put that whole mess behind her, but give her little family some financial breathing room," Emily sighs hopefully.

"I spoke with BJ earlier today and scheduled a meeting to catch her up to speed on the investigation and findings. I think that now, since it's out in the open and she is involved, we should be able to make quicker progress and settle this sooner.

28

"Look, Mommy!" Chumani holds out a flier from school. BJ takes it and looks at it. It is information about a Thanksgiving meal planned for their class this Wednesday, the day before the holiday. It reads:

> **Dear Parents,**
>
> **We, the combined Kindergarten classes of Cedarwood Academy, invite you to attend our annual**
>
> **Thanksgiving Feast on Wednesday at 11:30 a.m.**
>
> **Early dismissal for Thanksgiving break is at 1 pm. We look forward to seeing you.**
>
> **Sincerely, Cedarwood Kindergarten Teachers and Students.**

BJ places the flier on the front of the refrigerator.

"You'll come, won't you?" Chumani asks eagerly, with a touch of hope and worry in her voice.

"I'll do my best, baby girl. My lunch hour starts at 11:30, so I'll be a bit late, and I'll have to leave early, but I will be there for at least part of the time," she explains. "Is that OK with you?"

"Of course, Mommy. As long as you can be there for some of it, so you can meet my friends."

"I will be."

Chumani hugs her mommy tightly, then, seeing Riyon and RJ out by the pool, runs out calling, "Riyon, Mommy said she'll come for at least part of the feast."

"Yay," Riyon exclaims joyfully.

The children's conversation catches RJ's attention and redirects his path to go to BJ's door. "BJ?"

BJ comes to the door, "Yes."

"Do you have a minute to talk?"

"Sure, if you don't mind coming in and talking while I fix dinner," she replies as she heads back to the kitchen.

"I want to let you know that I scheduled a meeting with the lawyer at 8AM next Wednesday morning."

BJ whirls around, "Next Wednesday?"

Seeing the panic in her face, RJ holds up a hand to stave off her concern. "I figured it was the best time to schedule it so that we can be finished up there, and be over to the school in time for the Thanksgiving Feast by 11:30. Since I already intended to release everyone early from work, we'll be able to stay for the whole feast, and bring the kids home with us."

Her expression relaxes, and he continues.

"I also figured since you'd probably not be wearing work clothes to the lawyers, you'd feel more comfortable attending the feast after leaving the meeting than after working all morning."

BJ realizes he thought it out thoroughly. "Thank you. That is kind of you to plan it so well."

"You're very welcome," smiling, he winks, "I try."

RJ stands waiting by the truck for BJ. He looks up as she comes around the corner, inhaling sharply at the sight before him. She is dressed in a flouncy chiffon skirt revealing just the right amount of her long, slender legs. The pastel earth tones match her simple-styled blouse of similar material. She's wearing a coffee-with-cream colored shawl draped loosely around her shoulders. Her hair is in a high ponytail tied with a sheer cream scarf with tendrils of hair that float in wisps around her face and down her neck. She wears mid-heeled, ankle-high, strappy brown sandals.

With the many facets of the woman RJ has witnessed, this is one more to add to the list. His smile spreads slowly to encompass his face in complete appreciation.

BJ considers the many sides of her boss she experienced over the months she's known him, but the lanky man before her, clad in khaki trousers, topped by a cream button-down with caramel tie, and chocolate-brown full-zip cardigan, is a new vision of this man. He is always handsome, but today...? BJ thinks him wicked gorgeous. She smiles coyly, eyes demurely lowered. Both note the other's appraisal.

"Good morning."

"That it is," he replies as he opens the passenger door and assists her in. The short drive is made in silence, each with their own thoughts.

Upon arrival at the Law Office of Slatkin, Cohan and Jacobs, introductions are made, and they quickly get down to business.

RJ decides he needs to let tell BJ about his screenshots of the letters on her computer, knowing this may not go over very well, but hoping she is beginning to understand his sincere affection and desire to help her, has too often hindered his ability to maintain proper boundaries and caused him to act inappropriately.

"So before we get started I remembered something else I did that I need to tell you and ask for forgiveness for," RJ tells BJ.

"Sad that that doesn't surprise me," BJ chuckles. "Spit it out, Mr. Deceitful."

"Do you remember the day you left your computer open on the table and Riyon and I came over?"

BJ chuckles scoffingly, shaking her head. "Go on."

"Well, I screen shotted the message you received and your response." RJ looks down ashamedly.

"Well, I never sent the response because I didn't want them having a way to track and locate me."

"I thought that might be the case. However, I gave them to Josh, and he had his secretary retype your response verbatim and sent it for you from here so they couldn't."

"OK then, I guess I should thank you, Josh."

"We felt it was something they needed to hear from you and to be sure they knew you were not someone to be pushed around. Now that is settled, let's discuss the everything else."

An hour and a half later,

"...So, you see, Ms. McCallister, the private investor and the bank were out of line to pressure you the way they did.

"Unfortunately, you would have been responsible for paying back taxes whether you chose to keep the house or sell it, but a payment arrangement could have been set up for that. However, since the taxes have already been paid by the investor in order to proceed with the renovation, that is now somewhat of a moot point.

"There are several options you have in moving forward to settle this situation. For instance, if you would like, we can sue for the return of the house to you. You might have to repay the taxes to the investor who bought it. You'd need to take into consideration that it is now renovated, and you'd probably have to pay the investor for at least some of the renovations..."

"No." BJ puts up a hand to halt the possible methods to proceed. "I don't want the house back. I have no interest in it. I would have sold it in a timely manner had they given me time to get my head straight after everything and allowed me to birth my daughter at full term. However, they were too greedy and impatient. All I want is the simplest, least expensive method to get them off my back, and out of my life."

"This will in no way cost you another dime," Josh assures her. "In fact, if we proceed, you should receive a substantial amount of compensation for all they put you through."

"What is your best recommendation?" BJ inquires.

Josh proceeds to fill her in on his plan of action.

Satisfied, RJ and BJ depart for Cedarwood Academy.

Riyon and Chumani spot their tall, imposing parents as they enter the multipurpose room.

"Mommy!" Chumani calls out, running to her, arms open wide.

"Daddy," Riyon calls, filled with excitement, rushing to his father.

The mother, from the first day of school who, had felt the need to comment to them both, looked on perplexed. Being the busy body that she is and feeling the need to clarify things, introduces herself. "Welcome. I'm Mrs. Carmichael. You are?"

She approaches RJ first, hand extended.

"RJ," he replies simply, allowing a quick handshake.

"Your Riyon's parents, correct?" she inquires, looking from the adults to the children, "And Chumani's? But I didn't realize they were twins," she eyes them all, puzzled.

RJ, already annoyed with the nosy woman, inhales deeply, about to spout off when BJ extends her hand to Mrs. Carmichael.

"Hi, I'm BJ. RJ is Riyon's father, and I am Chumani's mother. You've evidently made some incorrect assumptions, which is the cause of your current confusion."

"Oh, but..."

"May I have your attention, please?" Ms. Whitaker calls out above the noise. Everyone quiets, effectively terminating the conversation with Mrs. 'busybody' Carmichael.

Ms. Whitaker explains the agenda for the day. Then, once the festivities are underway, two mothers approach BJ.

"Hi, I'm Susan."

"And I'm Mary Jane," they both extend welcoming hands, which BJ and RJ accept, responding in turn.

"I'm RJ, Riyon's father."

"I'm BJ. I'm Chumani's mother. Deciding to put rumors and curiosities to rest from the get-go, she continues, "I work for Mr. Fenton. Our children spend a lot of time together and are very fond of each other. Because of my work schedule, they also carpool together."

"Please excuse Mrs. Carmichael. She's basically harmless. Everyone knows she is the nosiest busybody. I think she's just bored and wants to find *anything* to gossip about," Susan explains.

"Yes, we noticed," RJ replies as they all chuckle.

"It's great how well they get along. We're room mothers, and volunteer in the classroom a couple days a week. They innocently fill us in occasionally, on a few family details."

Features awash with sudden pallor, BJ draws a fortifying breath. The sight and sound of which has RJ laying a comforting hand on the small of her back without thought.

The pallor and worrisome expression do not escape Susan, who continues quickly, "Nothing bad. Don't worry. Chumani tells everyone that you are a strong, hard-working mother. That she is very proud of you and that you rent an adorable house from your boss and his parents, whom she loves like family," she informs them, smiling.

BJ's eyes tear up at hearing that Chumani thinks her mother is strong and is proud of her.

Mary Jane supplies, "The two of you have two wonderful, insightful children who are a pleasure to know and work with. They are such assets to the other children. They actually bring about positive changes in a few kids who strive to behave better, like Riyon and Chumani."

Pride envelopes them both. "Thank you for your kind words," RJ expresses as the two subjects of conversation who rushed off moments ago now come rushing back to them.

"Here, Mommy."

"Here, Daddy."

They hand their respective parents the headdresses they created for them. Each is wearing their own. Chumani and BJ's are white construction paper Lady Pilgrim hats. Riyon and RJ have construction paper feathered headbands. Riyon's has only 3 feathers, but his father's has 12 colorful construction paper feathers. He explains proudly to the others. "I only have 3 because I'm still a young brave. Daddy is the Boss, which is the same as being the Chief, so he gets the full Chief headdress." They nod understanding, and RJ puts his on.

Most of the other fathers are holding their headbands rather than wearing them, possibly thinking them silly. Many, upon seeing RJ donning his, give in and put theirs on also.

Chumani explains, "We get to be the Pilgrim ladies. They started off being wishy-washy, weak English women that didn't do much, but later they became strong, independent women. Just like you, Mommy," she finishes proudly.

Tears spill from the brims of those standing around, as well as a couple of unintentional eavesdroppers.

BJ kneels and hugs the wonder-filled young lady before her, whom she is more than proud to have as her daughter.

The delightful feast the room-mothers made gets underway.

Later, as everyone is beginning to leave, Susan and Mary Jane approach BJ once again. "It was a pleasure to meet you, BJ. We know from Chumani that you work *'whole lots'* as she puts it, but we want to extend the offer that if you have some free time, maybe we can schedule a girls' day or at least go for coffee to get to know each other."

BJ realizes these two seem to be genuinely interested in becoming friends. "That would be nice. Thank you for the offer." The three exchange numbers.

Upon arriving home, the little Native and Pilgrim rush to fill Mémère, Misho, and Millie in on the day's event.

BJ takes Chenoa from Millie, nuzzling her youngest, eliciting giggles from the fast-growing little one. Looking around from the viewpoint of neck-nuzzling, BJ surveys the scene before her. Trying to decide if it is healthy to allow her girls to become so attached to, and feel as if they are a part of this family, or if this is a very bad idea, as she can only imagine how heart-wrenching it will be for them when the day comes that they have to leave. That thought begs an answer to the questions that next arise. Will they ever have to leave? When? Why? Lost in her own musing, she is caught off guard by Emily's approach.

"Earth to BJ," Emily whispers.

"Oh, I'm sorry, Emily. I didn't..."

"I know, dear. You were off in wondering land."

BJ looks at her quizzically.

"You were in the land of wondering 'what if' and 'when.' Your eyes are so expressive when you're not being guarded. The simple answer to all your questions is to live one day at a time. Just live in the moment, enjoy, and let the girls live and enjoy all they can. You are all loved and welcome in our lives, in your home forever." At BJ's narrow-eyed expression, Emily continues, "No, I can't read minds. However, I can look into your soul through those crystal-clear blue windows of yours, so I am able to read your thoughts pretty well." She pauses, "I see many things there that you yourself don't seem to." She finishes hugging BJ and Chenoa together, then swiftly changes the subject. About tomorrow..."

BJ returns her thoughts to the moment.

"I have been remiss with all that has been going on in the past weeks. I want you to know that we all would love to have you and the girls join us for our huge family Thanksgiving Day feast and celebration. However, we will all do our best to understand if you would prefer to have your own private celebration in your very own home."

Chumani, having come near, overhears that part of the conversation. BJ ponders, looking at her girls. "Well," she begins, "I figured it would be the three of us in our home so as not to intrude on your family." She pauses, seeing the expression that appears on Emily's face as well as the slight look of disappointment on her eldest daughter's face. She continues, "What do you think, Chumani?"

The girl's eyes light up. "I think we should spend the morning together at our house having Thanksgiving breakfast, then we can fix food to share with everybody else later for Thanksgiving Dinner," she announces happily.

"Sounds to me that you've already given this some thought," BJ states, and Emily concurs.

"Yup. Me and Riyon planned it all out. We decided. Breakfast is at our house, then spend the day cooking, and setting up for the big dinner."

Emily looks to BJ for her decision.

"Well, I guess the party planners have it all worked out," BJ announces. Riyon and the other adults tuned in to the conversation along the way, and all concur that it sounds like a good plan.

"Everyone will be so thrilled," she assures, then immediately turns to her husband and son. "That's settled. Now, to get busy with the setup and preparations. Please start by bringing the tables and chairs out from the garage and wash them. We'll need... let me think, I need to do a head count... oh, just bring them all out, and if we need more, we'll have the girls bring some."

Soon, everyone is changed into working clothes and pitching in on the preparations.

The men begin carrying out stacks of tables and piles of chairs. It strikes BJ; *everyone* is coming for dinner?

How many in total, she wonders, and begins her own count.

Seeing her counting on her fingers to keep track, RJ steps to her side, stating "Twenty-four," as he counts with her, "Mel, Zach, Austin, Aurora, Dehl, Nate, Jed, Nellie, Tanner, Ophie, Gil, Millie, Brady, Jake, Cheryl, Butch, his wife Glenda, Mère, Misho. Myself, Riyon, Chumani, Chenoa and you. That makes an even two dozen."

BJ's eyes continue to enlarge as the number grows. She now stands, jaw dropped. "Wow," she whispers in near disbelief. "That's a lot of people."

RJ looks at her. He waits for her to look up, "One Big Happy Family," he states. Looking directly into her cool blue eyes, he smiles, giving her a shoulder hug as he gets back to the tasks at hand.

BJ looks around at all the buzz. In that moment, a decision is made. She intends to allow herself and her girls to blend in with the family and enjoy this holiday as 'one of them', to experience this event like every other event in the past year. To accept this as the moment that it is, remembering that moments, whether good or bad, are not the end-all be-all of one's life. That bad ones need to be experienced as the life lessons they are, and good ones experienced as life rewards.

29

Thanksgiving morning awakens, filled with beautiful sunny skies. BJ looks all around her cozy little home. She looks into the faces of her precious daughters, realizing how very many things she is thankful for this and every day, but mostly for her two beautiful little girls.

"Good morning, Chumani. Good morning, Chenoa. Happy Day of Giving Thanks," she greets as she enters their room.

"Morning, Mommy, Happy Day of Giving Thanks to you."

"Tank oo Mama," comes a little voice from the crib.

"Chenoa!" BJ exclaims, "You said a sentence." She is at once over-filled with joy and self-reproach for not having been around as much with her youngest to help her learn to speak, and so many other things, as she had been for Chumani. BJ shakes away the negativity threatening to overcome her and remembers the vow she made to herself last night. "Let's get this party started," she announces, and they do.

Emily and Jason have been up cooking until very late. Family and friends begin arriving at 11:30. It appears they've also been busy cooking as everyone brings at least two items to share, which they place in the center of the tables. BJ contributes two big pans of cauliflower, broccoli cheese casserole, and a kettle of freshly made two-ingredient cinnamon applesauce.

Just before three o'clock, Emily stands surveying the tables, which have been set up and strapped together in four sets side by side then, end to end with 11 seats on either side and one at each end. She begins making check marks on the list she holds to be sure everything is set and ready. Everyone stands around taking pictures of the food-laden tables before Jason announces. "Let us begin, shall we?"

Everyone heads to the table to locate their name card, which Emily made, and had the children assist in placing, per her instructions.

Jason is placed at the head of the table on one end with RJ at the other end. Emily is to Jason's right, and BJ is to RJ's right with Chenoa between them in a high chair. Riyon sits to his father's left, and Chumani to her mother's right. All the other families and couples are clustered together.

Once all are seated, Jason stands. "Can everyone hear me?" he asks, feigning that the table is so long that he might not be heard at the other end.

RJ acknowledges affirmatively.

"First, let me say how happy we are that each of you is a part of our lives, and how joy-filled we are that you have all blessed us by being here with us on this Day of Giving Thanks. We have a family tradition that, while it may take a while with this many people present, we feel is still worth the time. That tradition is that we go around the table, and everyone must state at least one thing that they are thankful for this day. Let's begin so we can be finished before the food spoils," Jason jokes. "Who'd like to go first?"

BJ shyly stands. "If it's all right with everyone, I would like to go first because this might be a bit long." Everyone chuckles with her, and Jason sits, giving BJ the floor.

"Where to start?" she begins, "I figure by now most of you have in one way or another been filled in on some of my past." She looks around, seeing the nods. "One year ago, on this holiday, the only things I had to be thankful for were my beautiful daughter Chumani," she strokes her daughter's hair; "the impending birth of a second child," she repeats the action with Chenoa; "And the blessing that by this time on that day my husband drank himself to sleep which meant Chumani and I had once again survived made it through his morning drunken rage." She and everyone else choke back tears; she continues,

"In those moments of peace, she and I shared that afternoon, no one could ever have guessed at the turn our lives would take, mere hours, as well as one year later.

"I stand here before you, humbled by how welcoming, supportive, and loving you have all been toward the three of us. You were all total strangers one moment, and surrogate family to us the next. So..." she heaves a heart-cleansing sigh, "Today we are overfilled with abundant gratitude, and thanks to each one of you. You have filled our hearts and shown us how true family is intended to be. A lesson we shall carry with us all the days of our lives; we shall never forget these blessings, this sense of belonging you all have gifted us. Thank you."

Everyone is sniffling and drying their eyes.

Emily stands, "Normally we continue to the left of the person who starts, but I'm breaking the rules, and since I made them, I can," she states, smiling, bringing back a bit of levity. "I always have so many people and things to be thankful for: my adoring Husband, my fabulous son, my four amazing daughters, and their mates, my fantastic grandchildren, our collective health, and all our material possessions. However, this year I have something spectacular to be thankful for. That is, Breezy Jo McCallister! The strongest, most determined woman I have ever known. You have brought a new clarity of vision to me, and I dare say to all of us, through our knowing you. Learning of the life adversities that you have overcome, you have blessed each of us with a new understanding and gratitude for what we have. For all your struggles, my heart breaks. For all your strength, I applaud you. For all your blessings to us, I thank you."

Jason rises and raises his glass of sparkling cider, which they all have, "Hear, hear."

"Santé," Emily concurs in French. They all raise their glasses in salute.

The statements of gratitude continue in back-and-forth, across-the-table fashion until they reach the far end of the table, and Chumani's turn.

"I am thankful for my mommy, my baby sister and all of you. 'Specially for Riyon, Mémère, and Misho, but *most* 'specially for Mr. Fenton 'cause he showed me how a real Daddy is supposed to be."

Every adult at the table promptly covers their mouth to hold back the tears and sobs brought on by this honest child. Chumani looks to her mother, "I hope that's OK. I didn't mean that I love him more than you, Mommy. Please don't cry." Chumani climbs into her mother's lap to hug her.

"Oh, baby girl, that's OK. I know you love me. It's very nice of you to be thankful for Mr. Fenton."

Lastly, it's RJ's turn. He is still choking back the tearful lump in his throat as he stands, then kneels beside BJ and her daughters.

"I am grateful for every person at this gathering, and for everything I have in my life, but *'specially*," he uses Chumani's childlike term, "for this trio of women who have brought so much joy to my life, and the lives of all of us here today. These three ladies have affected so many changes in us, and taught us all so much about strength and gratitude. Thank you for touching our lives, my heart... I love you all."

More tears spill from every eye.

Jason stands once again. "OK, now let's eat before the flood washes away our meal. Let the feast begin!"

Everyone joins in the levity and begin to dig in.

Early Friday morning, RJ's cell rings. The caller ID showing Drew Conrad, he answers, "Hey Drew, Good morning. To what do I owe this pleasure?"

"Hello, RJ. I wanted to call to say Happy Belated Thanksgiving."

"Happy Thanksgiving to you, too."

"That and the fact that it's been a while since we've talked, I'm wondering how your lady is doing with tomorrow looming?"

"Wow. Thank you for asking and remembering. She is doing quite well." RJ fills his friend in on all that has transpired in the past couple months.

"So, it sounds like maybe you have realized how much she means to you? Maybe have admitted you love her?"

"Yeah, well, I did tell her when I finally admitted it to myself. Then yesterday, at Thanksgiving dinner, during gratitude rounds, I admitted in front of everyone that I love the three of them. Which, I guess, everyone else had already figured out," he chuckles.

"And?"

"I told her I didn't want to pressure her into saying something she doesn't feel or isn't ready to admit yet. She knows how I feel, and that's never going to change, whether she ever says she loves me or not. I know in my heart she does. I also believe he's scared. I mean, seriously, tomorrow is only one year since her whole world came crashing down around her. Doesn't matter whether that world was good or bad; it still was devastating. I don't expect her to be over that, or all the rest that took place, in only a year. She needs time to heal. I have time and patience. We have a lifetime ahead of us.

"RJ, my friend, you are a great man. I'm happy for you. Just don't forget to keep me in the loop, and if/when there's a wedding, I Dang well better get an invite. Better yet, I had better get an invite to meet her long before that!"

"What are you doing for New Year's Eve?" RJ asks.

"What do you have in mind?"

"I'm thinking with what we know about her past, I doubt she's ever had a great New Year's Eve. Thought we should have a big party here at my parents' and invite everyone."

"Heck Yeah! Count us in."

The two begin making plans for Drew and his wife to visit before ending their conversation.

Sunday morning's sunshine peaks through the window. BJ lies still, eyes closed, breathing steadily, trying to push the nightmarish memories of this day from her mind. She decided not to bring it up to Chumani. There is no reason for her to have to relive any of that. BJ wants to figure out a way to make this day memorable for some wonderful reason instead. But how?

'Tap, tap, tap,' sounds a light knocking on the front door. She gathers herself, grabbing and putting on a robe then goes to answers it.

"Good morning. I hope I didn't wake you," Emily whispers.

"No, I was awake trying to think of something to do today. Please come in," she steps back, allowing Emily to enter. "I'm about to have a cup of coffee, would you like some?"

"That would be nice, thank you. About why I'm here," she plunges ahead while BJ tends to the coffee-making task. "First, I wanted to check how you are doing today."

When BJ looks at her, she smiles, a knowing evident in her expression.

"I'm...doing OK."

"Good. The second reason I'm here is to ask if you have any particular plans for this day. If you have a certain manner in which you would like to commemorate or...?"

"I've decided not to even mention it to Chumani. It's not necessary to open old wounds."

"Wonderful!" Emily interrupts. "I was hoping you'd say that. I wholeheartedly agree. What I'm wondering is, there is this great Winter Carnival and Festival in a town just up the road a ways. I thought it might be a wonderful way to spend the day creating some happy memories for this day."

"That's what I was hoping to do. Though I didn't know of anything *to* do."

"Fabulous. Now, don't think that if you need some time to mourn, that you can't, I'm hoping that this might make things easier."

"When do we need to leave?"

Chumani walks around the corner right then. "Leave? No!" she almost squeals, shock evident on her young face.

"No, no, sweetie," BJ hurries to scoop up her daughter. "Not leave as in move out, baby girl. We are discussing going somewhere today, and I wanted to know what time we need to leave to be there on time," BJ comforts.

Chumani instantly begins crying at the thought of leaving, but brightens now at hearing they are going somewhere. She sighs, "OK, that's good. I don't ever want to *leave leave* here, only leave here, and come back. Where are we going?"

Emily supplies, "To a Winter Carnival and Festival in a nearby town. They have rides, games, food, craft items, and other stuff to buy for Christmas gifts, and they bring in a huge pile of snow and make a hill to sled on."

"That sounds like fun!" Chumani enthuses. "Can I go get Chenoa up so we can get ready to go?" Not waiting for an answer, she turns, asking, "Mémère, is Riyon going too?, and Mr. Fenton?, and Misho?, and you?"

"Yes, dear. We're all going. Riyon's Aunts, Uncles, and cousins will all be coming to meet up with us," Emily informs, looking to BJ to gauge her reaction.

BJ smiles broadly, "Wow, Chumani, that sounds awfully fun, don't you think?"

"Yippee!" she exclaims, running to get her baby sister.

"I hope that's alright."

"Sounds like a fun, joy-filled day. Perfect," she hugs Emily, who heads for the door to allow them to prepare for the day. "Is an hour long enough for you to be ready?" she asks as she exits. "Or do you need longer?"

"See you in an hour," BJ responds, smiling.

Entering the big house, she finds two men and a boy anxiously waiting. "Did she say they would go?" Riyon pipes up.

"Well?" Jason and RJ question in unison.

Emily's face lights up: "Yes."

"Yahoo!" Riyon exclaims.

"Great," Jason states, relieved.

RJ heaves a heavy sigh of relief. "How does she seem?"

"Actually, very well. She said she'd been trying to think of some way to create good memories for today. She is not going to bring up the anniversary to Chumani." She turns to Riyon. "I know we explained to you that this is the anniversary of Chumani's Grandparents and Daddy dying, but we need you to please *not* bring it up to any of them today. OK?"

"Yes, Mémère. I don't want to talk about that because that will make them sad, and I don't ever want them sad ever again. We need to always make them happy. Right, Daddy?"

"You got it, my little man," RJ tousles his son's hair.

"Men have always to remember, never leave ladies waiting, and never make them cry," Riyon announces proudly.

RJ bends to hug his wonderful son tightly. "Smart man you are, son. I love you."

Emily, Jason, and RJ all wipe tears of pride from their eyes. They are so blessed to have such a wonderful son and amazing grandson. Actually, all of their children and grandchildren are such blessings. *'Including BJ, Chumani and Chenoa.'* Emily's inner voice states as a matter of fact.

The weather is beautiful on this last day of November. All of the Fenton clan arrives at the festival. The day overflows with fun activities, food, joy, and Love.

RJ spots BJ standing off to the side of the group, who are all clamoring about which ride to go on next. He approaches. "Hello there."

She looks up, a soft expression on her features.

"How are you holding up with all this chaos?"

"I'm doing OK. Thanks for asking."

"How about on the 'unspeakable' subject?"

Riyon appears at his daddy's side as he is asking.

"Much better than I would have ever imagined possible," she pauses, looking at these two handsome men. "Thanks to your family," she concludes.

"We're *your* family too, now," Riyon interjects. "I think we adopted the three of you. Kind of like finding a family of dogs or cats that need to be loved, and rescuing them, but you guys are WAAAAYYY better than pets. Right, Daddy?"

Tears fill and spill from both adults as they kneel to hug this tender young man, bumping into each other as they do.

The trio laughs.

"Riyon?" She waits for him to look at her. "I love you," She informs him truthfully.

"I love you too, Ms. BJ. I wish you could be my mommy, and Daddy could be Chumani, and Chenoa's daddy. We pretend it's that way sometimes, but it would be so cool if it was real." Riyon throws his arms around BJ as the tears now stream down RJ's cheeks.

BJ, seeing this, tries to bring levity back, saying, "OK, enough of this mushy stuff for one day." She tweaks his nose playfully. "We're here to have Fun! Let's get back to it."

They rise, returning to the group. RJ takes BJ's hand as they walk.

Late that night, after all three exhausted kids are snugly tucked in their beds, BJ is sitting out by the pool, enjoying the cool last moments of this November evening. She is reminiscing and comparing how polar opposite this night is from one year ago. Hearing, or rather sensing, RJ's cautious approach as he wordlessly sits in the chaise lounge next to her, her eyes open to look at him.

"May I?" he whispers.

She nods, her eyes close.

After a few moments, his hand covers hers where it rests on the arm of the chair. BJ's breathing calms, allowing tears to fall freely and silently. They sit, not moving for about an hour, until the chill air is more than her sweater can ward off, and she shivers. RJ stands, taking her hand, helping her to her feet, then walks her to her door.

"I know this is far more than I have the right to ask," she begins, then hesitates.

"Ask me, Breezy," he encourages.

She swallows hard, "Would you mind...lying with me, and holding me tonight?"

"With pleasure and honor."

30

Josh submits the disclosure letter of findings and the proposed out-of-court settlement to the lawyers for the other parties involved, first thing Monday morning.

A decision is quickly reached by the other parties and their legal counsel to accept the settlement agreement in order to avoid court costs and the public embarrassment of a court case, which would outline the illegal wrongdoings of the bank and investors.

A mere two days later, Cheryl's voice comes across the intercom. "Mr. Fenton?"

"Yes, Cheryl."

"There is a messenger here with a delivery for BJ."

RJ doesn't even respond. He strides to the outer office.

"I'll sign for that."

"I'm sorry, Sir. I am only allowed to deliver to the recipient, a Ms. McCallister."

RJ steps through the door to the dock. Spotting Jake, Brady, and Butch nearby, calls out, "One of you find BJ, and send her in here immediately. Please."

"Sure thing, Boss."

"You got it."

"Will do," the trio responds. Everyone has noticed the positive changes between BJ and the boss recently, and it seems everyone approves. However, the look on his face right then is strained.

RJ returns to the office to wait with the messenger.

Butch locates BJ, telling her, "Boss Man sent us to find you, and send you to the office. Is something wrong?"

"Not that I know of. Why?" BJ inquires.

"He didn't look to be in as pleasant a mood as he's been lately, since…" at BJ's raised brow questioning look to the 'since' reference, Butch goes on, "Since you done what I said you'd do, and taught him a thing or three." He winks. "That, and since the two of you seem to be getting along better, is all I meant."

BJ smiles at the good-natured teasing tone of this burly man. "OK," she heads in the direction of the office.

Butch falls into stride alongside her. Brady and Jake see their approach and meander along with them. The action seems a bit like being escorted to the principal's office. She steps through the door, and the trio stops to wait, or stand guard, outside.

"You wanted to see me?" she inquires, taking in the sight of Cheryl and an unknown person in the room.

"Yes. This messenger has a delivery for you."

The messenger steps forward, "May I see your identification, please?" After he confirms she is the intended recipient, he asks her to sign for the envelope, then takes his leave.

RJ asks, "From their lawyers?"

She looks at the return address. "Yes," her voice, pallid as apprehensive pallor overtakes her features.

Both Cheryl and RJ take a step nearer to her as she inhales a steadying breath and begins to open it, then pauses.

"We're here for you, BJ. No matter what. If they decide to fight, we'll fight with you," Cheryl states, sounding bolder and more confident than RJ has ever heard her.

The three men outside the door are standing like three little boys, ears to the door, trying to hear what's being said.

BJ smiles at RJ and Cheryl, then continues to open the envelope, withdraw, and unfold the document.

BJ's eyes bug out, she gasps, "OH! Oh, my Gosh," she calls out loudly.

The trio of men listening in from outside the door rush in. RJ and Cheryl grab BJ's arms as she begins to waver.

"What is it?" Jake asks, coming closer. Butch grabs a chair and puts it behind BJ as she is guided to sit in it. Brady grabs a bottle of water from the mini fridge nearby and hands it to her.

BJ accepts the water, as she holds the paperwork in her shaking hand up to RJ, who takes it, and begins to smile from ear to ear, then reads out loud,

Dear Ms. McCallister,

We are pleased to inform you that our clients have unanimously decided to accept the settlement agreement in the full amount requested by your counsel.

On behalf of our clients, we would like to extend their deepest apologies for any and all adversity that you and your family have had to endure due to this unfortunate situation.

Furthermore, in retrospect, our clients have asked us to also extend our heartfelt condolences for the horrible losses you incurred, as their actions only compounded your pain and suffering.

The investor, having now been presented with the particulars of the tragedies, has seen fit to include a separate, additional sum to be used to set up interest-earning accounts for each of your daughters for their future higher education. i.e., college or trade school.

At your earliest convenience, please have your counsel provide us with the bank account information where you would like the settlement funds deposited.

On behalf of all of us here at McCormick & McIntyre and Conner & Cheetum, please accept our most sincere condolences and apologies for all you have been through.

May your futures be bright and filled with goodness,

Sincerely, Roger McCormick & Timothy McIntyre
Sincerely, Yul Conner & Larry Cheetum

RJ looks at the two checks for the girls, saying, "Holy Crap!" and hands them back to BJ.

Looking at the two identical amounts, she gasps, yet again. She ponders for a moment what all this means.

"I can't believe this is real. Is this actually over? Are they truly paying the full settlement amount Josh requested?"

Cheryl and the guys look at one another, then at RJ, who kneels beside BJ, responding, "Yes. That's what it says. It's over. No court battle, no more worries, and a whole lot of money for your financial losses, as well as compensation on behalf of both you and Chumani for Negligent Infliction of Emotional Distress. Plus, these two checks to set up educational accounts for both girls."

BJ looks up at him, then around at her friends. Her smile starts small, then spreads brightly. "It's over!"

Butch bursts out, "Whoo-hoo!" The others join his cheering. BJ turns to RJ, "Does everyone know?"

RJ looks around. "I thought only Jake and Cheryl knew."

Brady supplies, "Well, Emily told Millie, who of course told me. Don't know how Butch knows."

Hearing his name, Butch informs. "I got no clue what's goin' on other than what y'all just said that whatever *was* goin' on, is finally over, and our little Miss here is being compensated for whatever it was, and it brought a smile to her face, and that's worth hootin' 'bout."

Everyone laughs along with his exuberance.

"This calls for a celebration," Jake proclaims, "First round's on me after work," he says, giving BJ a big brotherly hug. "Congratulations."

Once they're out of the office, as the trio heads back to the dock, Jake assures Butch, "I'll fill you in."

In light of the good news she received on Wednesday, BJ decides to celebrate by splurging a little on Christmas, so at lunch on Friday, BJ asks, "Hey, Cheryl, would you like to go do some Christmas shopping with me tomorrow?"

"Absolutely!"

"I'll arrange for the girls to be cared for so we can have some adult girl time. Buying Christmas presents isn't something I was able to do much of before."

"We're going to have a blast," Cheryl bubbles enthusiastically.

They spend Saturday buying gifts for everyone. BJ buys a few extra for her girls, assuring herself that it won't hurt to spoil them a little this year. She even joyfully buys an artificial tree and decorations for their new home.

Cheryl notices BJ picking out streamers and balloons.

"What are those for?"

"For Chenoa's first birthday. I'm also going to get her a few separate birthday gifts. I refuse to let her birthday be swallowed up and rolled into Christmas just because they're only four days apart."

"I agree. That would suck, especially as she gets older."

Emily knocks on BJ's door one evening, a few days later, after she arrives home from work. "Hello, dear."

"Good evening, Emily. To what do I owe this pleasure?" BJ asks half teasingly.

"I would like to get something for Chenoa for her birthday and wanted to know if there is something specific that she needs."

"Not that you need to get her anything, but if you do, anything will be fine," BJ assures.

"I was also wondering if you have made any plans for a party or other activity for her?"

"No, I was just planning to bake her cupcakes and let her make a mess of herself with some, like I did with Chumani. It's Winter Solstice that day also, since I usually do some Solstice activities, I figured that would be enough."

"Well, my girls were asking if you didn't have plans already, if they could help plan a little get-together for all the children. Maybe play a few games. Nothing overwhelming. They figured the kids would all have fun. As you said, with it being Solstice, we could do a combo celebration. Do a nature walk or something of the sort, too."

"That would be great. I just didn't want to bother anyone, being so close to Christmas. I assumed everyone is so busy."

"I'll tell the girls to call you so you can make plans. I'm so glad I asked. It'll be fun for everyone. Good night."

"Good night, Emily."

Winter Solstice, the shortest day and longest night of the year, cum Chenoa's first birthday, arrives crisply cool with large white fluffy clouds half filling the azure sky.

The Fenton sisters and their children show up mid-morning to celebrate, and Chumani can barely contain her happiness at having a party for her baby sister.

The celebration gets underway with all the older children taking turns assisting baby Chenoa while playing Pin the Tail on the Donkey, Clothespins in a Bottle, Musical Chairs, and Duck-Duck-Goose before PB&Js with chips are served. Once lunch is complete, everyone gathers to watch the birthday girl open her first-ever wrapped gifts. Chenoa has such a blast opening all the wonderful gifts; she becomes so excited by the activity and discovery of the items inside that she squeals with joy. After all the gifts are opened, the cupcakes BJ baked and decorated are brought out. Both children and adults alike are pleasantly surprised as they look like little Cookie Monster faces with a mini chocolate chip cookie in the 'mouth' of each one. They are served with a side of ice cream and cup of hot cocoa.

Once the birthday activities are completed, they make peanut butter pinecone bird feeders for Solstice and take a nature hike to put them out and collect nature items to make Solstice wreaths. The afternoon is filled with children's laughter, rosy cheeks and noses from the crisp, cool December air. All in all, Chenoa's first birthday and Solstice celebration are a great success.

With Christmas preparations in the works, combined with the Kemps already working on planning the New Year's Eve party, an all-over excitement seems to fill every second of every day.

The whole Fenton-Kemp clan, along with the McCallister girls, gather during the day on Christmas Eve at Kemp House for their big family backyard barbecue and gift exchange. Those visiting leave mid-evening to ensure all children are in bed before Santa's arrival.

Christmas Day, the Fenton girls' families will spend with their respective mates' sides of the family.

After BJ gets the girls to bed and is sure they're sleeping, she puts out the few things Santa is bringing to them. She decides to go to bed at a reasonable time to get enough sleep herself to be fresh for Christmas Day.

Late in the night, a tall figure appears at the main door of her little home. The door is undetectably opened, and the shadowed figure slips in, near soundlessly, carrying a variety of gaily wrapped packages which are placed around the colorfully lit tree. The figure, then slips back out as stealthily as it entered, closing and re-locking the door behind.

Chumani wakes shortly after sunrise Christmas morning, she gets her baby sister up, hoping to instill Christmas excitement and wonder in her. As a gift to her mommy before waking her to go find out if Santa found them this year, Chumani changes Chenoa, who's now wearing pull-ups.

"Good morning, Mommy. Merry Christmas." Chumani whispers.

Chenoa squeals with joy as Chumani helps her up onto the bed with their mother.

BJ's eyes flicker open. "Merry Christmas, girls. Did Santa visit?" she asks sleepily.

"We're waiting for you to go with us," Chumani informs. "I changed Chenoa for you so you don't have to."

"Thank you, baby girl." BJ gets up, puts Chenoa down on the floor, takes her pudgy little hand, and Chumani's too, as the trio walks to the living room.

All three are surprised and amazed by the abundance of gifts around the tree left by Santa. BJ is momentarily puzzled, then realizes Emily has a key.

Chumani enthusiastically decides to help Chenoa open some of her toys first so she can begin playing while Chumani opens her own.

BJ pours a cup of coffee, loving being able to wake to it fresh and ready thanks to her programmable coffee maker. She begins making breakfast sticky rolls.

Sounds from Riyon and RJ out on the patio reach Chumaini and BJ's ears.

"But Daddy, I want to see what Santa brought them, and tell them Merry Christmas," Riyon pleads.

"I know, Riyon, but we need to let them have their special family alone time," RJ tries to explain.

"Mommy, Riyon and Mr. Fenton are here," Chumani calls, running to the door to let them in. "Merry Christmas Riyon! Merry Christmas, Mr. Fenton," she greets, hugging each of them in turn. "What did Santa bring you, Riyon? Come see what we got. We got way more than I ever did before. Probably 'cause my daddy never liked having toys around, and last year we just got out of the hospital 'cause Chenoa was born, so we didn't get anything 'cause Santa didn't think we'd be home. Now that we have a real home, Santa gave us more," Chumani rattles on exuberantly.

Through the window, BJ spies RJ shaking his head, grinning at the excited children as Riyon, following Chumani toward the door of the house, calls over his shoulder, "See, Daddy, I told you they wouldn't care if we come see what Santa brought."

BJ pours a second cup of coffee and takes both to the door, handing one to RJ in greeting. "Merry Christmas."

"Merry Christmas, Breezy," he says, accepting the cup, then gives her a light kiss on the forehead before they step in to join the trio of children, so filled with Christmas joy.

BJ excuses herself to change, then goes to tell Emily and Jason to join them for sticky rolls.

The day progresses in a comfortable, peaceful fashion with the children happily playing together with their new toys, alternating between the two houses and outside, the adults lying around chatting, relaxing. They have leftovers from yesterday's family gathering, so there is no need to cook. Emily and Jason return to the big house in the afternoon to rest and maybe catch a nap.

BJ asks RJ, "Would you like to stay and watch one of the holiday movies I recorded?"

Sitting snuggled on the love seat, watching the children and the movie, tears well in BJ's eyes. She sniffles in an attempt to hold them back.

RJ notices, he responds by wrapping her in a tender hug and drawing her closer, then kissing the top of her head gently, sensing these are tears of joy.

31

New Year's Eve is fast approaching. Emily has encouraged BJ to invite parents from school, coworkers and friends from the bar to attend the party.

BJ now informs Emily, "I invited the two ladies from school whom I've gone to coffee with a few times, and their spouses; Buddy, Josie, a couple other lounge co-workers and a few regulars from the bar."

Emily smiles, stating the now updated head count. "Wow. That's a lot of people," BJ realizes this will be a much larger event than the housewarming shindig.

"Yes, even a few of Rainier clients from around the country are flying in to attend, as well as local clients," Emily informs.

The next few days are a whir of activities.

Very early New Year's Eve morning, the caterers arrive to begin setting up tables, putting on tablecloths, centerpieces, streamers, and all manner of party décor. BJ isn't sure whether to stay out of the way of all the hustle and bustle or offer to help. She decides on the latter.

"Emily, is there anything I can do to help?"

"Oh, that is so sweet of you to offer dear, but the crews have it all under control. I'd rather you spend your day getting ready and rested for the evening. In fact, Mel called a few minutes ago to ask if I knew where you were. She called your cell, but you didn't answer. She was calling to say she is headed to the salon to get her hair, mani/pedi done, and wondered if you and the girls want to join her. I hope you don't mind, I told her that is a marvelous idea. That way, you can be away from all this hubbub for a bit, so she's coming to pick you all up in half an hour."

"Oh, umm..." BJ stammers.

"Don't worry, dear, it's my treat. The place the girls go has a play-room for the children. As a matter of fact, I think Riyon would like to go hang out with Chumani and Chenoa. That will keep him occupied and out of the way, too. I'll get him ready."

RJ's morning ahead is slated to be a busy one. He is up and off to get his haircut early New Year's Eve morning, then goes to the airport to pick up Drew, his wife Heidi, and two other business associate couples. While dropping them off at their hotel, RJ says to Drew, "I need to run a very important errand. Want to join me?"

"Is it a top-secret covert operation?" Drew teases.

RJ chuckles, "Yeah, something like that."

"I'm in."

They take off, leaving Heidi and the others to rest up for the big night.

While at the salon, Mel convinces BJ to get a few highlights, get her hair trimmed and styled, and have both a manicure and a pedicure. It is all a new experience for BJ, having never been to a salon or even had anyone so much as cut her hair; she'd always done it all herself.

"You deserve to feel like a woman and be pampered once in a while," Mel affords gentle encouragement.

The stylist is sweet, and for a small fee, she even trims Chumani and Chenoa's hair. They also have simple manicures done on them both. Riyon even gets in on the pampering, receiving a hair trim as well.

Upon returning from the salon with all the kids, BJ notes the intensified commotion, which is hard to believe is even possible.

Mel gives the four of them parting hugs, calling out to BJ as they head to their little house. "Tell Mère I'll be back later. See ya tonight."

Riyon is left in the care of Jason while Mémère is busy with the party arrangements.

BJ purchased a new outfit for the evening after Emily told her it is to be a bit more formal affair. BJ gets the girls dressed in the beautiful black velvet and electric blue chiffon matching dresses they got for Christmas, expressly for this event, then begins the daunting task of getting herself ready. Luckily for BJ, Kristen, and her best friend, Jenny, arrive to wrangle all the children for the evening. They come collect Chumani and Chenoa, leaving BJ to finish getting ready.

Amidst all the commotion, RJ arrives back at the house. He finds Riyon with Jason in the living room, hiding away from all the pre-party activity.

"Hey, Riyon, nice haircut, let's get you dressed."

"Okay, Daddy." Riyon complies without pause. Once dressed in his new clothes, Riyon heads off to join the other kids with Kristen while RJ showers and dresses.

BJ gives herself a head-to-toe assessment in the full-length mirror. She applied far more makeup than usual, but hopes she's kept it subtle. She's liking the new highlights and flouncy wavy hairstyle. Not that she'd do this for an everyday look, but it is nice to look in the mirror and see herself looking feminine on rare occasions.

The party is getting underway, with music and voices of people arriving waft in through the open sliding glass door. She hasn't seen RJ all day. Emily told her he was picking up clients from the airport and getting them settled at a nearby hotel.

"OK. Here I go," BJ tells her reflection.

'Tap, tap, tap' comes a soft knock at her door. "BJ? It's me, Cheryl," her best friend calls out, entering the house.

BJ steps into the living room. Cheryl gasps upon seeing her friend.

"Oh, BJ, you look Beautiful!" she compliments, in a reverent whisper.

Cheryl goes to BJ, giving her a big hug. "Spin," she commands, laughing blithely. BJ complies. BJ is wearing a black and silver, form-fitting, mid-thigh tank-style dress, and a shimmering, vibrant red shoulder wrap with mid-heeled red strappy ankle booties. Her hair is a tumble of long, silky waves, held back from her face on one side with a simple, elegant silver barrette. A silver herringbone chain graces her long neck, lying perfectly just below the hollow at the base of her throat, complemented by matching dangle earrings.

"Wow. Just...Wow. Emily said you went to the salon with Mel today. I saw how adorable the girls look, but ..." She pauses, then continues, "Has RJ seen you yet?" she asks, brows shooting skyward.

"Not that it matters, but no." BJ averts her eyes shyly.

"Oh, it *matters*," Cheryl assures her. "You're about to knock his socks off!" Cheryl grins at the blush that washes over her friend's face.

"I'm so nervous," BJ admits. "There will be people here I don't know. RJ's business associates, friends of Emily, and Jason. Not that it should matter. I mean, it's not like I need to impress them or that they'll even know I exist..."

"Trust me," Cheryl states emphatically, smiling hugely, "once you walk out that door, everyone will know you exist."

"Maybe I should change into something normal." BJ turns to go back to her room.

Cheryl takes BJ's arm, halting her retreat.

"NO," she states firmly, tempered with a caring smile. "You stand straight, head held high, and walk out there. Be proud of the woman you are. Now let's go. I'm right here with you."

BJ agrees, but steps to the bathroom mirror to reapply lip gloss and check her reflection one last time. Cheryl takes that opportunity to motion to Jake that they are on their way out. Jake catches RJ's attention. Nodding, he points toward the door as the beautiful duo crosses the threshold.

Family members who've been anticipating seeing BJ after Mel tells of the day at the salon detect Jake pointing, and turn to watch.

Hesitating, BJ halts. Seeing this, Cheryl takes her elbow, nudging her to continue. She scans the crowd until she catches sight of RJ standing stock still, brows raised, open-mouthed as if awaiting his next breath. He swallows hard the lump that overcomes his throat. BJ lowers her eyes, smiling demurely, then looks up to find RJ, as if in slow motion, striding toward her. He stops a few feet before her, giving her a slow and complete head-to-toe assessment before reaching out his hand to her, inviting her to come to him. She hesitates, then steps to him, taking his hand. The smile that creases his features outshines all the party lighting. He leans to her, brushing a soft kiss on her cheek, saying, "You're astonishingly beautiful. You literally take my breath away."

"Thank you," she replies coyly. Having taken in his appearance in fine black trousers, crisp white dress shirt topped with a charcoal gray V-necked sweater exposing a matching charcoal shiny silk tie, she reciprocates the compliment, "And you are devastatingly handsome this evening if I may say so." She looks up in time to witness the twinkle in his eyes.

"You may. Thank you. Shall we?" He extends a hand to her, which she accepts.

RJ flashes a grin at Jake, who comes to join Cheryl nearby.

As RJ and BJ walk away, Jake calls out, "Hey, bro?" When RJ pauses to look back, he continues, "Promise me no pool escapades tonight, OK?"

All those who had been present at the housewarming party laugh in understanding before returning to the festivities.

Both RJ and BJ blush. RJ waves off his friend's comment. They approach a couple that BJ doesn't recognize. She assumes it must be business associates.

"BJ, I would like you to meet Drew and Heidi Conrad. This is BJ McCallister," he makes the introductions.

They exchange handshakes and greetings. "It is an honor and my pleasure to finally meet you, BJ. I must tell you, Breezy suits you far better this night, for you are a breath of fresh beauty." Drew states, charmingly.

BJ wonders how this man has knowledge of her real name and what he means by *finally* meet her? RJ reads the questions in her expression, "Drew is the culprit who put me up to doing the background check on you," he supplies, laughing lightly to ease the tension before it starts.

Understanding registers in BJ.

"Breezy, please forgive me. I was only looking out for my old friend."

BJ looks from one man to the other, then at Heidi, who smiles, saying, "My husband is always trying to take care of others. I know he didn't mean to cause any trouble."

"It's fine. You're forgiven... this time," she teases.

"I have a few others I need to introduce Breezy to. Get some food and refreshment, and we'll catch up with you two in a while."

RJ places a hand on the small of BJ's back, guiding her through the crowd, introducing her to other business associates and family friends.

The parents from school arrive, so RJ and BJ greet them, then introduce them around so they feel more comfortable mingling.

Festivities are going well. Everyone is having a great time. A little before nine o'clock, RJ and BJ have Kristen gather up the children and take them into BJ's house, where they have a mini midnight celebration using Eastern time for their countdown and sparkling cider for their salute. RJ and BJ return to the party. Kirsten and Jenny take over getting all six kids changed into jammies so the slumber party and movie watching can proceed until the littles fall asleep.

Three hours later, the party is in full swing. The lead singer of the band announces, "Please, everyone, get your glasses of champagne ready."

A computer is connected to a movie screen on the patio, airing the rebroadcast of the New York New Year's Times Square countdown.

BJ stands at RJ's side. "Five, Four, Three, Two, One..." the commentator counts down.

"Happy New Year!" The entire party crowd calls out in unison as the band strikes up the tune Auld Lang Syne, and everyone turns to their partners for the traditional midnight kiss.

RJ gently takes BJ into the circle of his arms, draped loosely around her waist. He smiles sweetly as he bends to softly kiss BJ's supple lips. He draws back, searching her expression to gauge her reaction, wondering how she'll react if he deepens the kiss. He decides to give it a try.

BJ is swept away by the glorious sensations enveloping her in this moment. The cacophony, the throng of people swirling around them, yet at the same time, her sense is that the two of them are all that exists in this magical moment. When the kiss ends and their lips part, she becomes lightheaded, holding tightly to RJ for support a few moments longer. Her eyes open to discover him smiling down at her. "Happy *New* Year, Breezy Jo," he emphasizes the New.

"Happy New Year, Rainier Julian." Both use their proper names.

They stand there, side by side, watching the festivities. RJ nearly imperceptibly gets the attention of Jake and Drew and nods. The two know what to do. Jake motions to the band leader, who is also aware of what to do. The band winds down the song they're playing, and he lets the other musicians know what song to start next.

The song begins. RJ asks, "May I have this dance?" He takes BJ's hand, leading her to the dance floor without waiting for her response. RJ warps his arms around BJ's waist, and they begin to sway to the music.

"Breezy Jo?" RJ draws her attention. "I hope you truly know how much I love you." He pauses as the words of the song "Always and Forever," which he requested, float over the moment as they continue swaying to the music.

"I think I know you well enough to know that you are not yet ready for a marriage proposal," he pauses, sensing tension grip her, and waits for her to catch her breath before continuing, "However, I want you to know how very much in love with you I am. How serious I am about sticking with you through whatever life throws at you."

BJ looks up at him, a myriad of emotions flashing across her gorgeous features. The music softens, and BJ glances around, seeing the dance floor is nearly empty. Jake, Cheryl, Drew, Heidi, and three other couples sway slowly on the outskirts of the floor so that BJ doesn't feel like everyone is watching her. Even though they are. RJ now pauses their dancing. He reaches into his pocket and removes the item he picked up earlier today on his top-secret errand with Drew.

"Breezy Jo, I want to take this opportunity to commit myself to you. To promise my heart and soul to you from this day forward, for all eternity." He holds up the ring he withdrew from his pocket.

BJ focuses on the large heart-cut blue topaz, bracketed by two Chocolate Diamonds in a Bronzed Titanium setting.

RJ continues. "I don't want to pressure you in any way. I know in my heart you at the very least care for me. I am willing to accept only that if that is all you are ever able to give. I never thought I would, or could, love any woman, even a little, but I love you, Breezy Jo." He signals the band to strike up the Randy Travis song, 'Forever and Ever', which RJ sings to BJ, still standing there holding her hand and the ring.

The words beautifully speak his assurance to love her... forever, and ever.

"Breezy, will you do me the honor of accepting this ring as a token of my wholehearted commitment to you and your daughters. As my unbreakable promise to love you through all the days of our lives?"

Rivulets of tears flow unhindered. Heart constricting in uncertainty, yet bursting with joy, BJ looks around at all the smiling faces, feeling the love of each of them. Emily and Jason wait on bated breath to hear her response. Cheryl, Jake, Millie, Brady, the gang from work, the Fenton siblings, and spouses, the parents from school, Drew, Heidi and other business associates all stand motionless. Even the band members, though continuing to softly play the tune in the background, become still in anticipation. The photographer and videographer, whom Emily hired to photograph the party, are both now focused on BJ and RJ.

She looks back at the ring in his hand, then into his eyes. A shy smile begins to ease the moments before near panicked expression.

RJ's brows arch questioningly.

BJ's face lights up as she whispers, "Yes, Rainier, I will accept your token. I will accept your promise and your love, and I will reciprocate both equally for you and Riyon.

The collective sigh of elation expelled by the throng of people observing this monumental moment is about as loud as the near-deafening cheers and applause that follow as the band begins playing the song by Rhett Akins: 'She Said Yes.'

The ~~End~~ New Beginning

Author Remi Dayle

The spark to become a prolifically published author ignited in Remi Dayle at the tender age of 12. Remi has two wonderful daughters and is Mimi to three handsome grandsons and four beautiful granddaughters.
Remi is originally from Michigan, but lived more than half her life in Southern California. She has also lived in Indiana, Tennessee, and now resides in Nevada.
Remi is a character-driven author of clean, family-oriented romance, as well as other genres to be published in the future. She currently has two published novels and many more works in progress.

Author Remi Dayle

The following are two reviews of:
SECOND CHANCES

Second Chances shines as a tender, heartfelt story about family, resilience, and the unexpected ways love finds us again. Through BJ's journey as a single mother rebuilding her life and unknowingly stepping into the heart of the Fenton-Kemp family, you capture the quiet courage of starting over and the beauty of finding belonging where one least expects it. The emotional tension between BJ and RJ unfolds with warmth, humor, and authenticity, making their story both relatable and deeply moving.

Brenda A.

I've read and reviewed *Second Chances*, and it's a heartfelt, emotionally layered story that beautifully explores love, trust, and redemption. The chemistry between BJ and RJ, the warmth of the Fenton-Kemp family, and the themes of healing and new beginnings all make this story deeply relatable—and wonderfully suited for the screen.

Shelly V.

I trust you enjoyed Second Chances. Please consider writing and sending me a review of my work. Thank you.

Also, I'd greatly apreciate it if you would please visit my website@

www.AuthorRemiDayle.com

And please Follow me on:

Facebook.com/AuthorRemiDayle

Instagram @AuthorRemiDayle

TikTok / Booktok @authorremidayle

Patreon.com/AuthorRemiDayle

Amazon Author Central:

http://www.amazon.com/author/remidayle

I am a current member of Seirra Arts Literary Community- Reno and past SAG member.

Sneak Peek

Please enjoy these two excerpts from my Up Coming novel.

Our Guardian Angel

Love & More, Born in Storms

CHAPTER ONE

Kori Lambert

"We are gathered here today to say our final farewell to Ely Lambert. Beloved husband to Kori, father of Toby and Cody. Ely was wonderful in both of those roles and was well-loved in this community...."

The minister's words seem empty solace to Kori and her boys as they stand graveside listening to the eulogy. The bright, refreshingly crisp October midday is a stark contrast to the bleak hollowness they feel. Sniffling and muffled sobs emanate from all around them.

It has been three weeks since Ely's transition to the next realm. It has taken that long to wind up the preliminary investigation into the accident and deaths of Ely and Beau.

As neighbors and friends begin their graveside departures, they approach with comforting words and hugs for Kori and the boys.

Toby overhears a townsfolk comment, *'Poor Kori. How is she going to handle the ranch with no man of the house to take care of things?'* Toby decides at that moment, at the tender age of 7, *that he* is now the man of the house.

Kori and the boys drive up the long dirt driveway to their ranch house past the lush green pasture surrounded by split rail fences, the pipe-fenced paddock and corral, and the 10-double stall weathered barn filled with horses. The trio solemnly walks up the front steps of the wrap-around covered porch of their log-style ranch house and enter the front room.

"Please get changed out of your good clothes. I have to get the evening chores done. Then we'll eat."

The boys slink off to their room. Kori walks to the kitchen, where the table displays various dishes of desserts. At the fridge, she opens the door, displaying an array of casseroles. Letting the fridge door close, without taking anything out, she turns and goes to her room to change her clothes as well. Chores, then dinner, then off to the cocoon of her half-empty bed. One step at a time. That's all she can do…for now.

The bright rays of dawn, bespeaking a glorious morning, belie the bleakness of heart and sorrow of the Lambert family, filters in through the country floral, cotton window curtains, tickling Kori awake, urging her to begin morning chores. With lackluster spirit, Kori rises and gets the day underway. She wakes the boys, who exhibit the same lack of energy about beginning this new day, this new chapter of life, one without Ely; father and husband of the Lambert family.

CHAPTER FOUR
Kyle Elliott

Kyle stands surveying the vast expanse of lush green rolling hills dotted by a thousand or so puffs of white. He never thought it possible that he would have any reason to desire to get away from his family's sheep ranch on New Zealand's South Isle. However, that was before the 'Audrey Incident' as he has come to refer to it.

Standing there looking over his family ranch, he hears what he can only describe as a voice from within, telling him what he needs to do to be able to put that incident behind him and move forward with his life. In that moment, Kyle makes his decision final, to listen to that voice.

Kyle returns to the house to explain to his mother and younger brothers his need to get away for a while. "I assure you I have confidence in your abilities to handle the ranch while I travel in the US for a while to 'clear the mush for brains' I've had since the *Audrey Incident.*" He tells his brothers.

A few days later, Kyle boards a plane to the U.S., taking with him only his framed backpack filled to the gills and a bedroll strapped to the bottom.

It is fall in the States when Kyle arrives, and he spends the next few months backpacking to and hanging out in various towns across the U.S., doing odd jobs as he goes. He thoroughly enjoys meeting such a wide range of diverse people everywhere he travels and finds himself welcomed by most everyone he meets along his journey.

Five months into his journey, in early spring, Kyle arrives at the Do Drop Inn, a quaint local diner in Millerman's Creek, Tennessee.

The lunch crowd at the Do Drop Inn is bustling when the bell above the door jingles as someone enters. As is intended, the sound catches the attention of the staff, but also, patrons tend to take note of someone entering. The chatter of the locals softens as they observe a newcomer's presence. A tall, roguishly handsome man. Looking to be in his late twenties or early thirties, tanned, sun-bleached blond hair, sea-green eyes, carrying a framed backpack with a bedroll.

Kyle glances around the diner, taking in the looks of interest at his arrival, and smiles.

"Hello. Is a traveling man allowed to partake of a delicious-smelling meal here? Or is this establishment's fare only available to the local clientele?" his accent is noticeably not of American origin.

Irene steps from behind the counter, "Well, if the traveling man is as good-looking, complimentary and polite as you, I think we might could allow him to partake of a good hot meal," she smiles jovially as she indicates an available booth for him to take a seat.

The patrons return to their meals and conversations; some continue, while some start up about the foreign newcomer.

"Thank you kindly...Irene, is it?" he reads her name tag, which also states '40 Years of Service with a Smile'.

"That it is. I'm wonderin' where might that accent give 'way you'd be from? Iffin' I were a more worldly woman, I might would know?"

The broad smile that creases Kyle's face unveils bright whites encased in parentheses of dimples. It strikes Irene in the moment; they remind her of another pair of dimples she knows well. Those she hadn't seen much of late. Not since the passing of Beau and Ely.

"Not to worry. Most people who think that they know get it wrong anyway. I'm often accused of being Australian, which to a New Zealander is a bit of an insult," he winks at the older gray-haired woman.

"Ah, soz we have a Kiwi in our midst?"

"Aye, I see you're worldly enough to know to call me a Kiwi," he teases.

She hands him a menu. Saying as she walks back toward the counter to refill a customer's coffee, "Guess I learnt somethin' from watching that there, TV box," she chuckles, "Can I get you somethin' ta drink?"

"Water to start with would be fine."

Irene returns to the table with his glass of water and pulls out her order booklet and pencil, "I've of'en thought it unfair, workers need to wear name tags an' other folks don't. Kinda puts us at a disadvantage."

"My apologies, Ms. Irene. I must have left my manners on the road-side on my way into town. My name is Kyle Elliott," he extends his hand in greeting to this kind woman, who accepts the gesture.

"What, pray tell, brings you to our little town clear from the other side of the world?"

"That's a bit of a long story."

"Look at me. Ya must be starvin', while I stand here pryin' into yer affairs, which are nonna my business. What can I get ya ta eat?"

"No worries, ma'am. I'll take the day's special, Southern fried chicken, mashed, gravy and biscuits."

"Would you like anythin' else ta drink?"

"A glass of milk would be nice. Thank you."

"Comin' right up, sugar," Irene hollers as she walks back to the counter, "Beau Diddly! Fix me up an extra special of today's special for our foreign friend here."

Kyle smiles at the woman's vivacious personality. "Beau Diddly?"

"Yes, Sir. My late husband was Beau and our son, Beau Jr., some-where along the way got the nickname of Beau Diddly."

"I'm sorry for your loss."

"Thank you. It's been a bit of time now, soz it's not quite so hurtful anymore.

Irene serves up his delicious-smelling, homestyle meal, which Kyle polishes off in no time.

"How was that fer ya?" Irene asks as she pours coffee at the table next to Kyle.

"My most sincere compliments to the cook."

Irene offers coffee, which he accepts. Clearing away Kyle's dishes, "Could I interest ya in anythin' else? Perhaps some freshly baked pie for dessert?"

"You wouldn't happen to have any Kiwi pie, would you?" Kyle asks, half-teasingly.

Irene takes up the teasing tone, "The only Kiwi pie around these parts is you, cutie pie," she winks and they both chuckle.

"Well, then what kind of pie would you recommend?"

"My apple is always good, but my most recent flavor of the month is my strawberry, banana, chocolate cream pie."

"Oh my, that sounds wickedly delicious, even if a bit frou-frou, but I think I'm man enough to have a slice and not lose my masculine status," it was Kyle's turn to wink.

Miss Irene replies, "Believe me, I don't think there'd be anyone could ever doubt yer mascu-line status. If only I were younger...," she trails off as she goes to get his pie.

Upon her return, "Miss Irene, there is one other thing I'm wondering if you might be able to help me with."

"What's that, Sugar?"

"I'm wondering if you might know anyone around the area who could use some help with an odd job or two for a time in exchange for a place to set up my tent. Plus, maybe a meal now and again?" Irene's eyes nearly popped out of their sockets.

Seeing this, Kyle rushes on, "I can assure you, Miss Irene, I'm very trustworthy and able to do pretty near any type of work. You see, I've come to this country to travel around to see its diverse beauty and get to know about people from different areas. I find it easier to better understand people by working alongside them and immersing myself into their culture and lifestyle rather than just asking and being told about it."

"Well, let me see..." Irene 'pretends' to have to think about it for a minute. She looks around the diner to see if anyone is close enough to overhear what she has to say next. She leans close, whispering, "I do have someone in mind that I *know* needs help, but..." she pauses, looking the man straight in the eye, "No one, and I mean NO one, can know about it."

Kyle looks at her quizzically. "It's nothing illegal, is it?"

"Oh, no," she leans even closer to his ear, "It's a ranch just outside of town and... Well, they're in a bit of a predicament ya might say. I'm the only one who knows 'bout it. Not interested in 'ceptin' any help from any of us. What I'm thinkin' is maybe you could jus' 'happen by' and make your offer to help, not lettin' 'em know you an' I talked. I'm thinkin' maybe 'ceptin help from a stranger might be alright, but you have ta promise not to let on that I sent ya. I'm serious; ya can't tell no one else anythin' about it."

"OK, I won't. Where is this place?"

"That might be the only catch... It's quite a fer piece out of town. Not exactly sure how you could explain just happening across the place."

"No worries. I'll say I was wandering and chose that direction to see what I could see, and came across the place. That should work since that's exactly how I came to be here."

"Great! Tho' I gotta warn ya, they're a might bit of stubborn 'bout 'ceptin help, but *really* need some right now, as you'll see when ya get there."

"I'll just have to let my Kiwi charm win acceptance," he smiles broadly.

"Yer good looks might almost play 'gainst ya," Irene is thoughtful, "Might not trust ya. But iffin ya persevere, I'll be beholdin' ta ya fer life. Free food here anytime," she yet again winks at the young man.